DIVINE HOTEL

BY
NICOLE LOUGHAN

An Imprint of
Open Door Publications

Divine Hotel
By Nicole Loughan

ISBN: 978-0-9972024-1-0

Cover Design by Genevieve LaVo Cosdon, Lavodesign.com

Published by
Can't Put it Down Books
An Imprint of
Open Door Publications
2113 Stackhouse Dr.
Yardley, PA 19067
www.OpenDoorPublications.com

This book is dedicated to my father, Allen.
If I could find a way to step back into the past, I know I could
not resist visiting you one last time.

*The highest reach of injustice
is to be deemed just when you are not.*

Plato

CHAPTER 1

A long time ago, before most people can remember, a palace stood over Philadelphia. It was a place of refuge for the weak and weary of the city, a shining monument of marble, oak and brass that towered over the metropolis.

Good and evil were kept in balance there, until one day the scales tipped and evil won out. As the years passed, the marble and brass were stolen, and the oak was stripped of its shine. As the hotel fell into ruin, its inhabitants followed. All was not lost, though, for there was one chance to save the hotel—and its inhabitants—from this fate. Hidden not far away was an otherworldly gift meant to right the wrongs of the past, if only the right person could find it.

ॐ✖

2002

"You can't catch me," the boy shouted as he flung open the doors to the dilapidated dining hall. The room was lit by slivers of sun that peeked through the cracks in the high ceiling, and sporadic beams of light that shone through hastily fastened boards covering the room's many broken windows.

All that was left of the once great hall were water-stained plaster ornaments positioned high up on the ceiling, far out of reach. Everything of value was gone. The light fixtures, hardwood floors, door knobs, and every last bit of shined marble and brass had been stripped away. The floors were an uneven terrain of warped wood and broken boards. The edges of the room were a tapestry of trash, but the center of the great space, which had once housed long oak dining tables, was completely bare.

The girl in pursuit walked gingerly over the broken boards. She kept her eyes on the ground and squinted to keep the dust floating through the air out of her eyes.

"Slow down, Darrius!" she shouted.

She paused in front of a hole in the floor, which blocked her passage into the great room. She stared down and saw only darkness, which could mean the hole opened only down to the next floor, or could possibly reach as far down as all ten floors.

"Come on, Carol," he shouted. "You aren't gonna fall going over that tiny hole."

She watched him move with feline grace over the broken boards and gathered her courage. She involuntarily held her breath, took two steps back, and focused her eyes on a point just past the opening.

She ran as fast as her legs would carry her toward the gap. She pushed off and wobbled as a loose board slid away from her. She fell awkwardly forward and threw her arms out to catch herself. She scratched her palms reaching out for the ledge and only managed a precarious hold. If she'd weighed just a bit more she might have fallen in.

Darrius raced to her. The strain of holding on was too much for her, one by one her fingers were slipping, the pinkies first, then the ring fingers, and then all at once the rest gave way and she fell. Darrius grasped her wrist just before she slipped out of sight. He grunted as he pulled her up and out of the hole. As soon as he had her over the edge he fell backwards and she landed beside him with a thud.

Carol lay back and caught her breath as Darrius joked, "I could've made that jump with you on my back, you chicken."

She stared up at the ceiling and pointed at a plaster fruit basket. "Darrius, look, the ceiling. It's changed again."

He looked up and said, "I don't see anything different. You always think that ceiling looks different. Who do you think would get all the way up there and fix the ceiling?"

"It does change," she exclaimed. "It always looks like it's about to fall apart, then it's patched back up. Yesterday that fruit basket was just a hole in the ceiling."

He laughed so hard the ground shook beneath him. When he stopped he realized the floor was shaking without any work from him, and he bolted upright.

"What is that?" Carol demanded, as she jumped up and looked

2

down at the floor.

"It's somebody pounding," Darrius yelled as he, too, jumped up to his feet.

More knocks rang out around the hall, shaking up dust, which floated freely through the room. Suddenly a shout could be heard below their feet. "Keep it down," followed by a more distant yell, "Shut up."

When the pounding ceased they could hear the wail of sirens outside. Darrius jumped up and ran to peek through the boards.

"What?" Carol asked.

"It's the cops."

"What do we do?"

"We run."

CHAPTER 2

Sarah was startled out of a deep sleep when her phone rang, beating her alarm clock to its job. She answered the call and jotted down the important details. "Divine Hotel... woman arrested... little girl missing."

She was barely awake as she wrote. Then, out of the corner of her eye, she saw something just outside her window, and dropped the phone. It was him again, but as soon as she turned her head to look, he was gone. She leapt to her feet and ran to the window to try to catch a glimpse of him, but just like every other time, he was gone before she was sure of what she had seen.

She walked back to her bed, set her phone on the receiver, rubbed her eyes, and stared at the window. Her heart raced as she thought of him, because she knew it was going to be a bad day. He only ever came to her on bad days. She had seen him the morning her parents died. She saw him again just after a house fire, and once more when a childhood friend was in trouble.

He was so fast she could barely remember what he looked like. She didn't think he was particularly short or tall. He was slender with either blonde or white hair. She tried to recall what she had just seen, but again all she saw was an outline. She decided perhaps the light was playing tricks on her and he was never there at all, but she was anxious just the same.

She looked back at her piece of paper, snatched it off the nightstand and hurried to her closet. She quickly dressed in wrinkled khakis and a powder blue blouse. In her rush to leave she neglected her hair, opting to brush her big brown curls with her fingers so they wouldn't frizz with the interference of a brush. She grabbed a Pop Tart on her way out the door and ran to catch an early train.

She was the only person walking through the wide-open lobby of the Philadelphia Department of Human Services that morning. The gleaming white foyer was empty except for one security guard who barely glanced up from his newspaper as she walked past. She went to the turnstile by the elevator and swiped her card at the pad. The beep of the machine and creak of the turnstile as she walked through echoed loudly in the empty room. She walked into the elevator and began her ascent. She felt as if she had forgotten something and went through her pockets, finding her wallet, money, and I.D. badge. She pulled out her badge on its lanyard and placed it around her neck. She patted her front pocket and realized she had forgotten her can of pepper spray.

"Damn it," she said to herself. She opened her wallet, pulled out a ten-dollar bill and put it in her front pocket. This was a distraction technique taught to her by Ruth, her mentor. Ruth was a middle aged no-nonsense Caribbean woman, who the day she met Sarah said, "You look like Mary Poppins. You wear polyester shirts and flat shoes. Everybody going to know you ain't Philly, and that's bad. You need to protect yourself. Always keep ten dollars in your front pocket, and if somebody tries to rob you, pull out the bill, throw it hard on the ground, and run like hell."

Sarah got off on the sixth floor and jogged down the beige carpeted hallway to her office. She grabbed a fresh notepad, intake forms, and two pens. She booted up her computer to report the call she had received that morning. She scribbled a note to her cube mate letting her know she was going to the Divine Hotel, and rushed back to the lobby.

She left the building and walked briskly down the street to the gated parking lot reserved for state vehicles. When she got there the gate attendant was out of sight and the shack was locked. She looked around and saw the lot attendant at the end of the middle row filling a tire with air. "I'll be there in a minute, Sarah," he shouted.

"I'm kind of in a hurry, Herb," she yelled back.

"You're going to have to give me ten."

There was no rushing him. She was already going to be late so she darted across the street to the diner where she ate most of her daily meals. The small restaurant looked as if it was from another era, with shiny vinyl booths, Formica table tops, and chrome bar stools. The front of the store had an old-fashioned tin façade that announced the restaurant's name in neon. In good repair the neon would have said "Phillies Diner," but most of the bulbs were broken, leaving only an illuminated "P." Sarah liked the food at the little restaurant, but ended up there more often because it was cheap and close to work.

The booths and barstools were empty, and the only person inside was the elderly man behind the counter, polishing the mahogany bar to a bright shine. He was the same man she'd seen there every morning for the past year. If he wasn't working the register, he was sitting in the corner drinking a cup of coffee.

She stepped up to the counter and said, "Good morning. I need one cup of Joe, please."

"I'm sorry, but that's going to be a few minutes. We just started a new pot."

She groaned and said, "A Coke then. Anything with caffeine will do."

He turned around to the fountain and filled a large Styrofoam cup. He placed the lid on with shaky hands, spilling a bit as he handed the drink to her. She fastened the lid tight and handed him two dollars. When he tried to give her the change she pointed to the can on the counter and said, "No thanks. You can give it to the charity. Thanks."

She bounded out of the restaurant thinking she should have gotten a diet soda because her pants had been mysteriously shrinking. She got as far as the sidewalk by the street, went to take a sip of her soda, and realized she had forgotten a straw. She let out a huff, looked up, and turned to go back in.

"Oh," she yelped. The man from the counter was behind her, hunched over and reaching his hand out.

"Miss, you left this." He was holding a straw out to her.

"Thank you." Sarah was surprised he made the effort to come out to give her the straw. He looked so frail. She thought it must have taken a lot of his energy to walk out after her. "Thank you, mister... um, oh I'm sorry. I never got your name."

"I'm John. Thank you for asking, Sarah."

A look of terror spread over her face, as she realized she had never told him her name before.

"How do you..." she started.

He pointed to her chest. "You're wearing a badge."

"Oh" she said relieved. "I forget it's there. I'm sorry I've never thought to ask you your name. Sometimes I get so busy."

"Perfectly understandable, young miss. You're a social worker, right? Must be a tough job," he said.

It was a tough job, and she was starting to hate it, but she was not going to tell a perfect stranger that. She nodded her head and forced a smile. He smiled back. He was handsome for an old man. He had a strong jaw line and bright blue eyes, and though the skin sagged around his neck, his face was smooth.

He continued. "It seems to me it would take a person who had seen a lot in their young life to take on a job like that."

The hair on the back of her neck stood up. He said it like he knew about her. She looked to the ground and searched her mind for how he could know what she had been through, and determined that he couldn't. She looked back up and said, "Well it was nice to meet you..." but trailed off when she realized he was already gone.

She stared at the spot where he had just been, confused. She looked back into the diner and saw him standing behind the counter already. He waved at her and she waved back. She shook off the feeling that she'd missed something and started for the parking lot. When she got there Herb was at the gate holding up her keys. She checked them out, got her car, and left.

CHAPTER 3

"They've got Mom. We gotta get out of here and find Grandma," Darrius shouted as he watched the police through the slats.

Carol agreed.

Darrius turned away from the window and searched the floor of the room for a board big enough to make a bridge. He found one that was wide, long, and solid, and placed it over the hole.

"Go across," he said. "I'll hold it for you."

He placed his hands on either side of the board and steadied it for her as she inched across. She was nearly to the other side when she was startled by a deep voice from the corner of the room.

"Darrius," the voice echoed off of the empty space. "Your mother has my stuff and she looks like she's about to lose it. You're the man of the house now. You're gonna have to pay for it, little man."

"Hurry up," Darrius shouted, and Carol leapt off the board onto the other side of the hole. The board fell and bounced around again and again before it made a distant thud. Footsteps fell behind Darrius, and Carol squeaked in fright.

"Run, Carol. Find grandma and don't tell the cops who you are. Don't say anything. Just go."

She ran to the other side of room, past the broken elevator and into the dark stairwell. Just before she slammed the door she heard her brother scream. She turned around to run back to him when he shouted, "Find grandma and I'll find you."

❧❧

Sarah drove through the gleaming blocks of Center City, still golden with the light from the morning sun bouncing off of the skyscrapers. Hot dog and pita vendors were propping up their awnings and waving at each other. She loved Center City. It was her home. She was on her way to a place she had grown to loathe. Her stomach churned, and it only hurt worse the closer she got.

As she drove, her surroundings became more distressed. The grass and trees disappeared, giving way to uneven concrete sidewalks, and graffiti marred buildings. The streets appeared to narrow because the shoulders were littered with abandoned cars with flat tires and missing license plates. The golden light of Center City did not exist where she was headed, and she longed to get back to the light and the safety.

She passed the last of the gated-in alleys filled with trash and reached her destination. When she arrived at the Divine Hotel she parked on the street in front of a line of police cruisers. The officers were inside the ten-story brick building which announced its name, Divine Lorraine Hotel, with a tall sign on its roof in red letters that had once been lit. It had probably looked quite modern and fashionable forty or so years ago. The building stood out on Broad Street like a sore thumb. It was Victorian in style with keystone arches and castle-like towers capping its corners. She could tell that it had once displayed ornate stone adornments, but they had worn away.

She knew a little of the building's history. It was cherished by some in the neighborhood; they talked about it like an old friend. An historical marker announced its importance in history as the first high-class, fully integrated hotel on the East Coast, but the sign had been neglected just like the building, and left to rot. The hotel was officially condemned and meant to be empty, however people always seemed to find a way inside and squatted there.

Sarah walked past a man sleeping on a bench in front of the building. He was using a cardboard box as a sleeping bag. He had no covers or pillows, only newspapers balled up under his head for support. He didn't move as she approached. When she walked into the building she noticed there was not a functioning light in the lobby. The only light came from a dirty front window.

There was a small office, visible through a window, marked "*information.*". The darkened room beyond the glass held one desk and mounds of garbage. The desk was festooned with spider webs which reached to the walls and ceiling. It appeared the room had been out of use for many years.

There were also small tin mailboxes built into the wall. More than half of the doors were gone, but it looked like the carrier still delivered to the broken boxes, many overflowing with jammed-in envelopes. While she was looking at the boxes, trying to read the names, she was greeted by a heavyset officer trudging down the stairs, kicking garbage as he went.

He tipped his hat to her as he approached. "You must be DHS?"

"Yes, Sarah," She replied holding out her hand.

"We found the little girl we were looking for. We caught her running down the stairs. She hasn't said a word to us though," he said, making his way back up the stairs. "This is a nasty place; little girl and her mom living in here with all these scumbags. There's no electricity, no heat, no water. They just squat here. Mom stole food from the market down the street this morning. Grocer said she does it all the time. He's not having it anymore. We get up in here and we find all sorts of stuff: shoes, electronics, CDs. We have to take her in."

He stopped for a moment and took a few labored breaths before they continued up the stairs.

"Anyway, we arrested the lady. Her name's Linda, and she said she wants us to phone her mom. The problem is, the number she gave us is disconnected."

Sarah arrived at the threshold of the apartment and a pungent ammonia smell hit her nostrils. Cats, she thought. There was that and the faint odor of human waste. She must have shown her disgust because the officer said, "Oh yeah. They've been using a bucket in the bathroom. No running water."

When she walked in she found a young girl sitting on a bare mattress in the living room. Not that it was much of a room to live in. There was an opening in the wall for a fireplace, but there was no mantle and there were only a few tiles left inside the pit. The floors were untreated wood so warped the light from the apartment below was visible between the slats. The ceilings were high and pink insulation poured out of gaping holes. The mattress where the girl sat had little black dots in the crevices and clusters of similar flecks massing at the corners. Ugh, bed bugs, she thought as she shrugged her shoulder uneasily.

10

Sarah knew bed bugs were rampant in the city at this time of year. One of the other DHS cars was so badly infested the year before they had to wait for winter to come and leave the doors open overnight to finally freeze them out.

After the last run-in with bed bugs the department issued protocol to deal with them, starting with putting any clothes that came in contact with bed bugs immediately into a dryer on high heat. Sarah looked at the little girl, then around the apartment for clean clothes.

She bent down to the little girl and said, "Where's your bedroom, sweetie?"

She cocked her head to the side and held out her hand, sweeping it around the room.

The heavyset officer said, "There's only the one room."

There was nothing for children in the room. Just the mattress, a red ripped up couch, and garbage.

"Where's all your stuff?" she asked.

The girl looked to the kitchen table, then down at her feet.

"That bag?" she asked as she made her way to a duffel bag on the kitchen table. She went to it and brought it over to the girl.

"Can I look through this?" she asked. "I'm just looking for clothes."

The girl nodded and Sarah pulled out army toys, Barbie dolls, and finally some clothes, only pajamas and one t-shirt. No pants, no underwear. The pajama shirt looked too big for the slender girl.

She held it out and said, "My name's Sarah, sweetie. What's yours?"

When she didn't answer she said, "I just want to help."

The girl shook her head and Sarah turned over the pajama shirt in her hand. It had dinosaurs on the front and the tag had a name written with a Sharpie, "Darrius."

She pointed to the tag, looked to the little girl and asked, "Who's Darrius?"

The little girl's eyes grew big. Sarah watched her as she looked from Sarah to the door. Tears welled up in her eyes.

"Is he here? In the building?"

The girl sobbed and Sarah put her arm on her shoulder. "Sweetie, if he's here I have to find him. We can't leave him in here." The girl nodded and pointed up.

11

Sarah popped up and interrupted the police officers in the hallway. "There's another kid, a little boy named Darrius. Stay with her. I'm going to find him." The cop who had shown her upstairs offered to go up with her, and she accepted the help. She darted down the hallway, over broken boards and glass, back to the stairwell. The stairwell on the upper floors was pitch black with no windows or lights to guide them.

Sarah took the flashlight from the officer and shone it on the steps in front of her. They made their way up the stairs slowly to avoid stepping on trash and broken steps. Some of the concrete steps had broken away leaving a steep slope in their place.

Sarah moved faster than he, and was nearly a flight ahead of him when he slipped and fell. She rushed back down to him, and found that he had bashed his shin. The fall had ripped his pants, and she could see blood soaking through his pant leg.

"Are you okay?" she asked, flashing a light on his silver name badge that said J. Trudge. "Officer Trudge. I'm sorry…"

She stopped talking when she heard the sound of a door slam.

"That was the door we went in downstairs wasn't it?" she asked.

He nodded. "Go ahead without me. I'll make my way down."

She pointed the light at the steps and darted down them, quicker this time and knowing the terrain better.

She rushed down six flights of stairs, skipping every other step, and emerged in the grimy lobby she had been in before. It was still empty and dark, but she saw no sign of anybody in the room. She dashed to the front window but was unable to see anybody walking away from the building. She turned back to the room and noticed that some of the garbage behind the desk had shifted. She slid onto the desk, flung her legs to the other side, and waded through the piles of garbage. She walked to the back of the room and discovered a door near the moved garbage. It opened onto a long wide hallway lined with faded white columns, all crumbling and decorated with graffiti. The cracked slate floor led to an archway which housed a revolving door. The glass of the door was broken and the metal had bent under the pressure of insulation stuffed between the doors.

There were identical staircases on either side of the room near her. She flashed her light up each set, and found that they were boarded up at the top. She walked past the stairs and saw two identical sitting rooms. One was engulfed in black mold, the other held teetering piles of trash. She bypassed the rooms and ran toward the revolving door. On either side of the back wall there were two doors facing opposite directions.

She flashed her light to the floor by one door and saw that it was still littered with bugs and dirt, the other door the same. She turned around and ran back to the moldy room. She flashed her light in it and found many alcoves along the wall. She flashed her light in the alcoves one by one and found that the last alcove held a door. She pointed the flashlight to the floor and saw a cleared quarter circle in front of the door and a line of bug corpses along the outer edge of the circle. She pulled open the door and found herself in the courtyard of the Divine.

Balconies soared overhead in the courtyard, eight on either side reaching up to the top of the building. On the front of the building there were two large arches set in the brick, one on top of the other. The tops of the arches were open air bridges to get to the other sides of the building. The entire structure was built as two almost completely separate buildings held together by the walkways.

At the farthest end of the courtyard she saw a man walking with his hands on the neck of a young boy. They were walking away from the building.

"Hey," she shouted, running after them.

The boy turned his head, but the man holding him pushed his head back around and moved faster.

"Stop, right now," she shouted. The man quickened his pace, and she took off at a sprint in towards him. When the man turned and saw her running for him, he pushed the boy forward and looked as if he was preparing to run, but instead slowed down and turned the boy around. When Sarah caught up she saw a police car round the block and understood why he slowed.

"Just taking my son out for a walk," the large man said in a deep base. He bent his head forward to look down at her.

"What's your son's name?" she asked, smiling at the young boy.

"Kevin," the man replied.

She held her hand out, "My name's Sarah and I'm looking for a little boy named Darrius. Either of you seen him?"

The boy gave an almost imperceptible smile. The man refused to

13

take her hand and said, "Nope."

He turned the boy back around and Sarah saw the tag sticking out of his shirt, labeled Darrius. She said firmly, "Darrius, come with me."

The boy took a step in her direction when the man tightened his grip. Sarah felt the heft of the Maglite in her hands and made a split second decision. She yelled, "Catch," and threw the light as hard as she could at the chest of the large man. He took his hands off the boy to grab the light and Sarah yelled, "Run!"

CHAPTER 4

Back in the safety of the apartment, she bent down on one knee to stand eye to eye with the children. She held her hand out to introduce herself. "I'm Sarah," she said.

"Darrius," the boy said, holding out his hand. "This is my sister, Carol."

The little girl leaned into her big brother. He was slender, and Sarah guessed he was nine. Carol was thin as well, but she had chubby cheeks, which may have made her look younger than her years. Sarah thought she was probably six.

"I'm going to find you a nice place to stay tonight while we look for your grandmother. You guys want to come with me?"

They agreed. "I need to get you some new clothes, too; do you know of any stores nearby?" Darrius offered the flea market opening around the corner at nine o'clock.

Sarah and the children left together, leaving the police behind to search the rest of the building. It didn't take long for Darrius to lead the group to the flea market. He walked with the surety of a much older boy, knowing exactly where he was going. Carol walked slower and kept her head down. After nearly ten minutes in motion, Darrius was very far ahead of them. He turned and looked back every few moments to make sure he was not too far ahead. He finally slowed enough for them to catch up. Then he asked, "Is my mom going to jail?"

"I don't know," Sarah replied.

"Will we ever go home?"

"That's not my decision, Darrius. It's up to a judge."

"Our mom ain't bad," he said. "Please help her. We got no clothes 'cause she buys new clothes when ours get dirty. She don't like laundromats. People be gettin' attacked at our laundromat. They steal while you wait. They ain't nothing but common criminals, my mom says. Plus, these ain't even dirty," he said holding out his nearly clean, patterned shirt with a small smattering of food stains down the front and smudges around the collar. "She gets new clothes when ours are nasty. And she gets us everything we want. We never go hungry. Tell her, Carol."

Carol nodded her head in agreement.

"There's lots of kids hungry with holes in their clothes. We better than those kids. Our mom ain't like that. She never hit us neither." Darrius pleaded, "Please tell the police to be nice to our mom."

Sarah said she would, and she was telling the truth. She would add his statements to her reports. She also observed that the children didn't appear starved, mistreated, or dirty. Their clothes did look nearly new; that would go in the report also, but she knew it was unlikely to be enough to detract from their mother's multiple shortcomings and the state of their home. The kids would never be allowed to live in the Divine again.

"Who was that man who was trying to take you?" Sarah asked.

"Oh, that guy. They call him Runty. He's pretty mad about my mom gettin' busted by the cops. That was his stuff in our house."

"You should have told the police that, Darrius. They need to know. It might help your mom."

Darrius looked at Carol and then back at Sarah. "Nope."

"Why?" she asked.

"You wouldn't understand."

She spent the rest of the morning with the kids. First, they went to the flea market, which was hastily set up in a roped-off block. The merchants used folding card tables set up unevenly in long rows on either side of the street. The vendors stood behind the tables on the sidewalk leaving the center of the road open so people could walk freely. The market sold everything from live fish to knives, food, clothing, and even furniture.

Carol, Sarah, and Darrius stepped into the flow of patrons already making their way down the row of tables, bypassing those who stopped to make purchases. Carol tugged on Sarah's blouse and pointed to a table selling knock-off Disney and Nickelodeon products. "I like her," she said, pointing to a Dora the Explorer t-shirt with a smiling Dora decal waving at them. Sarah pulled out her wallet and purchased the shirt she was sure was not a legally licensed Dora product. She got a plastic bag for her purchase that said, King Chinese Buffet, and no receipt.

Darrius enjoyed looking through the bootlegged video tapes. The vendor assured them, "They are of the finest quality and are in English."

Sarah said no to movies but did let Carol buy a pinwheel from the man.

When they came across an enclosed aquarium with a frog Darrius said, "Sarah look. He's just like Kermit. I'll take great care of him."

She was not convinced and continued walking down the row. Darrius jumped in front of her, opened up his eyes as wide as he could and said, "I'm going to have such a rough night sleeping in a strange place. Don't you think it'll be easier if I had a friend to keep me company?"

She stopped, turned around, and went back for the aquarium. After a good amount of haggling, she bought Darrius a new striped Ralph Lauren polo and shorts from the man who also sold live aquatic animals, and talked him into a reduced rate for the frog. They took their purchases back to the Divine where the children changed clothes and then left, throwing their old clothes in the trash pile in the lobby on their way out.

Sarah pulled into IHOP and when the kids saw the sign they smiled ear to ear.

"Yes!" said Carol kicking her feet excitedly. Darrius held up his palm and she gave him a high five. They leapt out of the car and took off skipping down the sidewalk. Sarah let them run for a moment and then wrangled them into the building and ushered them to the bathroom to wash their hands. Sarah stood in the doorway to the bathroom, to watch the kids while still affording them some privacy. She noticed when they placed their hands in the water it ran dark brown.

"Wash your faces and your arms too, please," she said. "Behave in here; I'm going to make a call."

She stepped into the hallway, closing the door behind her. She could hear the two of them giggling and splashing. She worried about what the state of the bathroom might be when they were finished.

She pulled out her phone and called her boss to arrange housing. She jotted down an address and the kids came out, wet all over, but smiling and ready to eat.

They both ordered pancakes in the shape of clown faces and on the side they got chocolate milk. They ate everything on their plates as if there was a world record at stake. Once their plates were clean they both leaned back and held their tummies.

Carol rubbed her stomach until she let out a burp that was so loud people in the surrounding booths turned around. She covered her mouth and her eyes went wide with embarrassment, "Sorry," she said. "I never ate so much."

After pancakes Sarah got them back in the car and started for the address on the paper. She looked at the kids in the back seat, both smiling and staring out the window. "I'm going to take you to a nice foster home," she said. "I know this lady. She's very nice."

"It's just temporary, right?" Darrius said.

"It is. We will have to see if we can find your grandmother."

"What about Runty?" Darrius asked.

"What do you mean?"

He replied, "If Runty finds us, we're going to be in big trouble. What if the people we are staying with let him take us away? You need to find our grandma fast."

"I'll find your grandmother as fast as I can," she promised. "And I'll give you my phone number. If you need me, call anytime."

He seemed satisfied with that answer and continued the ride without another word. They pulled up to a row home neighborhood on the cusp of Center City and Sarah walked them up to the corner lot home. It was bright and inviting with a large grassy front lawn. They made their way to the front porch of the house and Sarah started to say her goodbyes, but then she remembered her file.

She pulled a Polaroid camera out of her bag and asked the kids to pose for a photo. When she got back to the office she would have to create a new case file for the kids, and the first entry in the file would be these photos.

She took Darrius's photo first. He wanted to look tough so he frowned and put his head down. After the photo he laughed. Carol smiled into the camera and said, "Cheese."

The foster mother walked out to the porch to greet the kids and

Sarah explained that Darrius came with a frog. The woman looked down at him and said, "I love frogs," and then invited them in.

Sarah took that as her cue to go. She found herself very sad saying goodbye to them. She was only with them for a few hours, but they had filled her with more joy than she had felt in a long time. She really wanted to make sure she took good care of them. When she pulled away, Darrius was already inside but she could see that Carol had run out to the curb and was waving to her with one hand and holding the pinwheel in the other.

CHAPTER 5

On her drive back to the office Sarah couldn't get the kids out of her mind. Other social workers warned her if she kept feeling so much she would burn out.

She remembered when she first started. She tried to save every person who walked through the door. She would give them the benefit of the doubt when they said they lost their rent checks, or when they said that they had never gotten their bus tokens. She would believe whatever story it was and give them money out of her own pocket. It didn't take her long to realize word had gotten out that she was giving away money and requests started pouring in. But worse was the attitude of her co-workers. The "seasoned" caseworkers would call her gullible if they were being nice, or idiot if they were not.

She remembered one rainy evening when the woman in the next cube over received a call from the lobby at closing time. A phone call from the lobby was usually a call to let them know a client had come in and needed urgent attention. If it was a standard visit they would send e-mails. The other worker heard her phone ring, checked the clock and, with five minutes left in the workday, she grabbed her purse and headed for the exit.

Sarah could hear the ring from her own desk and it nagged at her. The phone stopped ringing for a moment and Sarah stared at it, biting her lip. Then it rang again. This time she jumped up and answered the phone, "This is Sarah."

The operator said, "There's an old woman in the lobby, said her name's Anita. She's sittin' on a pile of trash bags that she's real protective about. She said she just got evicted and needs a place to sleep for the night."

Sarah said she would take care of it.

"Aren't you the Children's' Division worker?" the operator

asked.

"I am, but I don't mind helping out."

The next sound from the phone was something between a snort and laugh, followed by, "Good luck. We're closing up, come get her."

Sarah grabbed her purse and headed for the lobby. By the time she got there half the lights were off and the woman had fallen asleep on top of her bags. She gave her gentle nudge on the shoulder and the woman woke with a start.

"Let's find you somewhere to stay," Sarah said. "You're Anita right?"

The woman sat up and her grey wig fell forward, covering her eyes. She reached up quickly to put it back in place.

The woman looked embarrassed for a moment, but the smile on Sarah's face put her at ease and she stood up and pointed at her bags. Her voice was softer than her situation, "Can you give me a hand? Please be civil with my things?"

Sarah picked up two bags, which were deceptively heavy, and wondered how this woman had ever managed to get all of the bags there by herself.

She had a tight grip on the heaviest one when she felt something soft brush her hand. She looked down and saw a cockroach running up her arm. She shrieked and dropped the bag to the floor, slapping the bug off her arm.

"I told you to be civil to my things," Anita yelled. Then she bent over to pick up the heavy bag. "I'll carry it my damn self."

Anita managed to heft up each bag and keep up with Sarah as they rushed through a rain storm to the parking lot where the state vehicles were kept. When they finally reached Sarah's white Toyota, they were both soaked through with rain. Sarah directed Anita to put the bags in the trunk. Then the two of them made their way out of the city and out to the suburbs. City churches and shelters were always full on rainy nights, but the outlying suburbs had homeless-friendly churches that usually had open beds. Sarah drove Anita to a church she had been to before and gave her $10; enough to catch a train back to the city. There was no hourly report logged for pay and no expense report turned in. The car log simply said, Cherry Hill Homeless Shelter.

It was the old Sarah who helped Anita. She was changing and it worried her. She was running all of her recent interactions through her head and wondering if she was still doing all that she could for people. She wondered if she had met Anita in that moment if she would act in the same way.

She stopped at a red light and said out loud, "Stop worrying all the time and just do your damn job."

When Sarah got back to the office, she started a file for Darrius and Carol. Looking at their photos warmed her heart again; she knew she didn't want to lose her compassion on this case.

She affixed their photos to a brand new green file folder and grabbed her label maker, printing out their names on white tape. She affixed their date of Entry, Thursday April 6, 2002. Their files were brand new. This was Darrius's and Carol's entry into the system. She grabbed the police report, filled out in duplicate on carbon paper, separated the pages and slid a copy into each folder. Sarah would have to type up all of the events of the day into an intake report, but first she wanted to find their grandmother.

A search on her computer found that the kids' mother, Linda, and grandmother, Rosa Lee, were already in the system. She pulled both files and started flipping through them. Linda had lived with her mother Rosa Lee until middle school. She was pulled from the home for domestic abuse and adopted by another family. She stayed with the other family until the age of sixteen, when she requested, and was given permission, to go back to Rosa Lee. Sarah read that she had been arrested for prostitution shortly after she'd moved back in with her mother. Her mother's file was thicker, at least three inches of once-white paper tarnished to light brown. It was a file started before computers were used, so the words in the file were palpable, each letter raised from being struck with a typewriter. Rosa Lee's life was almost the same as her daughter's. She had lived with two parents until she was eight, in the same area of the city where she lived now. Her father had gone missing in the 1960s and her mother moved in with a man named Harvey who started abusing her and her daughter. Rosa Lee was brought into the court system because a school teacher had seen her with bruises; at least that's what the summary said.

She read through transcripts of Rosa Lee's statements. It seemed like she had been a bright child. She had done well in school until her father went missing. Her school file said she had a great interest in music and the arts.

Sarah was distracted by a green sheet at the back of the file. She knew the green form was for medical billing, it had been the same color for all of the years there had been files. Sarah flipped to the sheet and saw a grainy black and white photo of a young girl, a dead ringer for Carol, smiling with a missing front tooth. According to the detailed medical report, the missing tooth was the catalyst for the teacher's call to the police, not mere bruises. In Rosa Lee's interview notes she said it had been knocked out by Harvey over a dispute he had with her mother. The green sheet said the county paid to have the gums stitched up, but it said nothing about further repairs. The technology for dental implants did not exist back then, and Sarah wondered if Rosa Lee had ever had her teeth fixed.

She flipped back to the pictures. The photos followed the life of a person who had grown up in the system. The first photo of Rosa Lee, from the day her teacher called, showed a little girl with twisted pigtails on either side decorated with plastic barrettes. She was wearing a plaid, threadbare dress. She was skinny and her boney arms were wrapped in hand-shaped bruises. She had her mouth open as if asked to show her teeth. Sarah flipped through the pictures; Rosa Lee grew, the bruises faded, but the space for her front tooth remained vacant.

Sarah wrote down points of contact from the file; Rosa Lee was first. She searched the county records for Rosa Lee's mother and any possible siblings, but turned up nothing. She tried to find Darrius and Carol's grandfather. The file listed him as Kirby Holt. She typed his name into the computer and received one message, "Kirby Holt reported missing August, 1964."

She went to her computer and searched her data base for "Rosa Lee Holt."

Rosa Lee, or Ro as her criminal file called her, came up. She had been in the court system but never served time in prison. She had done a short stint in the county jail for check fraud in 1994, and that was the last mention of her. There was a number listed and an address from 1994. Sarah tried the number and was greeted with the shrill operator beep indicating service had been cut off.

She left the department system and connected to the internet. She flipped through papers while she waited for her computer to connect.

She often used internet search engines, which were sometimes handier than the government search engine. She had a hit: Several R. Holts were in the white pages. She printed off a list of thirty-two R. Holts and L. Holts in the greater Philadelphia area. No Rosas. She sat down at her phone with a red marker in hand and started calling.

Her mentor, Ruth, walked in as she had made her way in at around number ten on the list and looked over her shoulder.

"What are you getting into, child?" Ruth asked.

Sarah handed Ruth her file. "Trying to find some place for my new guys to stay. They really want to live with their grandmother."

"Did you check the county system?"

"Yes, there was nothing there."

"Then what ya doin' child?" Ruth said shaking her head. "I tell you true, there ain't no prize for all this searching that you do. I'm not telling you to hurt your feelings, girl. I tell you because you work too hard for the shit money the state pay."

Sarah and Ruth often disagreed on how much help was too much, but Sarah liked Ruth and she knew Ruth liked her, too. People said that the two of them would never get along when Sarah first started. Ruth was from Jamaica and at least twenty years' Sarah's senior. When the two of them were alone, Ruth was more herself than she was with the other girls in the office. She had a sharp tongue and came from a place where you never back down. Sarah was quiet and for the most part passive. After two years it made sense that Sarah was Ruth's longest running cube mate. For all of Ruth's tough talk she was a good person and good friend. Most importantly, she helped Sarah navigate the poverty stricken world of Philadelphia, a place Sarah had never known before becoming a social worker. She knew poverty, but she did not know Philly poverty, as Ruth quickly pointed out. Ruth understood the city in a way nobody else did.

She always told Sarah, "You remind me of me, honey child, before I knew how much I didn't know."

Ruth flipped through the papers on Sarah's desk and looked at the pictures of the two kids.

"Little lambs," she said kissing her fingers, then touching them to the photos. She turned her attention to Sarah who was covering the microphone on the phone as it rang.

"You know what, Ms. Sarah. I'm not here to cut you down pretty girl, you gotta do you. But I'm going to do me and get some lunch."

"Ms. Ruth, would you do me a favor and grab me something to eat?" Sarah said with a smile.

"Okay miss," Ruth walked out of the cube and gave Sarah a parting smile, showing her perfect, bright teeth.

Sarah continued to call all of the numbers, using the same script. "Hello, is this Rosa Lee Holt?" Then she would invariably get, "Who's callin?"

"My name is Sarah Davis from the Department of Human Services. I am looking for Rosa Lee Holt or a relative, are you her or could you direct me to her?"

She was hung up on, left a few messages, but no Rosa Lee. She only had two numbers left when Ruth walked back in. She placed her call and as soon as she hung up the phone Ruth burst out in laughter. "Girl, you not going to get anywhere callin' like that. They think you're a bill collector."

She continued holding her stomach and shook with laughter. Sarah huffed and turned back to her list and angrily scratched off R. Holt of Germantown Avenue with her big red marker.

"Girl, don't get pissy, let me help you with your list. Give me that paper." Sarah passed it over to her. She was getting frustrated anyway and did not want to look at it anymore. Ruth passed Sarah some chicken wings from the sports bar down the street, and said, "You eat and cheer up."

They were cold but still good. Ruth looked down the list and went back to one of the already crossed out numbers. She punched it in and dialed up her island accent and her volume. "Ehh, I be looking for Rosa Lee, you know de lady, ehh?"

Then Sarah listened to Ruth go "uh huh" a number of times. Ruth got even louder "Mind she business, ehh." Then "uh huh" again. She started writing on Sarah's list. "You see de girl tell her to call her girl Sarah at dis number." She gave Sarah's number and winked at her as she hung up the phone.

"What did you do? How did you know what number to call?" Sarah begged.

"Look at this list. Look at where Linda be from. What do you see?"

"I don't know." Sarah said, "What should I have been looking

25

for?"

"The neighborhoods, child; only two numbers on this list in that neighborhood where you pick up the kids. Nobody leaves they hood too far. Where the kids be, the grandma be. Don't you know your zip codes?"

Sarah shook her head. And Ruth said, "See, I tell you true, you don't know how much you don't know."

"What did they say?"

"She know Rosa, she staying with her and set up the phone in Rosa's name because she had better credit," said Ruth her accent slipping slowly back into the Queen's English. "Now you take this list and this address and you wait for girl to call. You got a meeting with permanency planning committee at three o'clock, and if you don't go, Yolanda going to break her foot off on you."

Sarah looked at the clock and said, "Crap." She wiped wing sauce off her face with the back of her sleeve, grabbed her planning committee file, and rushed out.

By the end of the night Sarah had failed to make any progress finding the kids a place to live. Rosa hadn't called back, and she had to stay late to record all of the events of the day with the children. She had to finish adding notes to her file, then log all thirty-two of her calls into the computer system. It took hours. She was again the last one to leave the building. Ruth left her at six and told her to call when she got home. Ruth always checked on her. They had a regularly scheduled evening phone call. She knew Sarah didn't know many people in the city and she watched out for her. Ruth, the unlikely cube companion, was Sarah's best friend and the closest thing she had to a parent.

By the time all of the information was recorded it was dark. Sarah left the building through the dimly lit, empty entry corridor. She swiped her badge again at the turnstile and the beep echoed through the room. She walked out into the night. It was darker than usual, without a star visible in the sky. There weren't any people walking around or cars in the street. It was eerily quiet and she didn't like it. Then she remembered seeing the man early that morning. She thought maybe meeting Runty at the Divine was the bad thing that was going to happen that day. But she wasn't sure. She decided it must be and let out a sigh of relief. She took another breath and started down the street towards the train station.

Her stomach grumbled, and though she was nearly to the station she decided to turn back and trek back to the diner. When she went in, the dining room was empty yet again. John was standing behind the counter and a young woman was standing in the back holding a balled up apron.

She walked up to the counter and said, "Hi, could I get a cheeseburger, please?"

"I'm sorry miss the grill is closed and I'm about to lock the door. I should have done it already."

"Can I get anything? I'm really hungry."

"Shakes, soda, or pies are all we have remaining."

She noticed a sign on the counter advertising cookie dough shakes.

"I haven't had one of those in a while," she said pointing to the shake.

The girl at the back rolled her eyes and tapped her foot. John said to her, "You go ahead."

The girl quickly turned and pushed through the back door. John hobbled to the shake machine and filled a disposable cup.

As he passed it over she said, "Thank you, John."

Sarah tried to pass money to him, but he said, "The register is locked so I won't be able to process your payment tonight. We have to throw out the leftover anyway."

"I can't let you do that. I'll give you five now and you can process it in the morning, keep the change."

"You can pay in the morning then," he said and passed her back her bill.

"I'll walk you out," he added. He limped alongside her. He was slow and it looked like it pained him to heave the door open.

"John, are you here every day?"

He chuckled and said, "Have a great evening and please get home swiftly, there is rain on the way."

She walked out the door and started for the SEPTA station. When she walked past the lot she noticed there was only one car in it, and it had a Tinkerbell decal in the back window. While she was looking at the car, lightning flashed across the sky and lit up the parking lot with bright white light; a loud crack of thunder followed.

Rain was on the way, but it was not there yet.

She felt a pang of guilt, thinking about John hobbling home alone in the rain. She desperately wanted to go home to sleep. She thought, haven't I done enough for people today? On the other hand, she still cared. She made the decision to check out her city vehicle and drive John home.

She turned to walk back to the light of the diner, but he was out of sight again. How is he getting around so fast? She thought. Then her mind wandered to the mystery man. The one she saw out of the corner of her eye on bad days. He always seemed to disappear before she could get a good glimpse of him.

By her calculation John should still be hobbling away from the door. She went up to the glass and knocked, but nobody came out. The lights were still on. He must have gone out the back. She continued banging on the door for over a minute, still no response.

She looked up and down the street but didn't see him anywhere. She walked around the back and noticed a walking path between two hedges.

She walked between the hedges until the path opened onto a street. It was a quiet street lined with trees and two story row homes. She caught a quick glimpse of John disappearing behind a house nearly two blocks away. She yelled, "John, wait!" and picked up her pace to try to catch him. She got to the house where she had seen him walking and saw another footpath. The path crossed into the yards of other homes, then wound through a park to a wooded area. She looked down the path and he was out of sight yet again. How is he so damn fast? she wondered aloud, her heart pounding with the thought that she might have found the man who has been following her for so many years. She knew she had originally set out to help him get home, but that quickly morphed into curiosity.

On the other side of the woods was a nicer section of town. There was no public transportation that she knew of. The diner and her car were a long way off, and she did not know where she was. She started to pay special attention to landmarks. As she walked through a park she noticed a fountain. She noted that she came from the path facing the plaque on the water fountain. "Plaque," she said out loud. As she was leaving the park she noted a gnarly oak tree, "Left of oak tree," she said. The iron gates of the park were still open and the path ended at a sidewalk that lined a wide street. The path was lit so she could see where she was going, but it was very dark between lights. Suddenly another flash of lightning rang across the sky, and brought with it the first sprinkle of the night. She considered turning around, having second thoughts about whether or not he was the man, but then she saw him again, even farther away than last time. She took off at a run in his direction, but soon lost sight of him again.

When she slowed down she noticed that the homes in this neighborhood were large old manors set back from the road. Many of them were gated.

"Am I all the way in Gladwyne?" She wondered aloud.

Gladwyne was a well-known area where all the old money lived off the main line. But she was sure she couldn't have gone that far.

Sarah looked up and down the street but saw no sign of John. No cars came in either direction, and there wasn't even a hint of movement other than the sway of trees. They were rustling in the wind, getting ready for the storm. She thought about picking a direction and giving it one last try. She took a few steps and decided to turn around.

The sprinkles turned into drizzle. She would be soaked by the time she got back to her train. The lightning flashed again, bathing everything in white light. She caught, in that moment, a quick glimpse of John far down the street walking toward an open gate immediately after the last flicker of lightning thunder shook the street and sent a car alarm into a frenzy. She turned toward John and headed towards the gate at a quick pace, when she heard a squeak and realized it was closing. She decided in an instant that she was going to run for it.

CHAPTER 6

Sarah slid between the gates as they came to a close. Now on the inside, she could see that the fence ran all along the property line. It was masked from the outside by well-manicured hedges.

She was officially trespassing. And John was nowhere to be seen.

She turned and tried to climb the fence, but there was nothing to climb. There was a lower rail a foot off of the ground, the iron bars were six inches apart and the upper rail was five feet off of the ground. She tried to pull herself up by that rail, but without a foothold, she was trapped. She turned to look at the house on the property; it was an expansive three-story brick manor. It had castle-like features, including turrets and towers. The windows were large and arched. The driveway, which she was standing on, passed the front of the house, circled around a fountain and flowers, and led to a five-car garage and carriage house. The lights were on in the main floor.

As she slowly examined her surroundings she regained control of her senses and decided it was stupid to think John might be her mystery man.

"What was I thinking," she said.

She started for the house, unsure of what she would say when she got there. She thought if John was in the house she might say she was planning to offer him a ride and had followed him. If he was not she would say she had accidentally got trapped when the gate closed.

As she drew nearer to the house she noticed two snarling gargoyle statues perched near the roof flanking the grand two-story entry. Some of the arched windows were filled with stained glass. She walked around the driveway to avoid trampling a garden of tulips that ran parallel to the pavement. She had to walk right by the front window. She started past it and stopped cold at she saw what was inside.

John was standing in the entryway of the grand house, not hunched over or hobbling. He was walking upright. In fact, he looked lithe. This change in his movement took years off him and brought back the thought that he was the mystery man. John threw the plaid shirt he was wearing to a young man who was also in the entryway.

The other man was wearing a suit and appeared to be laughing as John spoke. John was down to a pair of boxers and a t-shirt when he grabbed a robe off a chair, then said something to the young man that made him stop. When the young man turned around he had a serious, almost angry look on his face. She bent down so he wouldn't see her. He walked to the front door and opened it. Looking out onto the lawn, he said, "This is a horrible idea." Then he slammed the door.

"What's going on?" she whispered to herself.

White lightning lit up the whole property; she saw that the grass and gate went on for acres. She also realized if the men were still in the entry they would have a clear view of her. Thunder struck and the trickle of rain turned into heavy pellets. She was soaked. She ran to another window, which was protected by an awning, and tried to listen to what was going on in the house, but she couldn't hear anything over the sound of the rain.

She got down to her knees below the window and stood up just enough to peek over the ledge. John was right at the window looking out. His head was just a few feet above hers, but he was looking straight ahead. She dropped back down. Did he see me, she wondered. She squeezed her eyes closed and covered her mouth, afraid her heavy breathing would give her away. She was panicking.

"Like it or not it's happening today. I knew we had her today."

Had *her* today? Did he mean me? She started shaking.

"We have to rush it along," John said. "Don't worry, I'm sure she's who we have been looking for."

Lightning and thunder hit simultaneously. And a scream pierced the air. It escaped Sarah's mouth before she could stop it. She leapt to her feet and started running.

John threw open the front door and yelled out, "Turn on the search light, she's here. Finally!"

Sarah ran halfway down the driveway and darted off to the left, intending to try the side of the fence instead of the front. She was running with all she had and no visibility. Lightning struck again and she saw a shed mere feet in front of her. She slowed and held her hands out to stop herself from hitting it. Her hands smacked the shed, but she quickly pushed off and ran to the left, circling around the small building again as she ran for the other side of the yard. She heard sloshing footsteps closing in. She ran as fast as she could, the rain stinging her eyes as she went. She still had no visibility, but she felt something gentle brush her arm. It took only a split second for her to realize what it was. Tree, she thought, then immediately heard a smack and the world faded to black.

∾∾

She awoke sitting in a winged chair in front of a roaring fire. The room she was in looked like a medieval library. There were bookshelves built into the two-story room, in between the books the walls were paneled with dark wood and elaborate trim. The floor was dark blue, except for the area around the fireplace, which was a light marble that matched the six-foot-tall mantle. She noticed she was wrapped in a blanket and her hair was not as wet as it had been. She surmised that she must have been out for quite some time.

She heard a voice from behind her, "Sarah I knew you were coming. I didn't mean to scare you. I sent my man Winthrop to look for you, but we didn't quite know where you were," John said as he walked into view, followed by the young man. "I am quite sorry you are injured. Not my intent in the least. Please do not be scared, you have no enemies here, my dear."

"What's going on? Are you going to murder me?" She asked wrapping the blanket around herself tighter.

John furrowed his brow. "No, no, no. Why would you think that? There is nothing of that sort at play here. Ms. Davis you are as safe here as you will be anywhere in your life. I assure you."

"What do you want then?" Sarah asked. John didn't reply. He stood in front of her searching his mind for words.

"Have you been following me?" she asked.

"I have been keeping an eye on you this year, but let me explain…"

She interrupted, "No, not just this year. Every year. Always. Are

32

you the man whose been watching me?"

John and Winthrop exchanged a look.

"It was you, wasn't it?" she shouted.

"Allow me to explain," he said. Then she stared at him and waited for more.

"Go ahead and explain," she prodded.

"It's just too...." he went silent, then stared at her, lost in thought.

The silence was broken when Winthrop stepped towards Sarah and introduced himself, holding out his hand to her. She didn't take it.

He reached forward with his other hand and she threw up her arms in a self-defense pose. Then she relaxed when she realized he was holding a towel.

"You should dry off, ma'am." Winthrop said. "We have a spare room that is at your disposal if you should wish to use it."

The man started for the hallway, "Just down this way Ms. Davis, if you would follow me. I will allow you to dry off and change in private." He motioned for her to follow him.

"Am I a prisoner here?" she asked without following the man.

"Absolutely not," John assured her. "Get dry, warm, and dressed, and give me a minute to collect my thoughts; then we will take a drink and you can hear what this was all about. If you wish to leave, Winthrop will drive you home."

"Could I leave now if I wanted to?" she asked.

John chewed on his lip and looked down. "If you really want to go we will take you home. But I implore you, what I have to say is very important. We can talk somewhere else if you like."

She thought about it for a moment. She wanted answers about why he'd been following her. "Okay, I'll get dry and hear you out."

She followed Winthrop down the hall. It was bright with yellow paint, and elaborate crown molding lining the ceiling. The ceilings were very high. The hall was brightly lit by wall-mounted sconces and chandeliers. Winthrop opened a door for her and held out a towel.

"There is some aspirin in the medicine chest in the bathroom. You may want some to assist you with that bump."

"Right, like I'm going to take a drug in this house," she said sarcastically, snatching the towel from his hand without looking at him.

"Bye," she slammed the door on him. She locked it behind her and inspected the room. It was light green, with two high-arched windows straight ahead of her. There was a rolltop writing desk between the windows. A king bed was on the left wall of the room, and on the right there was a white marble fireplace. The interior of this room was much more modern than the gothic exterior of the house had led her to expect. She saw doors flanking the bed. She tried the one closest to the exterior of the house and found a bathroom.

She looked for other entrances and there were none. She opened the window; it was not locked or barred. She pushed the screen out for good measure and it fell a few feet to the ground. She was not trapped. She inspected behind the mirror to make sure there were no cameras. She peeked into the vanity under the sink and noticed more towels. She checked the medicine chest and there was only one item, a still-sealed bottle of aspirin.

She locked the door and started running a warm shower. The steam felt great against her cold, wet skin. She got so comfortable she planned to step into the shower without removing any clothing just quickly enough to warm up then she would jump back out again. She placed the towel by the glass door of the shower, so she could easily grab it. She got in and found the shower stocked with never-opened salon products.

"Oh, cherry almond mint smoothing shampoo," she said excitedly. She knew this to be a very expensive shampoo that she could not afford. She unwrapped the plastic protective top and opened the bottle to smell it. It can't hurt to wash my hair really quick, she thought. She rubbed her hands together and was intoxicated by the sweet smell. She decided to risk taking off her top, leaving on her bra to enjoy the shower. Six warm jets of water surrounded her. The white walls were so shiny it looked as if she was the first person to bathe there. It was nothing like the cracked yellow tiles of her antiquated bathroom, with a showerhead aimed directly at her sternum. She always had to bend over to wash her hair. Reveling in the joys of a full-sized shower led her to forget where she was. She snapped out of it, rinsed out her hair, and jumped out. She wrapped herself in the towel, her hair was sopping so she bent to the vanity to get a second towel for her hair. She let out a squeal when she looked again. The contents had changed. There were towels on one side of the vanity and clothes on the other side. She inspected the clothing and found neatly folded, brand-new clothing still tagged in her exact size. What the hell? She tried to remember if she only looked in one side of the vanity. She couldn't recall. She thought she would have remembered seeing clothing.

She decided if they were sized for her she would wear them. She dried off and pulled on a pair of jeans and a t-shirt from the cabinet. Her sopping wet clothes were left in a heap on the floor of the bathroom. When she bent over to grab her wallet out of the back pocket, she felt her head throb. She held her hand to it knowing she was going to hurt in the morning, but not enough to take a painkiller. She looked at her wet pile of clothes and suddenly remembered her cellphone. She couldn't believe she had forgotten about it. She grabbed it out of the other pocket and thought to call Ruth and tell her where she was in case something happened. She turned on the phone, which flashed blue before the screen went dead. "Great, water damage, the one thing the warranty won't cover," she uttered.

CHAPTER 7

When Sarah had finished, she wrapped her hair up in a towel and walked back to the hallway. Winthrop stood at the farthest end of the hall by the library motioning for her to follow him. She did, and just before she reached the door of the library he said, "You will leave here tonight with a changed outlook on the world. I guarantee it."

She walked past him into the library without saying. John was waiting in one of the winged chairs by the fire. He was holding a glass of caramel-colored liquor.

"Would you like a drink, my dear?" John asked.

"Nope. I want to know what's been going on and I want to know now."

He motioned for her to sit in the chaise by the window. She guessed that the chair she sat in earlier was still wet.

"Of course," he said and set his drink on a small table to his side. "Sarah, I have been watching you for a very long time. This you may have already surmised. But the reason is so complicated I hardly know where to begin. First, I did not choose you, but you were chosen for a task that I have at my door."

He took a breath. "It all starts with Plato and the story of Glaucon. In the book The *Republic,* I gather you have read it because I have seen it on your bookshelf, you will recall that Plato and Glaucon discuss a mythological ring of Gyges which grants its bearer the gift of invincibility."

She nodded her head.

"In the *Republic,* Plato's brother, Glaucon, says no man can wield the power of this ring without one day becoming unjust. Do you understand what he means by that?"

"If any man has the power to be invincible he will eventually be corrupt."

"True, true. But the ring, he says, does more than give you

invincibility. It shields its wearer from even the eyes of God himself. Meaning you can flout all laws, including those of space and time."

"What does this have to do with me?" she asked.

"Ah, you see it has everything to do with everything. A very long time ago my father and I poured over various translations and versions of Plato's *Republic*. At first we enjoyed the many interpretations of the lessons in the book. But in time my father became obsessed with Glaucon's story. He was convinced the ring was real, and he made it his life's mission to find it, even if it meant making him a stranger to his sons," John sighed and stared forward.

"I'm sorry, John."

"I know you truly mean that, Sarah, and that is why you are here." He sat back down and reached for her hand, but she pulled it away.

"My father followed stories of that ring to the ends of the earth, and I am convinced that is what finally killed him. I had not seen him for years when he passed. He was a stranger to me, and when I saw his body it was as if I'd never known him. He had aged a lifetime in just a few short years. I came to pay my final respects at his funeral and was frightened by what I saw. He was thin, gray, and weathered. The skin of his hands was nearly translucent and pocked with age; they were laid one over the other on top of his chest. I placed my hand around his and a shocking thing happened. I felt the shape of a tiny ring under his stiff hands. I knew in an instant what it was. I snatched it from between his fingers and made sure to hide it quickly in my pocket. I took it and told nobody. I wondered how it got there. Had he been found with his hands clenched, and it was under there all that time? Did my mother ask that he be buried with it? I still to this day do not know how that ring came to be there, but so it was."

He lowered his head and looked at Sarah intently.

"So, you are telling me the ring is real. Like the ring from *Lord of the Rings*? It's a real thing?"

John winced, and Winthrop let out another chuckle. "No, no, no. That is a work of fiction. However, the personification of the creature Gollum did resemble my father and his fascination with that ring. I don't care for the comparison otherwise; there is no such thing as a Hobbit."

"This is a very interesting myth," she said. "But what does it have to do with you following me?"

"Ah, well, last year Winthrop and I were driving home from the theater and unexpectedly, we saw a woman that we happen to be acquainted with transporting every item she owned in garbage bags. We followed her to make sure she would be safe, and we found her ascending the steps of your office. We were concerned for her, and so we parked our vehicle intending to assist her home, but before we made it back to her we found you bending over her, waking her with the gentlest hand. That was the day you came under our notice. We followed you and our dear Anita from that day, and found you had shown her the utmost kindness. We were quite happily surprised to see that you took good care of her."

"How do you know her?" Sarah asked.

"The story of Anita is a long one, but trust me. She is a good woman who deserves the utmost kindness. You would be surprised how many people try to take advantage of her. We have many times had to intercede in her life to ensure her safety. But I digress. That day you were known to us and since then I have been keeping a close eye on you."

"Is that why you were working at the diner?"

"I wanted to be in a place where I could hear honest opinions of you. I watched you and your co-workers without any of you taking notice of my presence. People will speak quite candidly around food service workers and their elders. My disguise as a feeble older gentlemen helped you and those employed with you let your guards down. I could eavesdrop with ease. Many of your fellows have broken privacy laws in that eating establishment, I might add."

"Hah," Sarah said. "If you heard my co-workers speak candidly of me I don't think you would be too happy with the results."

"Your co-workers can be vicious. However, I found that their comments about you tended to be statements about how unwise you were to be kind. They said you were a, what was that term, Winthrop?"

"I'm not going to repeat it," he said.

Sarah asked, "Couldn't you have spent one day in the restaurant to hear opinions?"

"My dear, I wish two favors of you, neither of which I would entrust to somebody whom I had observed for only one day. First, I must pass this ring on for safe keeping after my death. I do not trust it to be buried with me. Look what happened to my father. Anybody could take it. I don't trust it in a concrete vault, in the ocean or at the tip of the arctic. I need it to have a guardian. I need to make sure that I entrust the ring to a person I am sure would never use it to cause harm. This is why I have visited you at every step of your life. I had to know who you were and what you were made of. I became sure you were the one I had been searching for when I saw you on a summer night in 1984 helping Trisha ..."

She interrupted him shocked, "You know about Trish? Nobody knows."

"The ring, it will take you anytime, anywhere, and let you see anything, and it will let you make one change. It gives you the ability to do anything you can think of, and I know that you and Trish had bedroom windows that looked on each other, and one night you saw that she did not come to the window so you..."

She stopped him again. "Please, don't talk about Trish. I believe you. That's more than anybody knows. We don't need to discuss it. It's private. Get back to the second reason I am here."

He bowed his head and cleared his throat uncomfortably. "Secondly, and I am not proud to say this, I need your help. I have done something with the ring that needs undoing. I have been stuck in a cycle for years trying to repair a mistake I made long ago."

"What mistake?" she asked.

He hesitated.

"Okay, let me see this magical ring."

"Not tonight. There is much you must know about it before I let you in the same room with it."

"Well, then I would like Winthrop to take me home as promised," Sarah said.

John's face dropped. He looked as if he'd just been kicked in the stomach. He shook his head and said, "As you wish."

"Not forever or anything," Sarah said. "I'll come back tomorrow after work, but it's late, and I want to sleep in my own bed."

"Oh," John said happily. "Well then let us get you home. After tomorrow starts the weekend, and it would be my pleasure to invite you to stay at the Vandervelt Estate for some continued discussion."

"I'll be here tomorrow, but I'll be telling my friend where I am so nothing shady better happen to me. And I want a copy of both of your licenses to give to her," Sarah added.

"Is the friend you are going to inform Ruth?" John asked.

"Yes, why?" She responded.

"If you intend to give it to Ruth that is acceptable to me. Ruth appears trustworthy and loyal to you. Truth be told, I enjoy listening to Ruth, and I have considered asking for her help. Her knowledge of the city could be extremely valuable," he said, smiling to himself.

She had a feeling he knew a lot about Ruth, too. After a pause he said, "As you wish. Is there anything else we can do for you?"

"Yes," she said. "Can I have that shampoo?"

CHAPTER 8

Winthrop drove Sarah home. The ride took much longer than it should have by her calculation; she thought perhaps she was misremembering how long she had followed John earlier that evening.

She lived on the third floor of a modest apartment building in Center City, a nice neighborhood, but not one of the upscale buildings with a doorman. Her building was small and clean with old appliances. It was rented by young professionals with low incomes. Some of her neighbors were fellow social workers. Many were interns from the nearby pharmaceutical company. She had watched some of those interns find their way to permanent jobs which paid enough for them to move to the glossy new condos by Penn's Landing with views of the Delaware River.

She walked into her apartment holding her new high-end shampoo and copies of John and Winthrop's licenses. Technically, Winthrop was Addicus Winthrop, age thirty, and John was John Harold Vandervelt, age sixty-two.

When she finally crawled into bed it was late. She had to be up in four hours, dressed and ready for court. She had a hearing for Carol and Darrius first thing in the morning. She set her alarm and stared at the ceiling thinking back to what had happened with Trish when she was young. She had not thought of it in years, but as John had said, one would have to see a lot in her young life to become a social worker. He was right. She had seen Trish.

Sarah was from a town was known for being the only place in the state where mobile homes outnumbered stick-built homes. She lived in one of the nicest double-wides in her trailer park. Her parents were hard-working and very kind. Her father was a mechanic and her mother was a nail technician. They loved their jobs. Her mom spent her own money to take herself and Sarah to trade shows. She liked to learn about new painting techniques. She would practice her painting on herself, her friends, and Sarah. Sarah always had cute shapes painted onto her toes such as rainbows and hearts.

Some of the other park families were like them, but some were jobless or injured. Some were kind, others were very nasty. Her most direct neighbors were the Paddys. The Paddy home was a green single-wide surrounded by overgrown weeds. The inside had wood paneled walls, green-shag carpeting, and the kitchen was mostly yellow with discolored brown and yellow linoleum peeling up around the edges. Everything had an ashen tinge from cigarette smoke. The Paddy home was shared by Fanny, her daughter Trish and five miniature dogs.

Fanny seemed to love the dogs more than she loved her daughter. Fanny's days were spent inside eating chips, drinking beer, and watching daytime TV. The highlight of her day was petting her five yappy dogs. Trish spent her days with Sarah. Fanny never asked where Trish was going, and didn't care if she stayed out from sun up to sun down.

One day, Sarah and Trish had their toenails painted with yellow flowers. They went to the Paddy single-wide to get Trish a pair of sandals to display her designs and to show them to Fanny.

Fanny looked down at the floor over the two dogs sitting in her crowded lap. She had a furious expression on her face when Trish lifted her foot to show off her well-manicured toenails.

"Get that shit off your toes. You look like that whore stripper your dad took off with," Fanny screamed. Suddenly, she threw the can of Coors she was chugging at Trish's head. "You will not be a whore in my house. This is not a damn whorehouse."

Trish failed to duck her head in time to escape the beer. It got her right above her temple. She became disoriented and reached for her hair before closing her eyes. Sarah had never seen violence like this in person. She grabbed Trish's arm and pulled her out of the trailer. The spitting screams of Fanny grew as Sarah pulled Trish away. Sarah was sure she heard Fanny stomping to the door, but she was too heavy to catch up to them.

Sarah and Trish kept going until they got to the gas station positioned outside the entrance of the park. People from the park often hung out at the gas station. There were picnic tables and ashtrays outside for their use. Sarah and Trish sat across from each other at the table. It was littered with scratched lottery tickets. Trish had her head resting between her arms and was sobbing.

"She's going to kill me," Trish said. "I ran. It's worse now. She is going to be so mad by the time I get home she is going to tan my ass."

"I'm sorry. I was just scared," said Sarah. She was looking down, too. She was sad for her friend. She began picking through the spent lottery tickets. She started forming a pile of those she had checked and those she hadn't.

"I have to go back. The sooner I go back the less mad she will be. I'll give her a foot rub and give all the dogs a bath. Then she won't be so mad," Trish said, more for herself then for Sarah.

Sarah looked up. "No, I can fix this. My mom will talk to your mom. If she is still mad you can stay at our house. My mom will take care of you."

"My mom hates your mom. She says bad things about your mom. Actually, all the moms do," said Trish still looking down. Then she quietly said, "I like your mom. I wish she was mine. I wish every night for a mom like your mom."

Sarah was hurt to realize the other moms hated her mom. She was also hurting for her friend, who she never knew wished for a better mother.

Sarah decided not to ask what the other moms said about hers. She had completed her pile of checked lottery tickets. No winners. She started to pack up her pile to take them over to the garbage can. "I want to make things better, Trish. Let me go in with you. I'll apologize and maybe she won't be as mad if I am there."

Trish picked up some of the tickets and walked slowly to the garbage with her. "No," she said looking down. "It doesn't matter. I do everything like a whore. I don't know what I can do yet that won't make me a whore like that stripper my dad ran off with."

She said the stripper line like she had heard it a hundred times. Sarah reached up and rubbed Trish's back. "Tonight when you get to your room give me a wave so I know everything's okay."

Trish nodded her head. The two walked back towards their

homes, hand in hand. Trish rested her head on Sarah's shoulder as they drew nearer to her home. Dark was setting in, and the streetlights popped on. They walked slowly down the center of the dirt road that ran through the park.

They embraced each other one last time before they parted. When Sarah got home, her parents were in the kitchen hustling to get dinner on the table. Her mother set out spaghetti, and her father laid out a loaf of garlic bread. She was hanging her head, eating slowly and quietly.

"What did people say about the flower toes?" her mom asked. Sarah didn't answer she just shrugged her shoulders. "Darlin'?" her mom asked, "You okay?"

Sara was so worried about Trish she didn't feel like eating. She picked through her spaghetti then looked at her mother and asked, "Can I go to my room? I don't feel good."

Her dad asked her if she wanted to get out the Bible, which in their house had nothing to do with God. It was an old book which had the words Holy Bible written on the outside, but once it was opened it turned into a chess and checker board. The fake pages were actually drawers, which hid the game pieces. She and her father loved to play with the Bible, and just like the real Bible her father would often hold it in times of crisis and talk to it. The Bible was the only thing he had inherited from his own father, and he cherished it.

After Sarah declined the Bible, her parents knew she wasn't well and allowed her to go to her room. As soon as she was excused she ran to look out her window at Trish's house. It was fully dark. Lightning created the only light between the two trailers. No sign of Trish. At one point, Sarah's mom walked down the hall and knocked. Sarah didn't answer, and her mother moved down the hall to her bedroom. Sarah watched the clock tick by ten, then eleven. She couldn't take it anymore. She decided she had to take action.

She quietly cracked her window, which was just a few feet above ground level, and crept out. She crossed the length between the two trailers and looked in Trish's window. She couldn't see anything. She tapped on the window. No reply.

The bushes behind her rustled and her heart leapt into her throat. She turned quickly to see what was behind her and saw the outline of a man, lit from behind by her parent's porch light.

"You," she whispered loudly and took a step to him. As soon as she reached the bushes he was gone. After seeing the mystery man she knew she was in for a bad night. She had glimpsed the man before. And each time she had something bad happened.

She turned back to the trailer and crouched down. She went to the window at the front of the house. There was the glow of a television in the living room, which doubled as the dining room. There was no separation from the living room to the kitchen, either. It was just a walk-through, and then down the hallway to the rest of the house. She peeked in the window by the door to see Fanny sleeping, sitting up on the couch, surrounded by her dozing mutts. Sarah scanned the room for her friend and saw no sign of her.

She checked the window in Fanny's room, hoping Trish had got in good with her mom and been allowed to sleep in the waterbed in the big bedroom. She crept to the largest room at the back of the trailer and peered over the ledge of the window. Nothing. The waterbed was a mess of blankets and laundry, but no Trish. There wasn't anywhere else to check except the closets. Then she remembered the tiny room meant for a washer and dryer where the dog crates were kept.

Sarah kept to the side of the trailer and crept to the window of the tiny room. The window was very small, no more than a foot wide by two-feet tall. She stretched onto the tips of her toes and looked over the ledge. Her stomach dropped. She had found Trish. She was in a heap at the bottom of one of the locked dog crates. Sarah began tapping the window. Trish stirred and looked up. She could only see the top half of Sarah's face. Sarah was waving frantically. Trish shook her head at her and motioned for her to go away. Sarah shook her head.

Sarah went around to the front room of the house where Fanny was asleep, and quietly opened the door. It creaked as she slowly inched her way in. Once inside she realized that she was only a few feet away from Fanny, who was covered by her dogs. She thought what a disgusting mess they looked, curled up on the couch together. Fanny had tufts of hair all over her. They looked like one giant couch dog.

One of the dogs looked up as if it heard her thoughts. It growled, and the other dogs opened their eyes and lifted their heads. The little mongrel jumped off of Fanny and ran for Sarah with its teeth bared. The tiny fighter was laughable in size. Sarah pulled her foot back and gave the dog a kick that sent it a foot of the ground. It let out a bark, and Sarah was afraid Fanny might jump up. Sarah looked around. There were a lot more beer cans than there had been earlier. Fanny was deep in an alcohol-induced slumber. More dogs were jumping down to see what the fuss was. They ran circles around her, barking. She ignored them and focused on her task. As she walked toward the kitchen Fanny let out a loud groan. Sarah tensed her shoulders, turned and saw that Fanny was still sitting sleeping, mouth wide open. The kicked dog had returned to her lap to lick its wounds. Sarah was cautious, but convinced she would not be heard between Fanny's snores and the blare of the television. She reached the door of the "laundry room" and opened it. Trish still sat in the crate, crying.

"Go away. You shouldn't be here. She'll kill you."

"This is punishment for getting your toes painted?"

"No, I forgot to clean the crate. It was supposed to be done today, and I forgot 'cause we ran out. She said I got to stay here so I know how the dogs feel when they have to sleep in a messy crate."

"That bitch," Sarah said.

"You can't say that about grown-ups. She's right. I shouldn't make the dogs sleep in it. I know better. Go away. Everything will be fine in the morning, I promise. She is always nicer the next day."

"No. Why can't she clean the dog mess?" Sarah was filling a rage. "She likes those darn mutts so much she should clean up after them?"

Sarah had an idea. "Trish can you get to the lock on the outside of that?"

"No, why?"

"Try real hard to get out. I want to see what happens."

Trish reached for the lock and played with it, then pulled it hard. She pulled on other parts of the cage and nothing. Sarah could see it would be impossible to get out.

"Where's the key?"

"On the wall behind you."

Sarah turned around and grabbed the key. She knelt down and unlocked the cage. "Get out Trish. Your mom wants you to know dog mess, and I want her to know dog mess."

"No," Trish moved to the back of the cage.

"I'll do it without you then."

Sarah went to the bathroom and got toilet paper and soap. Trish crawled out after her and watched from the door of the laundry room. Sarah cleaned out the cage, then flushed the rest of the mess down the toilet. She grabbed the dog's messy blanket out of the crate and took it with her to the bathroom. She had Trish follow her, and she instructed her to rinse off and trade clothes.

"This feels wrong. I'm not supposed to disobey my mom," Trish pleaded. "When I say she is going to kill you, I mean it."

Sarah put her forehead to her friend's and stared into her eyes. "Don't worry about me. I'm worried about you. Now wash up."

Trish did as she was told. They went to her room. Sarah was now in the soiled clothing and carrying the doggy blankets. She crawled out the window with Trish and they walked over to her house. Trish stayed on the Davis's porch watching the living room window across the way. She was terrified her mom might wake up. Sarah went in the house and put the soiled clothing and blanket in the washer. She changed her own clothes and came back out with a plate of spaghetti and garlic bread and a can of Coke. The two girls picked at the food and shared the Coke.

"Sarah, I know you think you are doing good, but in the morning it's going to be bad for me. My life is not your life," Trish said. "Sarah, your trailer is the nicest house I ever been in. I've never even had food that tasted this good. You don't know what life's really like in the park. Your family don't live it. You're different."

"You won't be dead in the morning. Your mom's passed out drunk. Just tell her in the morning she threw you in there cause of your painted toes. Tell her you had washed the cage and went to the laundromat yesterday. You don't have a washer. How would you have gotten a clean blanket in there?"

"Huh," she said. "You're smart. I never thought that's why she's so nice in the morning. She's sober. Sarah, you're a good friend, but I want to tell you I say nasty things about your family, too. Everybody does it. I'm so sorry. You all never been nothing but kind, and I'm just a coward. I do what people tell me."

"It's okay," Sarah said, and she wrapped her arm around Trish. They stayed on the porch until the laundry was done and they swapped their clothes back. They snuck Trish into the house, and Sarah locked her back in her cage.

Morning played out exactly as Sarah had predicted, and Trish and her mother woke on good terms.

When Sarah reflected on that day she wished she had done more for Trish. She should have told her parents what had happened, or a teacher at school. Sarah's family moved away shortly after that incident, and she fell out of contact with her trailer park friends. She thought of how her life had changed. She never sat at a gas station going through scratch offs ever again. The kids in her new neighborhood had very different ways to pass time, like music lessons and swimming. Sarah changed when she moved out of poverty, but she never forgot about Trish and the people in the park. It was the same town, but a different world.

She was still staring at her ceiling, and a nagging thought popped into her head. I had seen my mystery man in the bushes that night. If John was there the whole time, why hadn't he helped me? Or had he?

CHAPTER 9

After just a few hours of sleep, Sarah had to get up for work. Her head ached, but her mind felt different. If she were to put a name on the feeling it would be hopefulness. She wondered if she had dreamed the previous day. She looked out her window and saw the steam rolling over the sidewalk from the manhole covers. The city appeared as it always did.

She went to the bathroom, and perched on the side of her tub was the expensive shampoo. She smiled.

She used her new shampoo that morning and it made her hair shiny and bright, out of place with her dull clothing. She put on her best turquoise-colored blouse; the edges around the sleeves were threadbare, and the khakis she wore in rotation with her black pants were starting to wear around the knees. She put her name badge over her shirt and let her dark, flowing locks hang loose. For the first time in years they weren't spoiled by frizz.

Her steps were lighter as she made her way out that morning. She strolled casually to the family court building, stopping for coffee and waving at everybody she passed.

She arrived at the mammoth-sized building and took the steps two at a time. She walked between the oversized columns that ran the length of the building and through the heavy oak doors.

The neo-classical building had soaring twenty-foot ceilings in the lobby, and the courtrooms were furnished with marble floors and gleaming chandeliers. The building was regal and formal. Walking into the lobby would have felt like going to a gala if it weren't for the modern additions: big white printed signs saying to check your cell phone at the desk and eight-foot tall metal detectors just inside the entrance.

The line of people waiting to be scanned at the metal detector flowed out the door. Sarah walked past the line up to the guard who checked her badge and sent her through ahead of everybody waiting. She asked the guard how long the docket was as he rummaged through her bag.

"By the looks of this line," he said. "It's going to be a long day."

His search of her bag was half-hearted, and he quickly moved it aside to grab another one.

Sarah checked the docket with the receptionist and saw she was scheduled for M Court on the third floor. She took the elevator up and saw there was already a line to check in. The guard had been right: it was going to be a long day.

After making her way through the line, she signed the sheet the bailiff kept at his desk to check-in for her case. With several names above her, she walked down the hall and grabbed a newspaper out of one of the machines. Then she went back to the waiting room and found a corner seat.

She was there to give testimony about what she had observed the day before with Darrius and Carol, and to assure the court they were safely place in a temporary foster home. She started to read the paper, but couldn't concentrate. Her mind was on John. She wondered if a magical ring could be real. Everything about the night before seemed surreal. She wondered if there was some other way he could know about Trish.

She let her mind wander to the possibilities of the ring. She looked at the people filing into the waiting room. These were people in peril. Most of them were represented by public defenders. Many of them had either lost their children or were on the verge of losing them. Many of the defendants called to this court had drug problems. Most of the adults involved in her caseload had had a drug problem at one point in their lives. When she looked closer she saw that the drug problems stemmed from life problems. She wondered if she would be able to really fix their life problems. If she would be able to go back in their lives and fix things before they went so wrong.

Her thoughts were interrupted when she saw Ruth scanning the room for a seat. When her eyes fell on Sarah, she made a beeline for her.

"Girl, where the hell have you been?" Ruth said in a loud whisper. "I called you and called you last night."

"My phone got wet. It's not working, sorry."

"You betta get a new one. Yolanda is trippin'. She said you didn't check your messages this morning. You check with me when we get to the lobby, ehh?"

"Yes, ma'am," Sarah said with a salute.

"Now, girl, what did you do last night?" Sarah had hoped she wouldn't ask. She didn't want to lie. She thought carefully about how to frame the truth in the right way. She also wanted to tell Ruth where she would be over the weekend so Ruth could look out for her. She decided to get it out really quickly.

"Well, my phone actually got wet last night because I was trying to help this old guy. I helped him, and he asked for more help this weekend, but I felt kind of weird about being at his house without somebody knowing where I was, so I really want to give you his information so that if something happens to me you can tell police where I was."

Ruth was raised one eyebrow and stared at Sarah as she passed her the IDs.

"What!" Ruth said loud enough for the whole room to hear. "Have you lost your damn mind? What are you talking about?"

"I just wanted to help this guy, but this younger guy lives there and I didn't think I should be alone with two men without somebody knowing where I am."

Ruth looked at the IDs, furrowed her brow and looked up at Sarah. "I know this man, this be John. He works at the Phillies Diner. I see his zip code, and I say to meself, 'How does this man live in this neighborhood?' What's going on, girl?"

"I can't say yet, Ruth. But I really am going to help this man."

"Why is he workin' at a diner? Look me in the eye, child."

"It's a long story."

Ruth sucked her teeth while she waited for more information. When Sarah offered nothing she looked down at the pages and said, "I'll take your IDs. I'll tell the police if you don't check in, but don't you lie to me, girl. If this ain't on the up and up I want to know. Somebody has got to look out for you."

"I'll tell you more after I know more," Sarah promised.

The DHS lawyer walked in and sat next to Sarah and Ruth. "I just got checked in. We should be called soon. Let's talk about

51

Darrius and Carol."

Sarah explained what she knew from the day before and asked Mr. Trent what happened with their mother and the grandmother, Rosa Lee.

Ruth chimed in. "Oh that lady called this morning. She said she would come today. She might be here." Sarah went to the bailiff and asked if anybody else had signed in with him on the Holt case. He said that a Rosa had. She turned her attention back to the waiting room and called, "Rosa." A tiny woman hidden by the crowd raised her hand. She had shockingly thin features. She was wearing a floral tank top that displayed her sharp shoulder and chest bones, and tangerine colored short shorts. Her clothes were falling off of her and completely mismatched to her age and size. Her knees were the most prominent part of her legs, and the rest of her skin was tight to her bones. Her cheekbones jutted out, creating extreme angles, and her hair was wiry and thin. She was continuously sucking her lips and making a guttural sound in the back of her throat.

"Are you Linda's mother?" Sarah asked.

"That's me," the woman said. Sarah could see that she only had two withered teeth left in her mouth, one on the top and one on the bottom. They were opposite each other. Sarah was sure from her appearance that she was a drug addict. Sarah waved for the lawyer and Ruth to come over.

The lawyer introduced himself as Mr. Trent and waved at her. Ruth stepped forward and shook the woman's hand. Then she bent close to her and whispered, "Girl, you using today?" The woman made the guttural noise, flared her nostrils and said, "No, I don't use. I'm too old to use."

"Girl," Ruth said. "You been usin'. I'm not your judge, and I ain't no cop. But you should get you in order before you come here. We take you to lunch today, ehh, get you a meal."

The woman shook her head. "I'm here to get my grandkids. Kids belong with family no matter what."

Sarah, Ruth, and Mr. Trent exchanged a look. Ruth excused herself and motioned for the other two to follow her into the hallway.

"She's not a viable placement option." Mr. Trent said. "We're going to have to push for continued placement. Let's ask the judge to order a drug test if she wants to push this."

Sarah asked, "What about the grandfather? Where is he?"

"All we have in the file is that his name was Kirby. We can't find any records of him after 1964. I looked around, checked court documents. There's nothing. He just vanished. There's nobody else in the family, just Rosa Lee, Kirby, and Linda. There's no dad listed on either birth certificate."

"Shouldn't we try harder to find him? Didn't the police ever look into his disappearance?" Sarah asked.

Before anybody could reply, the bailiff called their case, and they were ushered into the courtroom. Sarah and Mr. Trent sat at the table next to each other, and at the other end sat Rosa Lee and the court advocate assigned to the children. The advocate whispered a few words to Rosa Lee and when she whispered back he shook his head. Ruth sat at the back of the court in the observation seating.

The judge walked into the room and the bailiff asked all in the room to rise, and shortly afterwards started hearing the case.

Mr. Trent pleaded his case that the kids should stay removed from parent custody and he moved that the court should seek to terminate parent rights. The advocate wanted Rosa Lee to be named the children's guardian.

Mr. Trent said, "We have reason to believe that Rosa Lee Holt is using narcotics, and we move that before she proceeds with any custody plea that she be given a drug test."

Rosa Lee jumped up and raised her thin arm and tiny fist to yell, "I'll take your drug test, and get my grandkids. You racist. You think because I'm black I'm usin'? That's racist, you son of a bitch."

The judge pounded his gavel. "Sit down, Ms. Holt. You cannot act like that in a court of law, and based on your history I know you have some experience with the courts. Another outburst like that and you can wait in the hall. Further, I'm ordering a drug test."

"Good," she snorted. "That will shut up the racist pigs on the other side of the table."

"Madam," the judge said. "This is my final warning, stop shouting." Her advocate reached over, put a hand on her shoulder and whispered in her ear. She nodded and sat back in her chair.

"I am ordering you to be tested today, within one hour of these proceedings. The lab is on the second floor of this building in the East Hallway. The bailiff will give you directions and orders to take to the window. If you do not take this test within an hour I will consider its results invalid."

Rosa Lee jumped up and pushed her chair into the table. "This is bullshit," she yelled. "Why am I being treated like a criminal? I don't need fuckin' court. I got people who can find my babies for me. I don't need you sons a bitches."

Sarah rarely took notice of an outburst in court, where emotions always ran high, but she was taken aback by this outburst from Rosa Lee. The woman did not look as if she had that much fight left in her fragile body. Rosa Lee stomped out the door and Ruth scurried behind her. Her screams could be heard up and down the hallway. Finally, court resumed with the judge asking for information on the children's location. Sarah gave the court the information and testified that they were currently safe and could remain where they were until the next hearing in ninety days. It was the last case before the judge adjourned for lunch.

When Sarah left the courtroom she found Ruth waiting for her, hands on hips.

"Poor woman," Ruth said.

"Where'd you guys go?"

"To the lobby. I bought her a cup of coffee. We sat and talked. She's not takin' the drug test. She too proud to say she'd fail it. Better to be crazy than an addict."

"What can we do?" Sarah asked.

"She said she can get clean for her grandbabies," Ruth said. "Let's give her a little time to try." Ruth opened her phone and started to punch in some numbers.

"What are you doing?" Sarah asked.

Ruth rolled her eyes and replied, "I'm gonna pick her up Sunday and take her to the clinic."

"Aww," Sarah said. "You softie."

"Bah," Ruth replied without looking up. "Don't tell anybody. I got a reputation to keep up."

It was moments like this which made Sarah want to be more like Ruth.

They walked to the lobby and Ruth let Sarah check her messages on her phone. Her boss had been calling all morning. A lot of paperwork was due and she needed assurances it would be done by the end of the day. Sarah looked defeated; she knew she was going to be busy that afternoon.

"Why doesn't she call you and leave nasty messages and check up on your paperwork?" Sarah asked a Ruth.

"Because I don't put up with it. You act a pushover," Ruth said.

"I'm not a pushover," Sarah said bluntly.

"You don't need to prove it to me, girl. Where I come from we say certain people are lions, strong and proud. You're a lion, but a different kind of lion than where I am from. You are a cheery lion and nobody knows what to make of that. Nobody around here has ever seen a cheery lion. We need to get you to roar, little lion, so everybody knows what you're made of."

"Thank you. I will put that in your list of quotes, cheery lion." Sarah said smiling. Sarah kept a running list of island-related quotes from Ruth on the fabric board in her office. It was titled *Island Knowledge*, and when they needed a break they often went over the board of quotes for a laugh.

Sarah and Ruth continued outside and went to a street vendor for a hot dog. They walked around the fountains in front of the art museum, which was across from the courthouse, and ate their hot dogs together.

They stopped to watch the water and Ruth asked, "So what're you going to do with the Holt babies?"

"Change the plan. I'm going to see if the mom might be suitable in the future. Maybe ask for a continuance until she can get herself in order. I'll talk to the adoption coordinator this afternoon, after I finish Yolanda's paperwork."

She was lost in thought for a moment and then looked back at Ruth. "I really want to do right by them, Ruth."

"You'll do right by them. Have faith in yourself. You wish to do well, so you will," Ruth said. A young man holding a messenger bag walked by Ruth and bumped her. Ruth lifted her purse. She turned quick as a flash and grabbed the man by his bag. She pulled the bag to her, held her elbow to the man's throat and shouted, "Give me back my damn wallet." The man gasped for air and reached into his bag. He shakily handed over a light snakeskin wallet.

"You damn fool, get a job," she shouted and took her elbow out of his throat. After he took a breath, he ran away.

"He thought I might be an easy target, older woman, well dressed. He picked the wrong woman, baby."

"Are you okay?" Sarah asked.

"Fine," Ruth said. "I hate when people go looking for a handout. Damn fool. He's lucky I let him off easy. He made me drop my hot dog."

"Why don't you just keep your wallet in your pocket? You know it's harder for them to rob you that way."

"Hell no. This is designer. I bought it to show it off. If people want to steal that be their problem. You can live your life around the thief. I'm not."

They walked in silence to the tech store and then parted ways. Ruth had to get back to court and Sarah had to buy a new phone. When the new phone was activated and caught its first signal, Sarah called Winthrop and made plans for him to pick her up later that evening.

She went about her day doing paperwork and left her office on time for the first time since she had taken her job. Ruth was still there and made a face at her as she got up to leave. Ruth was on the phone so she couldn't ask questions. Sarah even left some paperwork in her inbox for next week, including Darrius and Carol's permanency plan. Ruth pointed to it; Sarah shrugged her shoulders and rushed to the elevator.

CHAPTER 10

When Sarah got home she put her day behind her and turned her mind to thoughts of the ring and John. She changed out of her work clothes and slid into a pair of jeans and twist-front top. She ran a brush through her hair and put a bit of gel in the front to give it life again. For the first time in weeks she patted a bit of foundation on her rosy cheeks and used a light coat of mascara on her lashes. She quickly threw together a bag, and ran for the stairs.

She was excited, but a part of her wondered if Winthrop would really be waiting for her. When she got to door of the building she saw him, right where he said he would be, and her heart skipped a beat. He was holding open the rear door of the town car. He had a warm smile on his face. She hoped her neighbors saw the display. She remembered that his license identified him as Addicus so she playfully said, "Thank you, Addicus," as she jumped into the back seat.

He winced. "I actually prefer Winthrop. I believe Winthrop, if possible, is less pretentious than Addicus."

He closed the door and went to the front to get behind the wheel.

"So you have issues with being pretentious, but you drive a Town Car to your boss's mansion. Are you John's son or nephew or something?" Sarah asked.

"Of those choices I will go with 'or something,'" said Winthrop.

"That's vague."

"It's complicated how I know John, but he is dear to me."

"Well if you won't talk about it, will you tell me, is the ring real?"

"Absolutely, yes."

"Why would John go through all the trouble of finding a successor to it if he knows you? Why not just give it to you?"

"That is a fair question," he said. He followed up with nothing.

"Not talking much today, huh, Winthrop?"

"I like to talk. It's just a long, unpleasant story. I don't really want to get into it today. But don't worry. I'm sure John will fill you in. He loves to tell stories. He is free to tell them where I don't have to hear them." There was nothing angry in Winthrop's tone. He was very matter of fact.

"So do you have a nickname or anything I can call you other than Winthrop? How about Winnie?"

"I have never gone by a shorter name. Winnie reminds me too much of a cartoon bear."

"How about Win?" she asked.

"If you must shorten my name, Win will suffice."

They rode the rest of the way in silence. Sarah stared out the window as they left the skyscrapers and concrete of the city and entered the tree-lined neighborhood where John lived. Sarah watched Winthrop drive and thought he was handsome. She found herself squinting at his ring finger. He definitely wasn't wearing a wedding band, but she was too far away to see if there was a tan line. He caught her staring, and she pretended to yawn.

When they arrived at the house John was waiting by the door.

"Marvelous! Now we can eat, drink, be merry, and learn a few things along the way."

"Marvelous," Sarah echoed.

Who says marvelous anymore? She wondered.

She threw her backpack over her shoulder and followed John into the house. Winthrop gently slid his arm through the strap of the backpack and tugged it off of her shoulder.

"Let me get that for you," he offered.

The foyer was cold with white walls and silver-flecked marble floors.

Winthrop disappeared down the hallway that led to the room where she had washed up the night before, and John came over to her with a tape measure in his hand. He wrapped the tape gently around her wrist.

"Six and a half," he said.

Sarah was perplexed. "What are you doing?"

"I am having you fitted."

"I thought that what you had was a ring?" She questioned.

"Oh, it is, but it's far too small to fit on a finger, and you would not want it there, besides. To keep it on one's skin at all times is absolute folly."

Winthrop walked back in the room, and John said, "Six and a half. Tell Petrov."

John then held out his arm for Sarah to take. They walked together down the center of his house passing a two-story entertaining room off of the foyer. It was filled with overwhelmingly beige furniture accented with dark brown rugs and pillows. It looked like the type of room you saw in an architectural magazine but that nobody actually used. To the right was his dining room, which, like the rest of the house, was overdone. The exterior wall was lined with highly arched windows; the walls were white-paneled wood in oversized squares. The ceiling was recessed; the inner most panels accented with light-gold-filigree. The centerpiece of the room was an elaborate many-tiered chandelier. The long, dark wooden table had seats for twelve but it was made up for three, with shining white dishes, the edges of which were laced with gold. Covered silver serving dishes sat on a sideboard and another covered dish rested on a dark wooden breakfast bar along the back wall. Sarah took a mental note to appreciate the grandeur of the moment. She had never been in a house so nice and had never dined in a formal dining room or eaten off of fine china. Earlier that morning she was dodging pickpockets and eating hot dogs in the park.

"Do you have a cook?" she asked.

"I do, but I have sent her and the rest of the staff home for the weekend so that we can have some privacy. We may see the gardeners tomorrow, but no staff in the house."

He motioned for her to take a seat, and Winthrop entered the room behind them. Once seated, Sarah noticed she was underdressed. Winthrop and John were wearing suits with ties. She was wearing jeans with a wrap top from Target. She suddenly felt out of place.

"Well," John said. "Let's dig in."

John and Winthrop grabbed their dishes and walked to the sideboard. When John removed the lids of the serving dishes, steam rolled out and the scent of spiced lamb filled the air. Sarah looked at the food, which was more or less identifiable. The second dish uncovered looked like snails; she bypassed that completely. The next was almost unidentifiable; it looked like potatoes but smelled like fish. Next was something that resembled white asparagus covered in a chunky sauce. The men filled their plates to the edges. Sarah followed along behind them, placing smaller portions on her plate. She didn't want to leave a lot on her plate if she didn't like it. When they returned to the table John and Win placed their napkins in their laps and Sarah followed suit. John played host, giving each of them a glass of red wine, though she never drank.

"We will dine here this evening," said John. "But tomorrow I would like us to go to the Country Club for brunch. Do you have something to wear there?"

Sarah realized that John was eyeing her underdressed state and felt defensive.

"I have nice things, John. I just thought we were staying at your house. Why dress up?"

"Oh, this time period we live in," he said. "It used to be you looked nice just for the sake of it. I see people wearing sweatpants on planes today. Sweatpants. I can hardly believe it."

"I own a pair of sweatpants, too," Sarah said, then took a hearty bite.

"I am sorry if I offended you, my dear. I was merely saying we could arrange for clothing if you need anything. You look lovely. I will withdraw my comment; it was inappropriate."

"So let's talk instead about why I am here. Reason number two, if I remember correctly, you did something wrong."

He hung his head, and let out all of the air he had been holding. After a moment he took a deep breath and started. "Yes, it's time to talk business. When I first got the ring I held onto it for a number of years. I dabbled with it a bit; requesting a sports car here, a gold watch there. These items showed up instantly. There was no lead time. The ring did not ask for specifics. You say you want James Bond's Aston Martin and the damn thing lands right in front of you, no questions. It was a fun trinket, but I learned quickly that the ring was too powerful to use cavalierly, and you can't keep it touching your skin. If one part of it makes contact with you, whatever is in your head comes to be.

"You could destroy many lives with one errant thought. It asks for no clarification on your thoughts. I only tested it a few times before tucking it away, scared of its power. I accidentally destroyed an entire wing of my home once. And let me tell you, destroying something is easy, but nothing can be so easily rebuilt. It only does things within your scope of understanding. You can't, for example just ask it to build a room for you. You must picture every nail, every board. If you don't have the knowledge to build a room, it will just be walls which will fall if unsupported. This I will explain in more detail when I tell you the rules of the ring. We will practice before I ever ask you to touch it.

"But, back to the point. When I was well into my forties I had forgotten about my magical trinket. I should have left it that way. It was tucked away in a vault where I intended for it to stay forever. However, I found myself at the beginning of what you call a midlife crisis. I found religion and started thinking about how frivolously I had spent my youth. I thought I owed it to the world to do something better with this gift of mine.

"The trouble began when I put my thoughts into action. I took the ring from its vault and attached it to a charm on a chain, making a necklace, which could be opened like a locket. I had already learned not to let it touch my skin directly without intention. I purchased a police radio and started to listen to reports of robberies and murders. I listened intently, awaiting an opportunity to start doing good with the ring."

John paused and smiled. "I was quite ridiculous, you know. I only knew what I had seen on television. I dressed in black trousers and a black sweater and placed a dark cap on my head. One night the scanner let out an alert. A silent alarm had been tripped at a bank. It was a bank that I used, so I knew the layout of it. I opened the clasp on my necklace touched the ring and thought for it to take me to the vault inside the bank. In that instant the vault came up around me, and there I was. When you ask the ring to take you somewhere, it's like time and space wrap around you. You don't go anywhere; the earth pops up under your feet.

"I arrived in the vault and found a well-dressed man stuffing bills from the shelves into a case. He was alone and took no notice of my arrival. He stuffed frantically, whipping around the room without stopping to take stock of what he was stealing. When I made a move toward him he saw me and startled. His face showed no anger. His look was one of terror, which took me by surprise. He asked who I was and how I had gotten there. I said nothing. I thought about handcuffs and tapped the ring. The man's arms slammed together and cuffs materialized to hold him. The man shouted with pain and when he regained his composure he asked me what had happened. I remained silent and tapped the ring to close the vault door. I left him in there bound with a look of bewilderment on his face, and then I thought of my home and tapped the ring again.

"When I was safely home I danced around my apartment, thrilled with myself for my daring feat. I ran to the scanner to hear how the events played out. The police arrived to find the man trapped, it was amazing. For a moment. I made plans to do more fantastic deeds on a grander scale.

"I continued to watch for stories of the man. I learned that his name was Harold and he was a clerk at the bank. His ruin played out in the papers, and I found out there was a lot more to his story than that one robbery.

"Harold's luck was out before he ever met me. He was in a great deal of trouble after a bad run of luck in Atlantic City. He had racked up a lot of debt. Casino owners were not like they are today. They would make you a loan, and if you did not pay they reacted with violence. I soon learned Harold had a wife and daughter that were discovered missing after his arrest and within a week they were both found bound and murdered, their bodies washed up on the shore, near to the casino he was indebted to. Heaven knows what else happened to them. In those days the paper did not tell you all the details like they do today. I was tormented by nightmares of what they must have endured. Harold, you see, intended to pay back his loans, save his family, and thereafter sacrifice his own freedom. I intervened and ruined... ruined so much."

John backed his chair away from the table. He had not touched his food during his story. He reached for his napkin and wiped away a tear.

Sarah asked, "Why didn't you just go back and stop yourself?"

"It seems this can't be done. I have tried every which way to go back and undo the events of that day. First, I tried to go back to the time of the incident, after Harold was in the vault alone and tied up. Once I was sure the previous copy of me had gone I freed him from his restraints and got him out of the building, but the police caught up with him shortly thereafter. I tried to go back and get him farther away from the scene, but the ring would not allow it. That is how I learned that I couldn't visit the same moment in time twice.

"I keep a notebook of all of my travels so that I might always remember where I have been and know where I cannot visit again. I have found that I can change that which happened prior to the event. I tried to go into Harold's past and undo his gambling problem. I found that with each attempt to help I ruined him even faster. I went to his past in as many points as I could before his entire history was dotted with my attempts to undo his fate. I could no longer go back without interfering with something else I had done. With each journey to the past I made the future worse, for all of us.

"I learned through this folly that the future is very hard to change in the way you would like. Many people, when they speak of time travel, talk of branches, where the future you change sets off a whole new branch of an alternate future. That is not the case. Time is more like a rope, a rope tightly set with a beginning and end."

He stood up quickly and walked to the drapes. He unfastened one of the golden ropes holding back the fabric and ran back to the table. He held it up horizontally with two hands. "First, the ring can take you no further than you have already been," he shook his right hand. "It will not take you to the future or to tomorrow, only to the past and the present. So, in one hand is the past and in the other is our current reality." He moved his left hand up and said, "See? I just changed the past but look what happened to now. It stayed the same. It is actually very hard to move the present. It can be rotated, it can be pulled a little forward and back, but to really move it takes a great deal of force." He pulled his left hand very hard and the rope popped out of his right hand and left a red mark in his right palm.

"The only way I have found to jar our current reality enough to make a great change is to take or save a life."

Sarah said, "But no life was taken in the past. Harold's wife and daughter were murdered in your present. It was probably going to happen anyway. Even if you hadn't bound him, the police were on their way. He was probably never going to get out. It sounds like your intervention mattered very little when it came to Harold."

John shook his head. "There is more to the story. As I said, I kept going to Harold's past. And while I could not change his fate I inadvertently changed it for many others. While I was in his past I got wrapped up trying to help him. I enlisted other people to try to set him on the correct path. One day when I was following Harold he attended a small church service. It was a service held by a man I had known from my own past, named Jim. I met Jim when he and I were both eager young volunteers at a place called the Divine Hotel. He was a very memorable man, tall and handsome. I thought he looked rather like a movie star. We both worked for the owner of the hotel, Father Divine. Divine was a good man, renowned for his generosity. I was so fond of Divine that I helped fund his church. When I realized that Harold was very nearly involved in Jim's small church, I thought..." John stopped speaking.

Sarah asked, "You thought what, John?"

"Well it made me wonder at the coincidence of such a thing. That I would run into Jim again. It was almost unbelievable. I tell you now the ring tries to set things right by coincidence. If something seems familiar or preordained, the ring pulls at you like a living thing, trying to steer you in the right direction. I can't explain it, but when you feel it you will know."

"So," Sarah said, "you thought this meeting with Jim was one of these moments where the ring was trying to steer you in the right direction after you went in the wrong direction. When do you think you went in the wrong direction?"

"I had given a great deal of money to Divine, assuring his dominance as a religious leader. But Jim had wanted to grow out from Divine's shadow and start his own church. I thought my actions in funding Father Divine had hindered Jim. The more I learned about Jim, the more I thought he was the key to Harold's salvation. He was charismatic and optimistic. His ideas for the future seemed so bright, and I was seduced by his words and his mission. I would be the first of many."

"I know the Divine," Sarah said. "I was just there yesterday. Do you believe that is too much of a coincidence, too?"

"It is," he smiled and reached across the table to hold her hand. "And it does not surprise me a bit. But the place you know to be the Divine Hotel is not what I knew it to be. It was very different in my day and in my reality. This is why I need you. It's not Harold who I am worried about now; it's the Divine. I'm convinced, as you said, that Harold's fate was sealed before my involvement. My actions that night were superfluous. But my actions with Jim and the Divine are unforgivable."

Nobody was eating anymore. The food had grown cold. Winthrop was watching, clinging to every word. She knew he must have heard this story before, but he was still listening intently to it again. "Go on, John. What happened?" Sarah prodded.

"I started going to underground meetings headed by Jim. I would sit on the edge of my seat listening to his sermons and theories on the world. I was sure that Jim was important to history and very afraid that my money had tampered with his success. I used the ring to visit the present and see what had become of him, and I was very disappointed.

I took a trip into Philadelphia to see what happened to Jim's followers. In the reality I knew, the Divine Hotel was still up and running. It was a jewel of the community surrounded by beautiful homes and shops. The empty lot next to it was a community rose garden, to honor of the late Reverend Divine's wife. The area was a favorite destination of tourists. The people of the church kept the streets safe, the homeless fed, and the neighborhood surrounding it peaceful."

This was a far cry from the Divine Sarah knew. She knew it to be one of the most dangerous areas of Philadelphia. "I've only ever known the Divine as it is today. I can see hints of its former grandeur."

"As I said, time is a rope. You were at the end when I intervened and pulled so hard that this new reality is where you have all now been set. You would never know it as anything else. Nobody would, except me. When I arrived at the Divine Church headquarters, I purchased a booklet on its history. Jim was a blip in the church's past. He was mentioned on one page; his name was mixed in with hundreds of others involved in the church during the civil rights movement. It took much more digging to learn that Jim and his movement had been crushed by Divine, for reasons unknown to me and his followers. Jim's small congregation was left aimless. Jim died young and that was the last of him. Harold and many others never joined the larger church and they found themselves without direction.

Many failed lives came after Jim's church faded out. This is when I decided to get involved.

"After months of observation and seeing how my money had steered Divine to more power I was convinced that I had unduly enriched Divine, and ruined Jim. I decided to even the scales and give Jim the same amount of money I had given Divine. It took me but a moment to learn that I had just made the biggest mistake of my life."

"Jim's movement was rightly crushed, I would find. The ideas I had heard were just a fraction of what Jim had planned for society. Once he had the freedom to pursue all of his beliefs, he turned to extremes. The moment I gifted him the money, the earth shook under my feet. I was tossed head over heels far into the air. There was no way to orient myself and no way to tell which way was up or down. I reached for the ring hanging from my neck for help and it burned me like a hot coal. In my panic I dug at the air trying to discern my direction, but before I could, I landed on my back in a dump, cushioned by mounds of garbage. I lay there for a time, my hand seething with pain." John held up his hand and there was a tiny circular scar burned into his left palm near his thumb.

"What happened?" Sarah asked.

"I had returned to a world I did not know. I changed the course of history so much the ring threw me to my new reality. I think it sought to kill me."

Sarah thought it was odd that he talked about the ring as if it were a living thing.

He continued. "I was mortified by my first look at the new Philadelphia. Poverty had grown; slums outnumbered the green spaces I had known. The Divine was a ruin. Today it would be easy to find out about Jim. Everybody knows his name. I am saddened to say even you will know it. Jim Jones."

Sarah put her hand over her mouth and gasped. "Jonestown, the cult."

"Yes, Sarah. My gift to him enabled him to found his own temple and with it he started a colony of followers. It seemed like a utopia until 1978. He convinced over 900 of his followers, including women and children, to drink Kool-Aid laced with poison and in his name and kill themselves. The pictures of the bodies, clinging to each other in their final moments just …"

John bent over and sobbed so hard his body shook. Winthrop stood and went to him. He bent down and whispered into John's ear. John nodded his head, and Winthrop said, "I'm going to put John to bed."

CHAPTER 11

Sarah went to her room to digest the information she'd just heard. She changed into yoga pants and a tank top, then sat at the edge of the bed. She noticed her nightstand held stacks of books about the Jonestown Massacre. She guessed that John or Winthrop must have put them there for her to study. There was also a spiral-bound notebook with a blue faded cover and yellow pages worn heavily around the edges. It was a Harvard Square notebook imprinted with a price of 29 cents. She flipped it open and saw that the first half of the book was a series of dates and times. Behind that was a series of handwritten notes. There was a divider, and the second half of the book was a long list of names. She counted twenty-four lines per page and almost fifty sheets filled in with names: first middle and last. Some had checks next to them; some had nothing. She guessed this must be a list of John's escapades with the ring and the people he had tried to help. She flipped through the pages quickly until she saw one familiar last name, but a first name she had never seen. "Winthrop, Ambrose." It had two checks next to it. It was the only name with two checks.

There was a gentle knock at her door before it was eased open. It was Winthrop, the one she knew. She snapped the book shut and looked up at him.

"I couldn't eat through any of that," he said. "It was a waste of food, really. I put everything away except the pie. Would you like to share some with me in the kitchen?"

"Sure," Sarah said. She noticed Winthrop had changed into navy silk pajamas. He seemed less regal now. His walk was even more casual. The lights in the house were turned down. The floors and walls were still shining, but everything seemed softer. She and Winthrop walked past the dining room, she in bare feet, and he wearing slippers. She could feel the cold of the marble floors as she followed him through the great halls. She thought people with marble floors must know to wear slippers. She followed him to a gourmet kitchen just past the dining room. It had a granite island in the middle and an oversized stainless steel refrigerator with a matching stove. The cabinets were dark cherry, and there were cherry stools at the island. She took a seat on a stool and Winthrop served her a piece of pecan pie with a fork and glass of milk, and then took the stool opposite her.

"If John's story is true, it's very sad," Sarah said.

"It is true, and it is sad," said Winthrop.

"But the one thing I don't get is if John came back to this time, and he didn't know any of what had happened before, what happened to the John who had been living in the world all that time? Did he just vanish?"

"I don't know. At different points in time John has come to me and asked what he has been doing, and I sometimes recall that he left just a few seconds before, and other times I don't recall him leaving."

"Well, what happens if, say, John had come back from the Divine and in the new reality he didn't have the ring so he never left? Would there be two of him?"

He looked lost in thought, "I suppose it's plausible."

"Wow," she said. "You guys really don't know much about this thing."

He smiled at her. "We know quite a bit, but certain things we have agreed not to test."

There were a few moments of silence when they both took a bite at the same time. Sarah was uneasy with the silence, and quickly gulped down her food so she could end it.

"Do you live here with John?" Sarah asked.

"I do."

Sarah waited for him to elaborate. And he didn't.

"If I can't talk to you about your relationship with John, can I ask what's with the way you and John got me here? Why the secrecy and the gate closing and you know, just generally trapping me?"

"You followed John. He didn't follow you, and you were never trapped. John was planning to talk to you soon. He was just waiting until the time was right."

"He should have talked to me sooner."

"You might have written him off as crazy."

She let out a chuckle.

"What?"

"I still think he might be crazy," Sarah said.

"He's a nice man and not at all crazy. He has done so much for me," Win said.

"Like what?" she asked.

"Like he took me in when I lost my parents."

"What happened to your parents?" she asked.

"I don't want to talk about it. Do you want to talk about your parents?"

She thought back to the last day she saw her mom. Upside down strapped into a car filling with water. "I saw John the day I lost my parents," she whispered. "Did he tell you about it?"

He nodded.

"Why didn't he save them?"

"Everything you just heard," he said. "You can't interfere. You don't know what will happen, and if he had he might have lost you."

Her eyes started to fill with tears. "I don't want to talk about my parents either."

He agreed.

She asked, "What did John see in my past that made him think that I was the person he was looking for?"

"He said that you were happy even when you shouldn't be. And you helped people when you didn't have the power to do so. He said you made your own power."

"Cheery lion," she whispered.

"What?"

"Nothing. It's just a joke a friend and I share. I have a question because I am just having trouble picturing it. How long did John really work at that diner?"

With a smile Win said, "A year."

"Why would he do that to himself?' she asked.

"It was a way to stay close to you. He said you were there more predictably than anywhere else."

She thought about that and realized he couldn't visit her at work because of security. Her cheeks flushed with embarrassment when she realized he was right. "That's horrible. As soon as I am done with this pie I'm going to start eating better."

Win chuckled, took a large bite of pie and said, "I make no such vow."

"So what do you do? Are you a butler or something?"

He nearly spit out his pie, "No, I'm not a butler. I do these things for John with matters pertaining to the ring. I help him look in on our friends affected by it. We keep tabs on all of the people that John could find that he wronged with the ring. You will find a notebook of those people in your room. But as to what I do for a living, I am trained as an attorney, and John realizes he is keeping me away from my profession. Therefore, he keeps me on a generous retainer."

She took a bite and sat in thought for a moment. "What do you do for fun, things that have absolutely nothing to do with John? Like, do you watch movies?"

"Of course I watch movies. Do you watch movies?"

"Of course," She said copying his tone. "It's a fair question for you though, Win. You act so hoity-toity I thought maybe you just sit in a rocking chair at night smoking a pipe and listening to a gramophone or something."

He pulled a napkin to his face to catch milk dribble. "No, I watch movies just like other people. We have some here. John has a screening room downstairs, but it's late to open that up tonight."

She was not interested in staying up late either. "What do you watch?"

"Old stuff, like Westerns."

They continued eating in silence and then he finally thought to ask her, "What kind of movies do you like?"

"Now that I think about it, half of the movies that I own involve time travel. *The Time Machine, Back to the Future, Somewhere in Time,* and even *Terminator.* I have other movies too; mostly comedies, but I watch the time travel ones a lot."

"I know," Win said. "John thought that was interesting, too. He felt it was a sign."

"If you knew, why'd you ask?"

"I wanted to be polite and make conversation. It's probably less creepy if I actually know things about you from you and not from John."

She agreed. "Next time I tell you something you already know, act surprised please."

"I shall do that," he said.

"Also, you're too polite. Work on that," she said standing and placing her plate in the sink. "Good night," she called over her shoulder, and left the kitchen.

CHAPTER 12

The next morning Sarah was awakened by the sound of a doorbell. She had no wish to crawl out of the luxurious bed. At home she slept on a worn mattress purchased at a big-box store, but she could tell this mattress was from a real mattress store. It was definitely top of the line. The sheets and blankets were so soft she hugged them. The bell rang again, and she finally decided to crawl out of her cozy den to see what was happening. There was a black car parked in front of the house. She pressed her face to the glass to get a better look at it. Win came to the door fully dressed and was speaking to a small, dark-haired man who handed him a little black box. Win opened it, examined the contents, and then shook the man's hand.

Sarah grabbed the robe and slippers that had been laid out on the ottoman for her. They were new additions to her room that had not been there the night before. She stepped out into the hallway and had started for the foyer when she bumped into Win. He was heading her way with the box.

He was not paying attention and nearly walked into her. She looked at the box in his hand and said in a high-pitched voice, "It's a little early in the relationship, Win, but yes! A thousand times, yes!"

He looked flustered and said, "No, it's not um..."

She laughed and said, "I'm just joking, Win. Lighten up. Is that the other type of wildly powerful ring that has the ability to destroy men?"

"Um, no," he said.

He opened the box and handed it to her. It was a bracelet. It had a solid gold band decorated with a large sapphire in the center flanked by a line of diamonds on either side. Win reached over her hands and said, "Let me show you something." He pulled the sapphire to the left with his finger and the gap between the diamonds closed to make room for the sapphire to slide. Under the large stone there was a round compartment which held the stone in recessed, firm prongs, like a jewel.

"Here, you can try it on," he said. He pulled out a small key and placed it in the hole at the side of the bracelet. The bracelet had a hidden hinge that opened on the other side. It opened just enough for her to fit her wrist in. "The key has a microchip in it. The bracelet can only be opened with this key," he told her.

She snapped the bracelet closed, and it was a good fit. She tried to pull it off over her wrist, but it was not possible.

"It's titanium, plated with gold, but it's stronger than a handcuff. There is no way to get it off once it's locked. It's a failsafe. When you are in the past you won't be able to take it off and nobody will be able to take it from you. It's the only way to be sure you don't get stuck. The ring goes in when the bracelet is off. Here, I will show you." He put the key in the hole again and gently slid the bracelet off her wrist, brushing her skin with the tips of his fingers. The touch made her tingle.

After he had the bracelet off of her hand he said, "I don't think wedding rings destroy men."

"The look on your face suggested otherwise," she said.

He smiled but offered no response. He turned the bracelet over and showed her there was a small silver panel on the underside. He slid it over. "You put the ring in this compartment. Then the bracelet is so tight to your skin there is no way to get it out again until you get back and open it with the key. It can't be dropped, lost, or stolen."

John yelled down from the landing at the top of the stairs, "Is that it?"

Winthrop said, "Yes, come down."

Sarah noticed John was dressed as he came down the stairs, making her feel uncomfortable in her robe and slippers. She offered to change.

"No, no, no," John said. "It's time to show it to you."

"Really, right now?" she asked.

"Let's go to the sunroom. I want to go over some ground rules with you before we go to the country club," John said.

He headed toward the west wing of the house. She had never been in that area before. The hallway was identical to the one where her room and the library were, but at the end of this hall was a large atrium instead of a library. It looked out over the backyard. The atrium was lush with trees and rows of green plants and flowers. The farthest corner had a waterfall. There was a white garden table and cast iron chairs in one corner of the room. John led them there and sat down. He motioned for her to sit, also.

"We take breakfast in here sometimes," John said. "But today we are going to practice. The first experiences with the ring can be messy. Better to be messy in here."

"The ring is in here?" She questioned.

"To be honest, it is always with me. I have had it on me since the first day I met you. I keep it here," he said, pulling up his sleeve to expose the solid silver band with a small red octagon in the center. He rotated the medic alert symbol and it gave way to a small compartment that hid a small golden ring. It was not exactly like the metal gold. It was lighter, and the outside had a brilliant shine to it, like diamond and copper mixed, but it was smooth. It seemed to be almost glowing and moving; it looked alive.

She reached for it, and John pulled his hand away.

"You have to be extremely careful with your thoughts whenever you touch this. Your thoughts must be precise. I don't recommend you think about any persons or great expanses of land. The ring interprets your thoughts without question. For example, if you were to think about lava and touch the ring you could be engulfed in lava in a matter of seconds, before you ever had a chance to touch it again. Let me show you what it can do."

He touched his hand to the ring. She heard a loud sound and the ground shook. John pointed to her right, and she saw a giant elephant next to her who trumpeted with his trunk. John touched the ring again, and it disappeared. He touched his finger to the ring again and held it there. The room went dark and glowing balls of light floated around the room bathing it in an iridescent glow. The water from the waterfall stopped babbling, left the enclosure and started to wind through the room. It came to Sarah and encircled her waist. She reached out and touched the flowing water. The balls of light danced around her while she touched the fall. John smiled at her, and the lights disappeared, the natural light from outside bathed the room again and the water returned to the waterfall.

Her mouth was agape as John reminded her, "It does more than

75

that. Those are parlor tricks. I want you to try something with it. But be very careful."

"I think I can keep my mind clear enough," she said. "I take yoga."

She moved her hand to the ring very slowly, clearing her mind by saying ohm then clearly picturing the Hope Diamond. She was nearly touching the ring when John suddenly grabbed her hand squeezed it to the ring and yelled, "Don't think of chickens, don't think of chickens!"

Chickens popped up all around the room. There were hundreds on the ground, one had landed in Win's hair, others clucked in the waterfall and circled her, John and the tables. The room was filled with the sound of clucks and the motion of white chickens jumping and flapping. Sarah was surprised that she was so easily tricked. She wanted to take her hand off, but John held her tight to the ring.

"Now think about making them go away," he said. Suddenly, they started popping and feathers were flying from the just popped chickens.

That's not what she wanted. She thought empty room.

Win, the chickens, the furniture and all of the plants slid loudly out the door and into the hallway.

"No!" she yelled.

"Focus, Sarah," John said, looking at her. He took her hand off, and she closed her eyes and breathed deeply.

She moved her hand back over to the ring and thought very concisely, no more chickens in the atrium. They disappeared. Return the plants to their space in the atrium. The plants slid gently back into place. Remove dirt from hallway. The dirt in the hallway faded away.

She knew she was doing well. John patted her hand. "You got it. And fast. I knew you would."

Win said, "It took me two days to clear my mind enough to stop destroying the house."

John hugged Sarah and said, "I knew it was you."

She opened her mouth to respond, but was interrupted by a knock on the glass of the atrium. Somebody was watching them.

CHAPTER 13

Sarah looked out at the atrium and saw a familiar face staring back at her. It was Ruth.

John saw her too, and shouted to Winthrop, "We need a better security system here, damn it."

Sarah walked over to the door of the atrium and opened it. Ruth came running over. "What is going on in here? Where did the chickens go? You all messin' with voodoo?"

"No," Sarah said. "It's much more."

"How did you get in here?" John demanded.

"Right through the front gate. I don't be sneakin' around. I came by this morning to check, because Sarah never checked in last night. When I drove by the gate was closed. I parked on the street and walked around the fence. When I came back around the gate was open and I walked right in."

John was still visibly angry and looked to Win. "We never closed the gate? We are getting better security starting tomorrow. Damn it."

Winthrop looked at his watch and asked John if he should cancel brunch at the country club.

"No," John said. "Add one more. I guess Ruth's in now; much earlier than I planned on telling her, I'll tell you that."

Win said, "Sarah, you should get ready. We have to leave here in twenty minutes if we are going to make it. We will fill Ruth in."

Sarah went to her room and went through the wardrobe. There were several outfits sized just for her. She grabbed a cream-colored pencil skirt and wrap-around navy blue top. She opened the lower drawers of the wardrobe and found one filled with jewelry and the other with shoes. The shoes still had price stickers on them. She grabbed a pair of navy pumps with a cream band over the toe. She went back to the jewelry drawer and found that most of it was too gaudy to wear every day. There was a small box in the corner that held a simple gold necklace with a sapphire pendant. She grabbed the necklace, which matched her dress, and then went to the bathroom to freshen up.

She showered quickly, jumped out and found a high-powered hair dryer and round brush under the sink, two items that had not been there previously. She dried her hair in minutes and topped off her look with a layer of pale pink lipstick. She stepped into her new clothes and looked in the mirror. Holy crap, I look rich, she thought. The fabrics of her clothing were like nothing she had ever worn before, soft and smooth. The fit of the shirt was crisp and tailored. The light it reflected made her think it must be silk, though she couldn't be sure because she had never worn silk.

The heeled shoes were coordinated with the shirt as if they were made to go together. She decided her hair looked out of place just being down. She went back to the bathroom and pulled out a drawer, finding it full of sparkling hair clips and pins. She took out a pin with three stones. She assumed they were rhinestones, and pinned back one half of her hair. Then there was a knock at the door.

"Sarah," she heard Win's voice. "We have to go."

She picked up her wallet and cell phone and carried them, as her dress had no pockets.

When she walked to the foyer she saw Ruth had changed, too. She had arrived in a velvet sweat suit, but she was now in a purple floral dress, complete with a hat and pearls.

"What the heck?" Sarah asked.

John pointed to the bracelet and said, "We took a shortcut."

Sarah handed her wallet and phone to Ruth, who tucked them into her violet handbag.

The four of them walked out the front door, and Sarah asked John what had happened.

"I told Ruth about the ring. I had thought I might bring her in at some point, anyway. This is sooner than I had planned, but there is no other option now. Her knowledge of the city is very valuable and I thought we might need her help."

"I will help, but I will not be touching that voodoo," Ruth said.

They started for John's Town Car. It had been pulled around to the circle. Sarah moved to sit up front with Win when he shook his head and said, "You need to sit with John and Ruth. He needs to talk to you before we get there, and I want to put the divider up." Sarah assumed they would be talking about Win's past, so she agreed and slid into the back of the car.

The seats were set up in an L so that all the occupants could look at each other. Sarah sat next to Ruth. Win got in and rolled up the divider.

As soon as the car started moving John started talking, "There are so many cautionary tales that follow the ring, but Winthrop's is arguably the most important. Winthrop is the son of a dear friend of mine, Ambrose Winthrop. Young Addicus is, to date, my only clear success with the ring, but he is also a testament to its great shortcomings.

"I knew Ambrose well, and sometime in the midst of all my trouble with the Divine, I met with Ambrose. After some number of months of his insistence that we have lunch I finally relented to his request for a meeting.

He wasted no time in telling me he was dying. He was a man very much like myself. He had spent his young life wealthy and never entered into a true occupation. He never married, had a real job, or gave up his bachelorhood. He told me he was going to die troubled. In the eleventh hour of his life he wished he had done more with it. That's always the way; I know now exactly how he felt." John took a breath and looked out the window.

"Are you dying, John?" Sarah asked.

"None of us gets out of here alive, Sarah. I will be leaving sooner than the rest of you, but I am not so close to dying yet as he was."

"Are you ill?"

"No," he said. "But I feel myself winding down," he shook his head and sighed.

"My health is of no importance. I need to tell you about Ambrose. He said that there was another path presented to him once, and he wished he had seen where it led. I asked him to tell me about it, and while he spoke I knew I would try to help him seek that path.

"Ambrose confided in me that he had had an opportunity to pay a kindness when he was young and he chose not to. It started when Ambrose was on his way to a golf outing at the very club we are going to today.

"As he approached he saw a young man, no older than 13, looking in the windows of the clubhouse. The young man was wearing untidy shoes, a threadbare shirt, and was thin as a rail. He explained he had taken a train to the outer suburbs, then a bus and finally walked three miles to the club. He was holding a crisp, typed resume in his hand like it was a precious object. Ambrose and his companions chastised the young man and one of the men reached forward and finally ripped the paper from the boy's hands. He reviewed its contents and tore it to pieces. After the boy was sufficiently deflated, they reported him to security.

"This never sat well with Ambrose. He wished he had been brave and stood up to his friends. He said if he could go back and do it again he would have stood up for the boy. He started his round of golf only to make an excuse to leave after two holes to try to find the young man and make amends. He had finally decided he would help the young man home and would offer to help him.

"He walked back through the clubhouse and found the young man sitting in the manager's office with a blonde woman at his side. She was looking at the boy as the manager yelled. He said the lithe woman jumped up waved her finger in the manager's face and told him off. She motioned for the young man to get up, and she stormed out of the office with the young man in tow. Ambrose watched the woman and boy stomp into the hallway and when she walked by him he felt his heartbeat quicken. She pushed past him, and he said he felt the air go right out of his chest. He described her as the most beautiful woman he had ever seen, her face was young, light and punctuated by bright green eyes. He immediately wondered who she was, why she was there with the boy. She stomped off so fast he had trouble getting words out. He followed to ask her name. 'Excuse me,' he stumbled.

"The boy turned to her and said, 'This is one of the men who tore up my application.'

"She looked back at Ambrose and shouted, 'You should be ashamed of yourself.' She continued on down the path, not looking back again.

"He couldn't regain himself to speak again before she was out the door. He went to the office to ask who the boy and woman were, and the manager said, 'Nobody, Mr. Winthrop. I'm so sorry you had to see that. Please have a drink in the clubhouse on me.'

"Ambrose persisted, 'I just want to know who the woman was.'

"'She was a looker, but not for you, sir. She is wrapped in unpleasantness; people not to be consorted with.'

"Ambrose tried to talk to the manager again to ask about her, but he either never learned her name or refused to let Ambrose have it. Ambrose thought of that woman and that boy every day for years. He said he felt as if his destiny was with them, and he missed it. He went to great lengths to find them, visiting schools and recreation clubs all over the city, but he never found them again. He begged me as his dying wish to help him find them. He needed them to know that he wished he had done it differently.

"I could help him find her. It would be easy. But I knew I would do more. My plan from the start of his confession was to rewrite history, and I carefully crafted how I would do it. I was going to give him a chance to do that day over again, starting from the morning he arrived. I would have him go alone. I was going to change the boy's attire, clean him up. Move up the arrival of the woman, all that. But as it turns out, my plan never went into action. I did next to nothing at all, and I changed everything.

"Ambrose told me before the incident he went on a streetcar tour of underprivileged neighborhoods with a charity group. They were trying to raise funds for redevelopment. I went back to the trolley tour to see what Ambrose was like to be sure he would help as he said he would. I had been fooled before by stories of what people said they would do. I sat behind him on the tour and said one line meant to bait him into conversation and give me insight into his character. As we passed a YMCA in the city with a line of young boys outside I said, 'I bet that some of these boys would benefit from a round of golf.'

"I felt the earth shake under me again, much like it did when I gave money to Jones. The bus disappeared, the streets melted away. I was sure it was going to send me cascading into the future again and try to throw me into the earth, but it did not. I did fly back through time. It was a soft landing, right back where I started, but I knew something was different. Something was better; I could feel it. Where I stood, the grass was greener. The colors surrounding me were more vivid than they had been before. I had done something, but I had no idea what. I called Ambrose and he answered, but he sounded different. He sounded younger. I set up a lunch with him as soon as possible at the club.

"When I walked in I noticed changes all around. The color on the wall was warmer; the chandelier in the entryway was smaller. I also immediately noticed a prominently placed plaque, with a picture of Ambrose on it with twenty well-dressed young men behind him. The plaque was a tribute to the tenth anniversary of the Winthrop Golf Cooperative and included commendations from state officials and the mayor. I read the attached article, which had been varnished into the bottom of the plaque, and found that Winthrop had started an inner city golfing program that paired seasoned golfers with inner city youth for mentoring. It talked of how it was a tumultuous beginning, but he persevered with the help of the former teacher and current Youth Violence Prevention League President, Diana Schubert.

"Before I could read any further, Ambrose tapped my shoulder and opened his arms to greet me. I gave him a hardy hug.

"'Reading up on me, John? That's old news and you know it,' Ambrose said smiling.

"I noticed an elegant blonde woman standing behind him wearing a blue suit. Ambrose turned and kissed the woman on the cheek and told her he would meet her after our lunch in the lobby. They both stared at me, and I felt it was my cue to say something. I attempted a stifled hello.

"She replied, 'Good lord, John. You're looking at me as if you've never met me!'

"'Of course I could never forget the lovely Mrs. Winthrop,' I said.

"She moved closer to me, and I could see she had bright green eyes. I knew this was the woman he had been searching for.

"'When have we ever been so formal, John?'

"'I'm sorry, Diane,' I corrected.

"She looked satisfied and kissed me on the cheek.

"In the new reality I created Winthrop had a wife, a son, and he was the head of a large national charity. He had a real purpose. He donated much of his fortune away. But he was better for it. Everybody in my life was better off. I couldn't believe I had done it right. It was my first and only success. I still can't make out why it was right. But it was. And somehow Ambrose had known the League and Diane were his destiny. He was right. People can feel where they were meant to be it seems. I have gone over this in my head a thousand times, but I don't know what worked.

"Unfortunately, it was only a matter of time before Ambrose's ailment caught up with him. It took longer than it had the first time around, but he did succumb. The worst part was that Diane had preceded him in death. She passed away from a tumor. The death of Ambrose left Addicus an orphan at just five years old.

"I immediately took responsibility for him. I did not tell him all of this until much later, of course. But I did groom him to be the next carrier of the ring. I thought it was his calling. The ring helped him come to be, so I thought it had chosen him. Unfortunately, at his first opportunity to use it there was a tragic accident, and he has refused to touch it ever again.

"I gave it to him in his own vessel, and asked him to take over correcting my mistakes. However, when he got the ring the first thought that came to his head was his mother, long since passed. He could not control it. He recalled her alive and was instantly taken to her alive in her youth. He had no memories of her except as photographs, because she passed when he was so young. He watched her live, walk, and talk. She was an amazing woman: kind, smart, and funny. It's no wonder he wanted to know her better.

"He stayed back watching her from afar for too long. I was in the present and knew nothing until he told me. He stayed in the past for nearly a year meeting with his mother throughout time. Eventually, he had decided he could save her. He went to her in an attempt to destroy the cancer that was brewing in her body. He asked the ring to eradicate the cancer in Diane's brain. The ring did as it was told. It destroyed the cancer, but destroyed her brain too, instantly. He said she was one moment smiling and talking, and then she went still and stared forward. Blood ran from her nose, ears, and eyes just before she fell."

Sarah whispered, "Oh no." And Ruth rushed her hand to her heart.

"Could you imagine what seeing that did to him? Diane died instantly and much sooner than planned. Addicus tried and tried to remedy this situation, but it could not be undone. He has to live with this gruesome memory forever and the knowledge he unintentionally ended her life early. It also sped up the death of his father. It devastated him and destroyed any taste he might have had for the ring. While he still had his memories, it changed the course of future events in his life. He was heartbroken when he returned to learn that many of his parents' possessions were now lost to him. They had no time to get their affairs in order before dying. Hardest for him was finding that a prized picture he had of his mother caressing him at his fourth birthday party was gone. In the new reality she died before it took place."

Sarah wiped a tear from her cheek.

Ruth spoke first. "John, that ring sound evil. It sounds like the Monkey Paw. The paw grants everybody wishes, but in the end they all wish they had never found the paw. Maybe you should count your losses and bury your ring. Better, wish you never found that ring."

"I can't un-wish things. I don't know all the rules of the ring. I have no idea where it came from. I wish the ring could tell me what I am supposed to do with it. I have learned what it can and can't do by horrible trial and error. I can't fix people. I can't raise the dead. There are just certain things it won't do. And I am afraid to change anything around Addicus because I don't want to lose him."

Sarah said, "I don't want him to die or the charity to disappear. But there has to be a way to do it all, John. We have to figure out why you were able to use it right once. Why this change stuck and why your other interventions went so badly. We have to figure out how to use it right."

"I think so, too," he said.

"Do you think the charity worked that time and the future was better because less is more?" Sarah asked John.

"I don't think that was it," John said. "I have done subtle things before, and they still led to strange consequences, did no good at all, or turned bad. Something about those words and that day just worked."

"Huh," Sarah huffed.

"While you are thinking, remember the cautionary tale in all of this. The inner workings of humans are tricky, and the ring follows directions very literally. It's as dangerous as it is great. Don't wish for ill people to be well, don't have it make people do anything. Try as best you can to never use it on a person for anything."

84

CHAPTER 14

They arrived at the club and pulled around the circular drive, Sarah took note of the three-story brick structure with large windows and dark green shutters. It had a green two-story entryway at the top of the stairs. The building was adorned with bright flowers that softened the otherwise stately exterior. When they walked in, the building felt especially warm, with cream paint and furniture with deeply set cushions. The entryway was grand and decorated with plaques and photos from various volunteer programs. It had the bones of a grand manor furnished with years of kind deeds. The people walking by held their heads high and greeted each of them with a friendly smile.

Sarah found herself staring at the walls. John placed his hand on her shoulder and said, "It's beautiful, is it not?"

"I have never been in a clubhouse before," she said. "The people here are nicer than I thought they would be."

"Yes," John said. "It is, as I told you, a kind place. You can feel the kindness that grew here from Winthrop's father."

They walked down a brightly lit hallway to the dining room, where the host greeted them. John tipped his head to him, and he replied, "Right this way."

They were escorted to a table near the center window, which looked out over the pool. It was filled with water, but nobody was swimming in it; given that it was early spring the water was likely quite cold.

After they were seated, John removed his napkin from his plate and placed it in his lap; the rest of the party followed suit. There was a pained silence for a few moments. Sarah felt intimidated by the surroundings, and thought Ruth might feel the same way. She stared out the window at the pool, wondering how they kept leaves out of it when trees surrounded it. John followed Sarah's line of sight and struck up a conversation. "I don't think I've ever set foot in that pool," he said.

"Nor I," Win responded.

Sarah asked," Why not?"

"It's always been a place for the ladies, I suppose," John said. "A place for them to sunbathe and for us to watch. In the summer you will find the balcony near the window crowded with young men who choose to take their brandy and cigars on the patio rather than in the study." John shook his head. "This will be a sad summer, I suppose. They are tearing it down."

"Really? What are they putting in?" Sarah asked.

Win responded, "A bigger pool with fountains and a waterfall. This one has been here for ages. It's been in need of an update for years. They can't even find filters for the old system anymore."

"Well," John said. "Dr. Glacier was quite attached to the pool, given that it was donated by his father. He sits on the board and refused to allow them to tear it down unless they named the new one for his father."

"The new pool will be Glacier Pool," Win said stifling a laugh.

"It's ridiculous," John said.

"I like it," Sarah said. "It sounds ironic."

"Exactly," John said, crossing his arms and leaning back. "Ridiculous."

The waiter had quietly come to the table and set out a plate with bread and gently placed a menu in front of each of them. Sarah looked through it and the only thing she was interested in ordering was in the kids' section. Chicken fingers sounded about right. She scanned the menu for anything that looked familiar and saw the word tilapia surrounded by a bunch of other words she didn't care to try to pronounce. When the waiter asked for her order she simply said, "The tilapia."

Ruth was next. She looked to the waiter and said with almost no accent, "Make that two."

Sarah wondered if Ruth was as lost looking at the menu as she was.

After the waiter was out of earshot John said, "We have to talk about business. You need to get the lay of the land here. I want you to see the grounds in case you need to arrive here. I want you to look for places to land, as Winthrop and I call it. You need to pick a place that is out of the way, where nobody will see you coming. I suggest the trees by the pool. Now that you have seen it if you have to appear here do you think you could picture it?"

"I do," she said.

"Don't picture the pool. It wasn't here in the sixties, just the trees. You have to be very specific."

"Understood," she said. "What else do I need to know?"

"I have pinpointed a date for your first jump. August of 1964. The first night I want you to visit is the night of Divine's annual fundraising dinner, just before I fund Jones. Three days from that date I will arrive at a party at this very club, just before midnight. I think your intervention should take place that night in this location, before I arrive. From the time of that jump I stay for a period of one month, which closes the window for any more interventions. If you are still there at midnight the ring will kick you out of that time. Do not trouble yourself if we fail on that night. We can try again. I have kept track of our windows to change what happened with Jones. We have many chances."

"I understand," she said. "How do we decide what to do that night? Should we start pulling records or going over notes?"

"I have two ideas of my own based on what I have observed in the past. My first idea was to fortify Divine with enough money to counteract what I gave Jones. My other thought was to try to direct Jones after I give him the money. Do either of my ideas sound like they would work, Sarah?"

"I don't know," she said. "I need more information. Is Jones the type of person who can be redirected? If we give Divine more money, will it be enough to overcome Jones? Is Divine a good enough man to entrust with more power and more money?"

"The same questions I asked," John said. "I would like you to go back and observe Divine and his followers, but from the periphery. Try to formulate another plan for us, but stay as far away from him as you can. Anything that involves Divine should only be attempted with extreme caution and only when absolutely necessary."

Sarah looked out at the pool again and started thinking. "John, why don't we just go back and tell you not to give him the money?"

John shook his head.

"I cannot make contact with my younger self. I had however tried to inform myself through a liaison not to give Jones the money, but it didn't work. I either didn't listen to the liaison or the damage was done in another way."

"I need to ask questions to get information. Can't that change history by itself?" Sarah asked.

John replied, "Yes, but you should try to make your interactions mundane, not memorable. You don't want to do things that will stick in anybody's memory or possibly change the course of history. Don't get attached to anybody, and don't let anybody get too close to you."

John stopped and dug into a pocket in his jacket, then looked up and showed Sarah a small, blue, spiral-bound notebook. "This is important, Sarah. This is a list of all the rules that I learned to live by when time traveling. When the time is right I will give it to you. You need to read the rules. Study them. They are exceedingly important."

"Understood," Sarah said as she reached out to take the book.

"Not yet" he said. "Not yet."

❧

As they started back to the mansion, Sarah was lost in thought, staring out the window. When she finally realized where they were she became uneasy. They were headed in the wrong direction.

"Something's wrong," she said. They should have been near John's neighborhood by now, but outside the car the streets were growing ever narrower and the homes were built tightly together. She felt claustrophobic, as if the lines of row homes with barred windows and crumbling steps were closing in around her. She knew this neighborhood. They were getting close to the Divine. Not a place for her in this car in these clothes. She furrowed her brow at John.

"What's going on?" she asked. "I thought we were going to your house. It looks like we're going into the city."

Ruth took notice as well and said, "What the hell?"

Win rolled down the divider.

"Why do you look mad?" he asked.

John lowered his hands in a calming gesture. "Everything is fine. I want to show you the Divine before it fell apart. It's important for you to see what we are saving. I want you to get the lay of the land

89

there so that we can start formulating a plan for your intervention."

"You don't need to show me the Divine. I've been there."

"John, I've been there too. This girl is right. We do not need to be here, especially not in a car this nice. We askin' to get carjacked," Ruth piped in.

Win looked back at them in the rearview mirror and said, "John, didn't you tell them we were coming?"

"No, I was getting to that. I got caught up in the other story on the ride over. But there is no reason to be worried. We are just making a quick stop. When the ring is with you, your mind can be at ease. I promise."

There were people on street corners eyeing the car closely. There was a heavyset man with oversized pants, a tight wife beater, and dark sunglasses standing in one of the vacant alleys. She took note of him because he was following the car's motion with his head. He grabbed his cell phone out of his pocket and started dialing. As they passed he stepped out of the alley and watched them as they turned.

"This is really bad, John," Sarah said. "We really need to get out of here. You don't understand this neighborhood. They are going to think you are a dealer they don't know. We need to go."

"Nonsense," John retorted. "If anybody approaches the car I will turn them up on their heads. I can freeze everybody in the block. You only feel fear because you have not experienced what the ring can really do. This is part of what makes it great. You never have to live in fear again. You can do whatever you want, wherever you want to do it."

Ruth was shaking her head. "John, I don't know the power of that thing you got, but I got a brain in my head knows more than you do. And if Sarah knows this area dangerous, you better believe it's damn dangerous. We gotta go."

"We are nearly there," John said. "We are making the briefest of stops. Sarah, I'm going to ask you to make a quick trip to a point in time before I changed the Divine. I want you to feel the energy, observe Reverend Divine and his congregation. I want you to go back to a date in 1964, three days before I showed up and started meddling. I want you to see the events that were unfolding at the time, and when we talk about the Divine I want you to know all of the players. I want you to understand the layout of the building and where you are going.

Go back to August 16, 1964 and enjoy the day. Walk around the Hotel, get a feel for it. When you return we will have only missed you for seconds, six seconds to be exact. It will take you three seconds to enter 1964 and three seconds to get back. The scene will change right around you. It is spectacular, I assure you. But you can't bounce around through time. You will come back to this time automatically. There is some sort of failsafe in the ring that forces you to go back to your time of origin before popping around again.

"I picked this date for your first jump intentionally. Firstly, I would like you to stay until the evening dinner and see if you can share space with my younger self. I have never been able to do so. Report back to me any accounts of that interaction, but don't say more than a greeting to me. I want to see if I am able to remember you. The ring has, to date, not allowed me to visit myself in other times at all. Also, if something goes horribly wrong, you will just have to while away a couple of days until you will be sent back automatically. That is when I use the ring to jump into the past again and if all of my research is correct, you will be kicked out, back to now, no harm done."

Sarah asked, "Why do we have to go to the Divine, John? I can just ask it to take me there from your house."

"No, when you first jump through time it's best to be where you want to end up. It's easier to set the scene around you and to land softly. You simply think take me to August 16, 1964. There is no muddling with the place. It can get complicated if you have to think more."

"I can just go to the past at your house, go back in time, and then ask to be taken to the Divine. There is no reason to be down here."

"I want you to see the transformation. Also, it means less time spent in the past traveling around. I'm going to show you one of the best parts of going into the past."

John reached for the ring and touched it. Sarah felt the shape and fit of her clothing change. She was now wearing a calf length navy blue dress with a square neckline. It had white piping around the edges. It was a tight fit. Her shoes were changed too, with thicker and higher heels, and she was wearing nylons with a line running up the back. John had a proud smile on his face.

"You should see your hair," Ruth said, failing at suppressing a laugh. Sarah reached up and touched her hair. She could tell it was smoothed and pieces of it were pinned away from her face. It felt like the front was a loose curl.

"You better be able to change it back, John. I spent good time getting that hair right," Sarah chided. She leaned toward the front seat of the car to talk to Win. She felt even more vulnerable now that she was wearing a skintight dress. If she showed up dead in this outfit in this neighborhood they would think she was a hooker earning her way doing theme gigs.

She tried one last time to get Win to leave. "Win, this is not a good idea. That man back there in that alley is a lookout. He is telling bad people we are up to something. There will be people watching us. Is this thing bullet proof?"

"Sarah, you are overreacting." Win said with a smile. "John is right about having the ring. We can be out of here in a second if we have to be."

"Here," John said. And he held out the bracelet box to her. "Wearing the ring will make you feel safe, I assure you. And if we get it ready now we can be in and out in just six seconds."

She opened the box, and John moved to put his key in the lock on the side. The bracelet beeped and the lock disengaged.

"Now hold the bracelet door open," he said. She turned over the bracelet and placed her pointer finger on the silver door on the underside. She slid it aside. John put the key in a tiny hole on the side of his bracelet; it was a match for the hole in her own bracelet. The clasp on his bracelet beeped and opened just like hers. She could see that his wrist was encircled with a lily-white tan line. It was worn very tight to his skin and clearly never moved. She could see he was not exaggerating when he said he always had the ring with him. He stretched his arm around in a circle after removing the bracelet as if he was free of a shackle.

"I have a little feeling of panic myself right now," he said. "I can't remember the last time this ring and I were parted. I think I could get used to not having it for a while. Now hold that up so I don't drop the ring."

He opened the compartment on the underside of his ring and placed his hand in a cup over it. He tipped his hand back and held the ring in his palm. He quickly pincer-grasped it with the other hand and placed it in her bracelet. She closed the door quickly and John grabbed the bracelet and snapped it around her wrist.

Sarah and Ruth simultaneously let out their breath. Neither had realized they were holding it. It was as if somebody was juggling molten steel in the car, and now it was safely away so everybody could move again.

"It's on you now, my dear. And I know it could not be in a better place." He held her hand tightly with his own and put his other hand over the bracelet. He held her very tight and kept patting her hand. She thought he was either sentimental or he was having trouble letting go of the ring.

She began to feel jittery as they got closer to the Divine. Sarah had her hand next to the bracelet, ready to make a move if anything happened. She noticed that there were still men on the side of the road checking phones along the way. There was also a dark green, low-rider Cadillac not far behind them with overly tinted windows all around and garish chrome and gold rims that spun opposite the motion of the car. She was watching that car intently, trying to decide if she should ask the ring to drop it in the middle of a field somewhere.

John broke the silence. "We are just going to pull up and stop for one moment. You don't even have to get out, Sarah. Just think of the jump. Think of the date we discussed. It was a safe time to be in this neighborhood back then. You will be fine. Do you remember it?" She nodded. "We don't need to worry about them, Sarah. When we stop, immediately touch the ring and think of the date. You will go and be back in six seconds in this reality. If you want to try to disguise your arrival, you should try walking as you land."

John let go of Sarah's hand and moved to the back seat by Ruth.

"Look around closely, Sarah. Watch the Divine. Watch what happened through time. Are you ready?"

She was not ready. It was happening too quickly. She wondered why John was forcing the use of this so fast. She wanted to go home or to the safety of John's house.

"Sarah!" John said. "Watch the Divine. As soon as Win stops, use the ring."

Win pulled up to the Divine Hotel, right where Sarah had been a few days earlier when she picked up Darrius and Carol. The car came to a stop, and Win turned around. "It will be fine," he said. "It's an adventure."

Sarah opened the clasp on the top of her bracelet. She noticed that the ring looked different than it had before. It still stirred, but the movement was different. It had appeared to be slithering on John's wrist, but now it was gliding. She reached with her index finger to touch it and thought, August 16, 1964.

Everything went quiet and the motion around her slowed. She watched the brick façade of the Divine brighten, buildings were disappearing in the distance and trees were popping up. The movement around her had slowed almost to a stop. Sarah could still see John and Ruth in their seats, moving ever so slightly. They jostled to the left and right almost imperceptibly. She could see the green car was passing them on the side, its movements at a crawl, and she suddenly saw something that made her panic. The back seat window was open a crack with a gun barrel pointed out from it. The gun was fixed on the back window of the town car, which meant it was aimed at John and Ruth. Sarah saw a trace of smoke escape the barrel of the gun and a bit of silver edging from the tip. She reached her hand back for the ring, but before she could touch her finger to it, Win grabbed her by her wrists and pulled her hands apart.

"No, don't!" he shouted.

Sarah tried with all her might to get her arms away from him. She elbowed him in the face, and shouted, "Let go!"

But he didn't budge.

The car started to fade around them and without the car to hold them Sarah began to fall. Quickly, a pink Cadillac came up underneath her and stopped her descent. She was on the hood and Win ended up above her on the roof of the car, still holding her arms awkwardly.

"I have to go back to Ruth!" she yelled. "Let go!"

Her voice was the only sound filling the space it was otherwise completely silent; buildings and scenery were silently fading in and out.

He responded, "You don't have time. Stop fighting me."

New scenery slid into the foreground: trees, grass and benches. Their car was completely gone. Ruth and John were gone.

The cracks in the sidewalk around them closed. The windows of the Divine were mending and the brick turning from dull dusty dark brown to light tan with bright white trim all around. The neighborhood changed from garbage and dirt to grass and clean sidewalks. Fences disappeared. Graffiti faded away leaving gleaming surfaces. Time sped back up, gravity returned to normal and sound resumed. Sarah felt the cold steel of the car on her backside, before she slid to the ground.

CHAPTER 15

1964

Win followed to the ground, only his fall was higher. She felt a dull ache in her back but was so angry she barely let it register. She rolled onto Win and punched him on the shoulder.

"They're going to die! Why did you stop me?" she yelled.

He moaned and held up the palm of his hand to block any additional blows, "Calm down. I stopped you because you didn't have time to stop the bullet. It would have taken three seconds to rebuild the world around you and you would have watched John and Ruth die in slow motion. We can't go back until we change everything enough to save them. You couldn't stop it then, so we have to change everything now."

"What do you mean, change it all now?" She said still on top of him.

"Ahem," a deep voice boomed behind Sarah.

She pushed off of Win and dusted herself off. She looked at the source of the interruption. It was a young man with big dark eyes and a smile that looked familiar. He was wearing a pressed, navy blue uniform with gold trim and a matching hat.

"Now lady and sir," he said. "I'm not here to judge, but you being on each other outside the Divine, is not the best idea. Father Divine doesn't look kindly on mixing with the opposite sex."

Sarah pushed herself off of Win and slid off of the car.

The young man continued. "He especially wouldn't like it in the street right outside his hotel. You need a hand, sir?" He held his down to Win.

"We're not doing anything untoward, I assure you sir," Win said accepting the man's hand. He stood and stretched. At his full height he towered over the other man by at least a foot. "This young lady and I were just heading this way. We found we were both going to be staying here, and she kindly just helped me out of the way of a car and uhh..."

He was interrupted. "Well, I'm not saying you are a liar, sir, but take a look up and down this road here." He pointed down the street. There were no cars driving down the street in either direction. "Don't worry, sir. Your secret is safe with me. My name's Kirby. Kirby Holt. I help out around here. I can help you with your bags," he said, then began looking around for bags.

Sarah grabbed Win's arm tightly out of shock. She knew Kirby, from Darrius and Carol's file. He was their missing grandfather. Was this a coincidence?

Kirby made a face at her as she grabbed Win's arm and said, "Well, see that's exactly the sort of thing Reverend Divine does not appreciate. No mixing sexes, no touching outside of marriage, period. If you stay at the Divine, you all have to stay separate. Also, just so you know, you have to attend every service held in the great hall on the top floor."

Sarah let go of Win and apologized.

"Do ya'll have any bags then?" Kirby asked. Sarah realized they should have some bags or that would look strange.

"Yes," she said, and Win played along. "Just there on the other side of the car," he said.

Sarah walked around the car, tapped the ring and thought luggage. Two wheeled bags showed up at her feet. Then she smacked herself in the forehead, realizing there was no wheeled luggage in the 1960s. She pictured leather suitcases, like she had seen in the movies. She pictured one brown and beat up with stickers from all over the world plastered on it. She pictured the other bag plain and black. The luggage shifted into the form she pictured. She couldn't think about what type of clothing they needed, so she just thought heavy.

She picked up the first bag; it was indeed heavy. She struggled and made a grunting sound as she tried to move it. Kirby came around and said, "Let me get that for you miss."

Win grabbed the black suitcase. He lifted it and a look of pain crossed his face. He mouthed the words, "Lighter." But she didn't catch it.

"Well, I'll just carry this in myself," he said straining.

Sarah suppressed a laugh. As they walked, with her leading the

97

pack, she looked back at Kirby. He was still moving along at a good pace but Win was struggling. He swayed back and forth along the pavement, almost losing his balance a few times. She took pity on him, touched her ring and thought, lighter. He straightened immediately and almost fell backwards. Kirby turned around and said, "Sir, if you having trouble just leave it there."

"No, it's fine really." Kirby turned and went back for it anyway. He reached to take it from Win's hand. Win said, "No, it's not even heavy. It's uh…" Kirby took it and lifted one eyebrow at Win. Sarah held her hand over her mouth looked away from him.

With the bag removed he ran ahead to catch up to Sarah.

"I don't know what money looks like from this time," Sarah whispered. "Do you?"

The door man waved his arm, gesturing for them to come in through the revolving door, now in full working order.

"Ladies first," he chimed Sarah walked through. She walked into the Divine and nearly held her breath at the sight of it. The hotel was gleaming with marble flooring, polished wood banisters and towering white columns. The two staircases were open at the top and flanked with golden banisters. The ceiling was inlaid with pink and brown stained glass, which shone from behind, casting a soft glow on the floor of the room.

The two rooms, which in 2002 she had dubbed the mold room and the trash room, were identical, and made up as elegant sitting rooms. They were both furnished with pink brocade wingback chairs and fainting couches arranged around low marble-top coffee tables. The right sitting room had a white grand piano, and the left sitting room had a long white hutch filled with pictures and curios. Both rooms were alive with people, one man at the piano padding softly at the keys, and others lost in conversation in the chairs.

She saw Kirby in the right sitting room, by the piano. He had Sarah and Win's bags on a pushcart. He smiled at them as he pushed forward the cart, which also held a plump little girl, not school-aged yet. She was wearing a long sleeved purple print dress that came to her knees. It was edged with a lace collar and lace cuffs. She wore white socks under white shoes adorned with purple flowers. Sarah saw the girl's smiling face and instantly knew who it was. Rosa Lee, Darrius and Carol's grandmother. Sarah recognized the girl's ear to ear smile from her photos. Her smile was genuine, her hair was styled with love, shining and twisted into neat pigtails kept in place with matching white and purple barrettes. She beamed at Kirby as he pushed the cart, and he beamed right back. Sarah knew this was not a man who would have left his daughter willingly, and soon he was going to vanish.

As she walked along behind Kirby, the click clack of her heels on the shimmering floor shocked her. When she had been here just two days ago the floor was battered wood.

Win noticed her staring at the floor and whispered, "A developer stripped this place a few years back. They took everything of value."

They walked to the check-in counter. It was made of dark mahogany and trimmed with a shiny brass foot rail just off the ground. The top shone with fresh wax, and was adorned with flowers. The front of the desk had a brass chair rail just off the ground. It was a far cry from the battered, Formica-topped pine desk that would occupy the space in the coming years. A bubbly blonde greeted them warmly.

"Good morning and welcome to the Divine Lorraine Hotel. How long will you be staying with us?"

"Three days," Win said.

"Are you familiar with the Peace Mission?" she asked. They hesitated, and she started her speech. "The Divine Lorraine is the hub of the International Peace Mission Movement. It is the first fully racially integrated hotel on the East Coast and it is the highest caliber of integrated hotel anywhere. We provide anybody of any race with lodging and food at a reasonable price. But you must follow the rules of the hotel. Men and women are to remain on separate floors and dine apart. Please refer to this brochure for all of the rules." She held out a brochure titled, "Universal Peace Mission Movement, Divine Lorraine Hotel Rules," and continued. "You must also attend services in the Grand Hall on the top floor at meal times. Meals are twenty-five cents. We invite the homeless of the community here to dine with us, and we expect that you will treat them with respect and dignity. There are also a number of preplanned activities for guests of the hotel. Please refer to the concierge for any further assistance with activities. He is the gentlemen over to the left."

They looked over and saw a young man sitting at a desk labeled concierge. He was wearing a black hotel uniform similar to Kirby's with brass shoulder adornments and a brass name tag that said Randy.

"Please sign in here," the blonde said, passing a bound leather ledger to them. Win signed in under his own name. Sarah followed suit and did the same. "The total for two rooms for three days will be four dollars apiece for room with a shared bath or six dollars for a private restroom."

"Private," they said in unison. "Great," the woman said and turned the ledger to write it. That will be a total of $14. There is a $2 deposit which may be refunded after you leave as long as the room is in good condition."

"Paid upfront?" Sarah asked.

"Yes."

"I need to use the restroom. Could you point me in that direction?" Sarah asked.

"Sure," the woman said. "It's down the hall past Randy there. You are free to use it as soon as we settle the room." Sarah looked at Winthrop. He reached into his wallet and looked through the bills in it. Sarah had no idea if money from the 1960s looked the same as money from the 21st century. The woman looking over the counter lifted her eyebrows at the number of bills in his wallet. Sarah was a little surprised, too. She could see from where she was standing a number of $100s. He was covering those with one hand. He pulled out a $20 and handed it to the woman. Sarah looked closely and noticed the bill was from sometime in the 90s.

The woman barely glanced at the bill before stuffing it in the register and making change. After handing him the bills she reached behind her and pulled two large brass keys off of a peg board.

The woman motioned for Sarah to move close to her. She did, and the woman leaned in and whispered, "I just want to let you know we expect a certain level of modesty in your attire. Please, make sure that you find something in your suitcase that hits a little lower on the leg and maybe doesn't fit so snug."

Sarah's cheeks burned red.

John picked the damn thing, she thought. Maybe he didn't remember exactly where hemlines were supposed to fall in the 60s.

"I'm sorry" she said, "I thought..."

"It's all right. Now you know. Just check your brochure for

100

guidelines." The woman gave her a perky smile and passed over their keys. It was easy to know which keys went to whom. Sarah's said Female in big letters over the number 605 and Win's was 705, no words over the top of his number.

They walked over to Kirby, still standing at the cart with their bags, with Rosa still swinging.

Kirby said, "You don't mind if my baby girl joins us for the ride up, do you? She loves the elevator."

"Of course not," She said, bending down to talk to Rosa, "Should we ride together?"

Without hesitation Rosa smiled back and nodded. Sarah could see Carol in that smile, but there was something different. Rosa had an air of innocence and trust that Carol lacked.

Kirby pushed the cart, and Sarah and Win fell in line behind him. Rosa went to the back of the cart and hung from the back bar staring at Win and Sarah.

"Where y'all from?"

"I'm from Michigan," Sarah said.

"Y'all know HOMES then?" Rosa asked.

Win shook his head, and Sarah nodded.

"I do know HOMES. Everybody in Michigan knows HOMES," Sarah replied.

"What's home?" Win asked.

Rosa jumped in and sang, "Huron, Ontario, Michigan, Erie, Superior."

"It's a verse taught to school children from the Midwest to remember The Great Lakes," Sarah replied, before returning her attention to Rosa. "A lady as young as you, from Philadelphia knowing about HOMES, must mean that you are either very bright or well-travelled."

"Daddy knows HOMES. He's from Detroit." They piled into the elevator, and Kirby pushed the button for floor six.

"Where are you from?" Rosa said, pointing to Win.

"From here," he replied.

"Oh," she said, looking disappointed.

"Sorry it's not more exciting, like Michigan with lakes."

"Why you dressed like that then?" She said pointing at his suit.

Kirby chuckled before issuing her a very soft scolding, "That's not so nice, sweetheart. Some people dress different. He's got his reasons."

The elevator dinged for the sixth floor, and Kirby held open the door for Sarah.

"I will help her with her bag first," he said. "Then I'll meet you with your bag in a moment on floor seven."

Win blushed and grabbed his bag off the cart. "I really can take care of it myself. I just lost my footing. I'm fine."

He pulled the four dollars he had just received from the desk clerk out and held it out to Kirby. "Here, for your trouble."

"Whoa sir. I ain't no charity case, thank you," He passed the money back.

"Let me give you something, especially for your advice outside." He passed the man back a dollar.

"That's more my speed. Don't think I don't appreciate it, but don't go throwing charity my way. I work hard. I earn my money. And mister, you be careful. Don't go flashing your wallet around."

Kirby pushed the cart down to Sarah's room, opened the door, and placed the suitcase on the ground for her.

She stood in the center of the room basking in its comfort. The walls were clean, white, and over twelve-feet high. There were two floor-to-ceiling French doors along the outer wall capped at the top with a round half circle window. The floors were a blonde hardwood, keeping the room light. There was also a fireplace in the corner to her left. The surround of the fireplace was made up of small, rose-colored tiles, and the mantle was tall with pillars. Above the mantle was an oversized mirror. Around the fireplace was a sitting area furnished with a white couch and a white armchair. There was also a black and white television on a rolling cart between the fireplace and the window. The ceiling was the most detailed part of the room. The simple light fixture was surrounded by an elaborate floral plaster medallion. On the right side of the room, opposite the sitting area, was a full-sized bed with a white canopy. The bedspread was pink and gold. The only other splashes of color in the room were from pink, purple, and green fresh flowers on the mantle and the dresser next to the bed.

"This way's your bathroom, Miss," Kirby said, opening a door by the fireplace. He opened it and exposed a blue-walled room with white tiles and a claw foot tub. Every surface gleamed.

"I'll be on my way, then," Kirby said. Rosa gave Sarah a hearty wave as she rolled out of the room on her cart.

Sarah ran after them into the hallway. "Is Rosa always here with you?" she asked.

"I have her with me as often as I can," Kirby said. "And Father Divine don't mind family stayin' together."

"I hope to see more of you during my stay," Sarah said to the little girl. And Rosa gave her a big smile.

Sarah went back to her room and looked out her window observing the attire of the people on the street below. She noticed some women were wearing pants. She checked her Divine handbook to see if this was acceptable and found it was absolutely not allowed. The picture showed a woman with a much longer hemline than Sarah's, a few inches below the knee. It looked like knees were out. The basic drawing on the brochure showed a woman wearing a loose blouse, buttoned to the top, and a long plaid skirt. The word that came to her mind was frumpy. She decided to give it a try. She touched the ring, looked at her bed and pictured the ensemble on it. She pictured the colors as brown and red plaid with a plain white shirt.

"Ick," she said out loud. She changed the skirt to a light blue plaid and took up the hemline. "Still ick."

She scrapped that project and went over to the mirror by the fireplace. She pictured the dress she was wearing in a peach plaid. It was a little busy with the piping, so she pictured the edges finished with satin and puffed out the sleeves a bit. She also pictured the hemline lower. She could not see the bottom of the dress. She conjured a floor-to-ceiling mirror along the back wall by the entry door. A mirror showed up, and she took a mental note to remember to make that disappear before she left. Her ensemble needed a belt. She pictured a brown belt and a pair of brown, heeled shoes to match.

"Better. Now I have to help Win out."

She looked out the window at a man walking down the street in a green tweed suit. She could not see him very well because of the distance, but she got the idea of what the suit should look like. She found a rotary dial phone on her dresser next to the flowers. She dialed zero and got a hotel operator. She asked for room 704 and was put through.

"Sarah," Win answered with a questioning tone.

"Yes," she said. "Are you alone?"

"Yes, please come up. We need to talk."

She touched the ring and thought about room 704. She emerged at the door of the room, instead of in as she had intended. She quickly knocked and heard footsteps on the other side of the door. Win whipped it open and rushed her in.

His room was almost identical to hers, only it was accented in yellow and gold. As soon as the door closed she found her anger again.

"What's going on, Win? Is this a test or something? What happened back there with the car and the guns? Was that planned? Did John plan on you coming with me?"

"I don't know what's going on. I know John wanted you to do a time jump today. He wanted to spring it on you and see how you did, but the car and the guns, he never planned for that. We didn't even know two people could jump at the same time."

Sarah retorted, with her hands on her hips. "What did he have in mind?"

"John had a plan. He was going to train you, go through all the books, all the history of the Divine and Jones. He never would have wanted you to be trapped here without the rule book," Win said.

"Then why did he want me to jump the first day I had the ring?"

"He trained me for years before he ever let me jump. And it was wasted. At the first opportunity I proved myself untrustworthy. He needed to be sure you were stronger than I was, that you wouldn't do what I did, and at your first chance at the ring you wouldn't choke and end up chasing your parents, trying to save them… like I did."

"It never even occurred to me to try to save my parents," Sarah said.

"Only an idiot would do that, right?" Win said.

She softened her tone. "I think if I hadn't heard your story that would have been my first thought. If I believed I could save them I would. But knowing what happened to you, I would never risk it."

"Well, that's why John didn't train you more. That's why he took us to the Divine. He didn't want to complicate your jump since you weren't trained. He wanted to keep it simple. But everything's different now."

She went to the window and looked out. She saw the beautiful green of the neighborhood and children playing in the park across the street. "How could he have destroyed all this? I don't understand. He should have given me more information so I know how to fix this. He should have given me at least a few days of lessons on how it works. He barely knows me. How could he trust me to have this ring?"

Win stood straight and walked to the window by Sarah. "I thought John made it clear. He knows you. He has known you for years. He has been everywhere in your life. He is running out of time, and he said he couldn't die without fixing this. Everything's changed now. Sarah, *we* have to do everything."

"Everything?" She questioned.

"We have to change the past so we can save John and Ruth. We have to change everything enough so that the neighborhood is different. We have to make a change in the past strong enough to change the future so there is not a gun pointed at John and Ruth. If we were to go back right now they would be lost to us. We have to tread carefully. Remember, John said that one thing he changed, talking to my dad, sent him on a whirlwind back to the present?"

"Yes," Sarah agreed.

"If we change something too big we, well you, will go back instantly, and we won't get a second chance. You go back to the time you left. There is no way around that. We have to make the right change."

She said, "We have to figure out how John made that one good change with your dad, and I have to ask. Do you believe John's story about how he got your dad and mom together? I feel like he left something out."

"I've always thought that, too. We need to find out what it is," Win said.

"There's one other thing," Sarah said. "The man who found us here, Kirby? I know him."

Win cocked his head to the side, "Coincidence?"

"Two days ago I was assigned to place his grandchildren in foster care. And the coincidence doesn't stop there. I picked them up here at the Divine."

Win's eyes were huge.

"And Kirby is about to disappear."

CHAPTER 16

2002

Officer Trudge was called to the scene of an unusual murder scene outside of the Divine Hotel. He was needed for crowd control as droves of onlookers had come to see what had happened. An unidentified white, senior male and a middle-aged African American woman had been found gunned down in the back of a limousine. The driver had fled the scene. The man in the car was wearing a medic alert bracelet with no medical information on it. The plates on the car were forged, and there was nothing in the car to identify the man. The medics were baffled by his bracelet, pressed tightly to his skin with no visible clasp.

Trudge was still limping from his fall two days earlier. He had a new, heavy Maglite on his hip, after his last one was lost by the overzealous social worker he met just before he injured his leg.

He tried to hide his limp as he walked up and down the police barrier trying to keep people out, while also trying to hear what was going on inside the unusual crime scene. He overheard talk that the woman in the car was from DHS and that they found identification for another DHS worker, Sarah Davis, in her purse. Trudge's ears perked up at the mention of the social worker responsible for his current ailment.

"Can I help you?" the detective looking at the ID said after he noticed Trudge eavesdropping.

"I, uh, heard you say Sarah Davis. I met a Sarah Davis a couple of days ago here. She was with DHS on a call," Trudge reported. "You said her stuff's in that car?"

The detective called him over and showed him the ID.

"That's her," Trudge said.

"Where do you think she is?" the detective asked.

"I don't know. She seemed pretty nice the other day," Trudge said. "I don't think she's involved in this."

The detective jotted down the information from her ID and handed the wallet off to another officer.

He walked to Trudge holding out his hand, "Detective Cooper with the State Police." He introduced himself. "Let's go see if we can find her."

1964

Win stared at Sarah as she looked out the window. He was trying to piece together what all of this meant.

"John must have known something about Kirby. This all has to be connected: John, the Divine, Jim Jones, and Kirby. For it all to come together here it has to mean something."

Sarah turned to him. "So we have three days. What's our move?"

Win replied, "We get more information. We need to find out more about John and what he did with the Divine. We also need to learn more about Kirby. We need to try to find out what happens to him and see if it's connected to what's about to happen with John and Jim. And before our three days are up we need to come up with a plan to make a huge change to save John and Ruth."

"So, in the meantime we just don't talk to anybody?" Sarah asked.

"No, we can talk to people. We have to. We just need to be careful not to stand out too much. Not to change people. Don't give any advice. You can ask questions, but try not to make them too strange. Nothing that would give somebody too much notice of you. We just need to lay low."

"Well speaking of laying low," Sarah said. "We need to get you into period attire."

He looked down. "The three button suit is timeless."

"If a child can tell you are out of style you need to do something. I saw a guy on the street earlier, and he was wearing a suit. I paid attention, so I can replicate it. You are going tweed," Sarah said.

She reached down and touched her hand to the ring and pictured the suit she had seen on the man earlier. Win's suit changed around him, the fit around the chest was tighter, the fabric changed from a blue pinstripe to tweed brown.

He looked down. "Ugh."

"It will help you blend in, and that's what it needs to do. Suck it up. I'm going back to my room and then heading to lunch. We have to arrive separately," she said.

Sarah started to reach for her wrist when she stopped and said, "Before I go, there is one more thing we have to decide. Do we tell John from this time who we are or not?"

"Why wouldn't we tell him who we are?" he asked. "He might be able to help us out."

"There are a lot of coincidences right now. I think John must have known about Kirby, and I find it strange that he didn't mention it. We might have better luck finding out the truth if we follow him. John asked me to introduce myself to him in the past, which means young John has no idea who we are or that we will be here. It's our best chance to find out what really happened."

"I see your point," Win responded. "We can meet with him and talk to him, but let's wait it out before we tell him who we really are."

Sarah shushed him. "Do you hear that?" Footsteps approached their door, followed by a quick knock. They looked at each other nervously, and then a newspaper slid under the door. They heard the steps continue down the hallway and then another knock on a neighboring door.

"I guess they have newspaper service," Win said, picking up the paper. He placed it on his night table and looked at the front page. "Look at this. There is a reception at the Franklin Institute Friday night to display the newly remodeled human heart exhibit."

"I've heard of that. You get to walk through a giant model of a heart. I didn't know it was this old," Sarah said.

"According to this it's already ten years old. It was just refurbished," Win informed her. "I've never been to the Franklin Institute. My parents were more into government and history so we went to Independence Hall and the Betsy Ross House, but not to science museums."

"I've never been, either. So let's agree if we get back in the same shared reality, the first thing we will do is go to the Franklin Institute together."

"Sounds like a plan," he said. "If we get back and survive I will take you to the museum."

"Well then, it's a date," Sarah said smiling at him. "I am going back to my room; meet me in the dining hall, top floor."

Sarah tapped her ring and was back in her room. Another copy of the newspaper was on the floor just inside her door. She walked over to the door and picked it up. She looked at the article more closely. She noticed that the Vandervelt family was listed as one of the major contributors to the heart project. She digested this news for a moment and decided it didn't amount to much. The Vandervelt family probably donated to a lot of charities. It was likely just another coincidence. She set the paper on the mantle over her fireplace and headed down the hallway to the elevator. She walked along the clean brightly lit corridors of the Divine and was passed by a young woman who was brightly dressed in a floral print dress. Her hair was pinned neatly up. Sarah thought on how different the current occupants of the Divine were from the Divine she knew in her time.

Sarah continued down the hall to the elevator and was greeted with a smile by an older Latina woman, also neatly dressed. They rode in silence as the elevator went to the top floor of the hotel. When the doors opened, Sarah entered a wide foyer large enough to be a ballroom itself. The hardwood floors were protected by a bright white rug. The wall of the room opposite her, which abutted the dining room, had six heavy oak doors, all propped open to welcome people into the larger room.

Sarah entered the dining hall, and the sight of the room took her breath away. The apex of the ceiling towered at least thirty feet overhead but fell into a gentle curve, rounded all the way to the floor. The walls, which blended into the ceiling, were painted an elegant shade of Tiffany blue. Cream-colored molding accented the walls and the arched windows, which bathed the room in light.

At the head of the room was a polished oak buffet, which ran the length of the wall. There were three long oak tables that ran the length of the room, with matching oak chairs surrounding them. The room had seating for hundreds of people. Each place was set with china and silver. Sarah recalled what the woman at the desk had said about the lunches being open to the homeless of the city. It was a surprise to her that somebody with a building like this would open it up to the homeless and serve them lunch on china.

At the head of the room, near the buffet, she caught her first glimpse of Reverend Divine. He was shorter than she had expected.

His wife was seated behind him, her blonde hair beautifully coiffed. She recalled from the history of the Divine that they were considered controversial in this time because they were a mixed-race couple. Nobody in this room seemed to take notice. He was impeccably dressed, with dabs of silver on his cufflinks and tie. His hair was speckled with a bit of silver as well, hinting that he was edging away from his prime.

Divine stood and walked up a short set of steps to a raised platform set up on the center of the stage. From that vantage point he towered above everybody in the room. Just above his head, almost as if it were by design, was a word painted on the wall in gold letters. "God."

Sarah was still standing just inside the door when a blonde woman with a bouffant hairdo and a blue plaid dress waved at her and motioned for her to come over.

"Hello," the woman greeted. "I see you're looking around the room the same way I did when I first saw it. I'm going to go ahead and guess that you have never been here before?"

"No, I haven't. Can I sit where ever I want?" Sarah asked.

"Well, you can sit anywhere you want on the ladies' side of the room, which is over there."

She pointed to the left. Sarah noticed an empty seat next to Rosa, who saw her in the same moment and gave an excited wave. Sarah returned the wave with a smile and walked over to take the seat next to her.

"Hi," Rosa said. "Was your room pretty?"

"I loved it, thank you. Has my male friend arrived yet?"

The two scanned the room and then Rosa pointed him out and started giggling.

"What?" Sarah asked.

"You'll see," Rosa said.

Win was sitting at the end of one of the tables. He was in the seat closest to the podium. He had the best view of the room from that vantage point. At his table were many men in tattered clothing, mixed in with the well-dressed patrons of the hotel. They were sitting in an elegant room surrounded by china and silver and none of them made a move to take anything. None of them looked like they were anxious to get their food and run. There were untouched baskets of rolls on all of the tables. When Sarah visited the soup kitchen down the street from her office the mood was somber; people shuffled down the line, holding their trays close and hunched over their food, protecting it.

Win caught Sarah's eye across the room and waved at her. She waved back. She noticed that nobody was sitting by him. There were three empty seats between him and the next man. And the four seats across from him stood vacant as well. She pointed to the empty seats and he shrugged.

Organ music filled the room from a pipe organ at the far end of the stage. A white-haired woman played a familiar Bible hymn. When the song concluded, the room quieted and the doors at the back of the room closed.

As soon as everybody was seated again, Divine spoke.

"Peace to you all, my brothers and sisters," he boomed in a loud voice that betrayed his size. The smile on his face and the magnanimous gestures he made as he spoke drew them all in.

"Know your place," he shouted, and the room was silent as he scanned each table. Then he continued. "Today we are going to talk about your place and where you belong. Can any man put you in your place?"

"No," people shouted around the room.

"No, I tell you. You can have a place, there can be a place, but on this earth and in this world there is no man who can put you there. He can put your physical manifestation in a place, but no man can put your mind anywhere. No, I tell you only God can put you in a place and keep you there. God can take you from a place where you are and raise you up. He can keep you there or he can let you fall. Your place is with your state of mind. Only you and God determine your place. Pray brothers and sisters, to be in a better place. Pray to him and do the work he asks of you. When he calls, answer and put yourself into a better place." The sermon continued, but Sarah stopped listening. She decided instead to look around the room for familiar faces.

She found one right away. At the farthest end of Win's table, in the very back of the room, was Jim Jones. He had a too-bright smile painted on his face as he stared at Divine. He was wearing a cream-colored suit, which played against his dark hair, which was wilder than the pictures she had seen of him in history books, but there was no mistaking him. He had striking chiseled features and piercing eyes.

He rocked back and forth with the rhythm of the sermon. When Divine would raise his voice for emphasis Jim would close his eyes and lower his head, as if physically taking in the words.

Sarah continued to watch him. Then there was a silence in the room, and she turned her attention back to Divine. He was staring ahead intently and then said, "With that, I keep you all well and hope you are as I am. Well in mind, body, and spirit. And remember, while no man can control where your mind is in this world, some men can physically move you, and must do so, especially when you are sitting in their seat." He looked down at Win and the room erupted in laughter.

Rosa looked up at Sarah and said, "Told you. I knew it would be funny."

Win's cheeks flushed, and he jumped out of his seat and moved over. Divine stepped down from the podium and continued to laugh and slap his leg as he found his way to his seat. He sat down next to Win and the other seats around him filled in with ushers who had been standing around the room. The female ushers found seats near Sarah and the organ music began again, quieter this time. The noise level in the room started to dial backup. A side door opened at the back of the room, and men in white uniforms wheeled in carts full of food. Steam rose from the dishes that were placed in the center of each table.

Win sat quietly next to Divine, lowering his head to try to convey his embarrassment. Divine leaned over to him. "I did not mean to embarrass you, son. Every once in a while a new guy comes in, bypasses the seating attendants and ends up in my seat. And I just can't help myself but to zing him."

"I understand," Win said.

Divine bumped him with his elbow and said, "Pass the potatoes, son. I'm starving. Get yourself some on the way over."

Win grabbed the potatoes and scooped some for himself before passing them on to Divine.

"Now young man, what brings you here?" Divine asked.

Win wanted to say as little as possible. He knew he shouldn't be talking to Divine, lest he say something that could send him back. He wasn't even sure if he would be sent back as he didn't have the ring. "I'm traveling with a lady friend," Win answered pointing across the room to Sarah.

Sarah noticed them pointing at her and she gave Win a stern look.

"That beauty sitting next to our youngest congregant over there?" Divine asked. Win nodded, becoming ever more embarrassed. "Well, then you came to the right place. You see, you need to be in a place like this with a girl like that. You can't fight the devil of temptation when you share your space with a beautiful woman. Do you understand my meaning, young man?"

"Yes," Win said. "She's just a friend, though, I assure you."

"Friends can become more than friends when the devil is involved. Now you stay friends and let the relationship of your mind develop. And let your relationship with God develop before the relationship of your physicality develops. Unless..." Divine leaned in closer to Win and said in a voice only Win could hear, "physicality has already been developed."

Win was taken aback and sat straight up, "No, sir."

"Good for you," Divine said and slapped him on the back.

Lunch went on, and Sarah and Win ate little, though the food was amazing. Throughout lunch, Rosa went on about starting school and wanting a piano and a pony. She talked to Sarah and the other women at the table freely. She seemed to be well-known.

Win stayed quiet through the meal while Divine and his friends talked. After lunch Divine stood and tapped Win on the shoulder. "I am sorry my young friend, but I never did get your name?"

"Winthrop," he answered.

"Solid name, sir. Solid name. I find it within myself that I should ask you and your lady friend to help me with a project. You see I find that the word of God is best received when it comes from the mouths of young people such as yourself. I am asking a small group of dedicated servants of God to come to a dinner party this evening. Come out with your friends and enjoy some fellowship and assist me in my mission of spreading the word to other young people. Could I persuade you to join me?"

Win thought on it, "Can I ask my friend and get back with you, sir?"

"Certainly. I don't want to upset your lady friend," Divine said. "When you decide to come you just call the front desk, and they will make sure to direct you to the right place."

Divine started for the door and stopped at Jim, who was standing, eagerly awaiting his turn to speak with Divine. Win and Sarah watched the interaction. Divine said something to Jim, who had a paper in his hand and appeared to be reading something off it. Divine cut him off and said something; Jim smiled and bowed his head in deference.

Jim said, "Thank you" loud enough for Win to hear it. Win thought Jim had just been invited to the dinner as well. Jim's invitation quelled Win's fears that Divine just wanted Sarah at his house.

CHAPTER 17

Win and Sarah stepped into separate elevators. Sarah was alone in her elevator and as soon as the door closed she tapped the ring to go to Win's room. After a short elevator ride, Win arrived at his door and opened it to find Sarah standing on the other side, waiting for him.

"Did you get any information?" Win asked.

"Nada, unless you want to hear about ponies," Sarah replied. "I know you got something. You sat with freakin' Divine."

He told her about their brief conversation, leaving out the physicality question, and told her about the invitation to dinner. "I think he invited Jim to it. Did you see them talking?"

"I did. We have to go and see if there is something we can use to change Jim," Sarah said.

Win walked to his phone and dialed the front desk. "Hi, this is Addicus Winthrop. I just checked in with my lady friend today. Father Divine invited my friend Sarah and me to dinner and asked me to call the desk to confirm my attendance."

He hung up the phone and turned to Sarah. "There will be a bus waiting for us in front of the hotel at six o'clock. She said the attire is formal."

"What does formal attire look like for this time?" Sarah asked.

Win looked to the television in the corner. "Let's find out." He pulled over the small white set, which was on a wheeled cart, and turned it on. He flipped through the dial, but it appeared there was only one working station. On it was the opening theme music to a television show called *Dobie Gillis*.

Sarah watched it for a minute and shook her head. "It's in black and white and they're only showing people from the waist up. I can't get anything from this."

"We have a few hours before we have to go to dinner. Let's go do some research. Meet me in front of the building in ten minutes. I know a place," Win told her.

"How do you know a place?" she asked.

"There is a store downtown I used to go to with my mom. It's been around forever," he told her.

"All right. Let's go shopping," she said and tapped her ring to bring her back to her room. She washed her hands in the bathroom, materialized a purse and a hat to match her recently created peach dress. Once dressed properly for a '60s outing she went to the lobby and then through the double door entrance to the building. She sat at one of the benches outside the hotel. It occurred to her this was the same bench that she had seen just a few days ago acting as a bed to a homeless man. Then it was strewn with newspaper and surrounded by broken concrete and dirt. Where she sat now was a bright white bench surrounded by lush grass and shaded by a willow tree.

While she was enjoying the sunny day and manicured landscaping, Win exited the doors of the hotel and walked over to meet her. He held out his hand and she placed her own in it.

"You looked lost in thought," he told her.

"I was just thinking about how great this place is...was?"

"True," he said to her. "Maybe we can bring it back."

The two of them walked together down the sidewalk and along the street.

"Do you know where we're going?" she asked.

He smiled and raised his eyebrows at her. "I am looking for one thing in particular. It's something I always wanted to do, and I think I hear it."

She heard a dinging in the distance.

"Yup, that's it. Let's go!" he said excitedly. He squeezed her hand tightly and pulled her down the street after a trolley car.

"Come on," he shouted hurrying her so they could catch up. She placed her hand on her hat as they ran to keep it from blowing off her head. Her heels clacked along the flawless cement as they chased the car. The trolley stopped at the corner and the riders by the windows waved their arms trying to rush Win and Sarah. As they got closer they saw the driver turn around in his seat and open the door. They jumped on the car and the smiling driver welcomed them as they breathlessly climbed the stairs.

116

The driver let out a chuckle and said, "I hate to make you run, but we gotta keep on schedule, folks." Win handed the man some coins and the two of them sat behind the driver.

"Where are we going?" Sarah asked.

"We need to go to Jewelers' Row to get some cash," he said to her. "It's not right for us to materialize things and give people fake money. It can create problems to make fake things. We'll sell my watch; it's from the '30s so it can actually exist in this time. Then we are going shopping."

Win leaned forward to the bus driver. "Does this car take us near Jewelers' Row?" he asked the driver.

"No sir, it won't get you near. It will put you right on top of it. You will be up in it in near ten minutes. Do you need a cue to get off, son?" the man asked.

"Please, sir," Win said.

Sarah asked, "Why would materializing things with the ring make problems?"

"Everything that you make actually comes from somewhere; it does not just get pulled from the cosmos."

"Holy crap," she said loud enough for everybody on the bus to look at her. She lowered her voice. "Why didn't you tell me that sooner?"

"It didn't seem important in the grand scheme of things. You are taking very little; most people won't notice," he said.

"I've never stolen a thing in my whole life. I won't start now. I will not materialize another thing," she swore. "Wait, what if what I created doesn't even exist like the dress today or the suitcases, what happens if what I pictured isn't made?"

"The raw materials will be taken, thread, fabric. There is probably a fabric store missing a yard or two of peach fabric right now," he said plainly.

"If I wish it away does it go back?" she asked.

"It depends on how you think of it."

"Well, with the chickens I just pictured those away. Does that mean they went back to their farms?"

"Maybe, but not the ones you exploded, they probably just exploded."

"What a mess," she said, thinking about the implications of all

117

the ring use she had been engaging in. "Wait. How do you know this?"

"When John wished for very specific things he learned they were missing. James Bond's Aston Martin, for example. John really did wish for it and read in the newspapers the next morning that it was reported stolen. He said he wished it away and the authorities said it mysteriously reappeared."

"I wish you had told me from the beginning that I was stealing."

"I'm sorry. I never thought of the small amount that we take as consequential. A little fabric here and there," he said.

"It's consequential to me. I never had much of anything, so to take a little, to me, is a lot. I only ever had one dress. What if one thing I materialized was the dress of a single mother? Her only nice outfit," she said.

"I never thought of it that way. Perhaps this is why John and I were such failures as keepers of the ring," Win said. He held his hand up and placed it over his heart. "No more using the ring for material gain, Scout's Honor."

They continued their ride to the city, enjoying the sights. Everything looked new. The dull worn edges of the city buildings from their time were now sharp. Nothing in this neighborhood looked rundown. The city felt like it was on the edge of a boom. But Sarah knew from her time that this was the peak. Not long after this time crime would skyrocket and continue to grow for the next forty years. New building development would slow to a crawl, and the city would be known as one of the most dangerous places in the country for decades to come.

After a short ride the driver gave them the signal to get off the bus. They stepped out onto a tightly packed street crowded with people. There were signs on every corner advertising jewelry, gold, watches, and diamonds.

"This is the diamond district," Win told her. "Let's pick a trustworthy place and sell my watch."

"But if it's from the 30s, it's an heirloom, right? Maybe we should sell something else, like my necklace," she said.

"I have no idea how old that is. It could be a lab created stone, and if they didn't have those in this time we could dupe some poor jeweler. Better to sell something we know is old. Besides my watch is just a watch. I'm sure I owe a few to the cause, as I have materialized before."

They picked a small, family jewelry store, Fernando Jewelers, with a friendly-looking staff. Win fetched a good price for his watch, and with period-appropriate cash in hand they headed out on the streets. Win handed Sarah some of the bills and she tucked them into her handbag.

"Let's go to Wanamaker's," he said. "I know my dad and mom used to shop there so it's at least relatively high end."

They continued walking down Market Street towards City Hall. Sarah asked Win if he had been to this area of town recently. He hadn't.

Sarah said, "I used to come here a lot because it's so close to my office. There's this really cool underground mall. I used to love it till I got pickpocketed there."

"You say that so matter of fact," he said with a laugh.

"Yeah, it was a really cool place with a big tile mural. Sometimes I would buy food in the mall and sit in the train terminal looking at the mural and watch the people getting on and off the trains. One day I was sitting on a bench with a cinnamon bun, staring at the mural when somebody lifted my wallet. They took cards and cash and returned my wallet to my purse without me knowing. Ruth has since informed me that marveling at the beauty of anything in the city marks you as a tourist. I didn't know anything was missing for days. When I realized my card was gone and being used I pinned it down to that guy who seemed so nice sitting near me at the Gallery terminal. Ruth said at least I was pickpocketed by a pro. She said idiots take all the cash and cards so you cancel them as soon as you realize. The really good ones only take a little so you don't know and they can rob you blind over time."

"Comforting," he said sarcastically.

"It's better than a violent robbery," she said.

"Has anybody tried to rob you like that?" he asked.

"Well, one attempted robbery, but without success," she said. "I was on a social work visit in a very rough part of Kensington. A group of men were walking in my direction. I ignored the voice in my head that was telling me to switch sides of the road. I was stupid not to trust my instincts. I stayed where I was, with my head up, and adopted an 'I'm not afraid of you walk.' Ruth does this all the time and it works. But with me it was a flop. They knew I was afraid. I thought I was about to pass unnoticed, but one of the men turned and gave me a smile that made the hair on my neck stand on end. His face was twitchy. I knew from Ruth that people with twitches are usually high. As a rule, most people leave social workers alone. It's one of the unspoken rules of the street. But on drugs people often forget the rules.

"There are a lot of rules like that. You don't mess with kids, pregnant women, old women, or social workers. Anyway, there I was passing this group of men, teens really, and one of them reaches out and grabs my arm. He was holding it very tight and this other guy steps in front of me and says, 'Give me all your money.' I did exactly what Ruth taught me. I reached into my front pocket and pulled out a ten-dollar bill I always kept there. I held it up so the guy could see it, elbowed the guy holding me as hard as I could and when he let go I threw the bill on the ground and ran like hell. I headed to the house I was scheduled to visit. The boys chased me, but they were too far behind after fighting each other for the ten dollars. I got to the house and the father of the child I was coming to visit was standing on his porch. He yelled for me to hurry up. Word had gotten to him in that short amount of time that somebody was trying to rob his social worker. He stood out on his porch as the boys approached. He gave them a steel stare and patted a bulge on the front of his hip. They looked at each other and walked off as if nothing had just happened."

"Wow, all this stuff happened to you and you weren't scared?" he asked.

"I was scared as hell at the time. But I try to think about the good stuff about the city instead. I met Ruth, who taught me how to protect myself. I met a man who was willing to protect me even at his own risk. I learned a cheap lesson about watching my belongings from a man with no interest in hurting me. It all could have been worse."

"Or people could not rob you at all, don't you think?" he said.

"Well, there's always that. But look at where I am today. I am, in this moment, the most powerful person in the world. I'm walking through time with a handsome man about to go dress shopping for a dinner party at a mansion. I'm starting to think that keeping your head up has its perks."

Win smiled at her and found he didn't want to take his eyes off of her.

"Amazing," he said.

"Amazing what?" she asked.

"Sometimes life just surprises you," he said. "Let's go shopping."

Wanamaker's was an imposing multi-level department store with a brilliant façade lined with columns from the golden era of department stores. There were actual models in the windows. They were wearing jewel-toned glittering fabrics, with skirt lengths shorter than Sarah was able to get away with wearing at the Divine. The models' hair was teased high. Their eyes were brightened by fake eyelashes and thick eye shadow. Sarah thought they were very beautiful in a way that her modern world wouldn't appreciate, though she did. The women flirted with passersby by giggling and blowing kisses. Men flirted back and mothers covered their sons' eyes as they passed.

Win and Sarah entered the store. Sarah marveled at the three-story foyer. The room was glitzy, like a ballroom, with polished tan and white marble floors and chandeliers drawing the eye to the ornate ceiling several stories above them. There were perfume and cosmetic counters in the foyer, not like the open glass cases of their time, but actually set in marble. Golden chairs upholstered in tan brocade fabric faced the counters for women to be coiffed by the employees. Past the entry were racks of clothing and beyond the racks were private dressing rooms for the more upscale fare. Win told Sarah they should shop off the rack as couture clothing would draw a lot of attention.

"I have never been able to put an outfit together on my own," she said. "I just buy off a display."

"Well, that's bad news," he said. "I can't dress myself either. I was relying on you for help." The two walked through the store looking at displays. Finally, a store clerk took mercy on them and asked them if they needed assistance.

"Desperately," Sarah exclaimed. "We have a formal dinner party tonight and we're not sure what to wear."

"You are both so adorable. You can get away with wearing anything. Except tweed," the man said picking at Win's jacket. "A man built like you should be in a solid. You're too tall to get away with all that busy-busy."

The man picked a solid black tuxedo with bowtie for Win and set Sarah up with a black and white diagonal striped dress that hit just above the calf. It was a one-shoulder number, a little risqué for the Divine. She told the clerk she needed something more conservative for the party she was going to.

"What party are you going to where this wouldn't be conservative enough? You need to show off the shoulders. It's all the rage," the clerk told her.

Sarah said, "We are going to a party at Father Divine's, and he is very picky about attire."

"Hah," the man said. "There may be strict rules about dressing at the Divine Hotel, but everybody knows high fashion is the order of the day at his house."

"Really?" Sarah asked.

The clerk chimed in. "Trust me, modern and off-the-shoulder is on the mark for a Divine party."

"What happens at these dinners?" she asked.

The man smiled. "The best food, the best wine. Anybody who is anybody is there. These parties are the place to be."

He held out a dress and looked Sarah, "I recommend this one."

He switched his focus to Win, "If you want to make sure this beautiful lady comes home with you. I recommend you keep her close and buy the matching cover-up on floor two."

2002

With some trouble, Trudge made his way slowly up the steps of the Center City apartment building where Sarah Davis lived. His shin was calling for him to stop, but he didn't want Detective Cooper to know he was in pain, so he pressed on.

"No elevator, I guess," Trudge yelled back. Cooper didn't respond, so he continued up the stairs.

When they reached her apartment, they gave a hearty knock, which yielded no response. After a long wait the detective called the building supervisor, who soon ascended the stairs and unlocked her door.

The apartment was sparsely furnished, but clean. The kitchen had one small round table with two worn out wicker chairs. On the center of the table was a vase with three wilted daisies. An old yellow sofa, a small television, and a radio perched on a buffet table were all the furniture in the living room. In the one and only other room a cheap looking double bed was made up with a mismatched comforter and sheet set. The detective went through the drawers, which were half empty.

Trudge opened the closet and found one black dress, six shirts,two pairs of pants, and five feet of empty rod. The top of the closet held a flat black pair of inexpensive shoes and a small Bible.

"She doesn't have much does she?" Trudge said to the detective. Cooper responded with a grunt as he looked through the drawers.

Trudge pulled down the Bible from the top shelf and opened it, finding it was not a Bible but a game. He opened the secret compartments of the Bible and flipped through the black and red painted wood pegs and crudely carved black and white chess pieces.

The detective made his way to the bathroom attached to the bedroom and said, "I've got something."

Trudge closed the Bible, placed it back on the shelf and walked to the bathroom.

The detective handed him the two pieces of paper which had been sitting on the sink. They were photocopies of two licenses.

"Is that the guy from the car?" Trudge asked looking at the paper which held the information of the older man.

"Looks like it," the detective said.

Trudge held up the picture of the younger man. "So who's this guy?"

CHAPTER 18

1964

Win filed out of the hotel with the other men from his wing and found Sarah waiting on the lawn with the other ladies. She was easy to spot as she stood half a head taller than the women around her. She had a white wrap pinned loosely over her shoulder to mask her curves. When she saw Win she smiled and boarded the bus.

It was filled with mostly women, all young like Sarah. Win was one of the oldest riders. The collective attire on the bus was up a few notches from the lunch dress code.

While walking through the aisle Sarah took notice of Jim, seated in the back of the bus, alone. Sarah sat in the middle of the bus on the women's side, and Win sat opposite her on the men's side. As soon as the bus pulled away, a chorus of hymns erupted from the other occupants of the bus. It started with *This Little Light of Mine*. Neither Sarah nor Win knew the words. Win looked to Sarah, who was doing a poor job of lip syncing. He smiled at her, and she smiled back. She gave up the attempt and just swayed with the tune. He swayed along with her. The young woman next to her gave her a light jab with her elbow and asked, "Is that your beau?"

Sarah smiled, "No, just a friend."

The other girl's smile grew. "Mmm hmm. I got friends like that."

The bus pulled up as dark set in. All of the occupants were glued to the windows on the side of the bus that had a view of Divine's home. It was a grand estate, much like John's but even larger. The walls of the great manor-style mansion were built of light brick. The home had at least three floors, more if one counted the spires and towers, which punctuated its tallest points. The windows on the front of the home were arched and contained red and gold stained glass. Candles were lit in every window, evoking a feeling of warmth from within.

The bus traversed a circular driveway which afforded them a second look at the mansion, before it settled under a brick awning which led to an expansive porch. The occupants of the bus were greeted by a welcoming party of tuxedo-clad staff. When they had disembarked, a young man in a dark suit stepped forward and welcomed them with a warm smile.

"Welcome to the home of The Great Father Divine. He has generously opened his home to all of you tonight and I hope you will return his generosity. Please follow me as I show you what rewards await you if you allow yourself to become Divine."

The man led them up the steps of the porch and they all fell in line behind him. They were a jovial group, walking, talking and laughing as they made their way into the house. As they were ushered through the opened double doors of the home, the click-clack of women's heeled shoes could be heard mixed with the din of chatter. Woman and men mixed together after departing the bus.

They were escorted down a wide hallway flanked by dark oak walls. It could easily be a dark space, but the bright white floor, red carpeting, and exquisite gold chandeliers made it seem warm. The welcoming crew opened a French door to the dining room at the end of the hall. The room held a long slim dining table decorated with overflowing vases of dark-pink roses, carnations, and chrysanthemums. The sheer number of flowers was overwhelming to Sarah, who had never seen anything so grand. In the few breaks between the blooms ere overpowering; the only break was gleaming silver candelabras gleamed in-between the vases. The places were set with china and the serving dishes were polished silver. Sarah thought this would be the third time in her lifetime that she would eat something served out of silver.

At one end of the great room was a bar surrounded by vacant space meant to allow people to mingle. There were hors d'oeuvres on small tables along the exterior wall of the room. It looked as if they were placed in such a way as to keep people moving. The tables were placed between the multiple sets of glass double doors that led to a patio. The doors were closed, but the heavy cream jacquard drapes that covered the windows were drawn back.

Sarah and Win went to the bar and stood near Jones, close enough to hear him if he said anything, but not so close as to speak to

125

him. While they were near, he said nothing. He didn't drink. He stood next to the wall and occasionally walked down to the table to sample the food. He seemed awkward in this setting. Shortly after their arrival, Divine, his wife, Mother Divine, and another young man, who looked vaguely familiar, entered through a different door on the far side of the room. Divine was sharply dressed in a tailored tuxedo. Mrs. Divine was equally exquisitely dressed, in a rich, rose-colored fabric that complimented the flora in the room. The younger man's dress was more informal than the rest of the group, light khakis and a polo shirt. He had a V-neck sweater casually draped over his shoulders. His walk was cocky, and he held his head too high for his age. Sarah and Win looked at each other. There was no mistaking the bright blue eyes on that man. It was John.

John circled the room making conversation with each group. Halfway through he stopped and talked to Jones. Sarah and Win moved closer to hear what was being said, but had no luck.

Their proximity to John made them the next logical recipients of a visit from him. "What do we say to him?" Sara asked.

There was no time to plan as John had already turned and set them in his sights. "Well, hello," he said to Sarah. He took her hand and kissed it. His gaze completely avoided Win.

"I've never seen you around here. Why is that?" he asked.

"I'm not from here," she said, pulling her hand away and making a great display of wiping the back of it on her dress.

"Where are you from?" he asked.

"Michigan," she said.

The smile faded from his face, and he stared at her intently.

"Where in Michigan?" he asked.

"You wouldn't know."

"Try me," he said curtly.

She held up her right hand, to form the shape of state, and pointed to the center.

His eyes grew wide, and he moved his gaze to her neck. She reached up to cover it instinctively.

An awkward moment passed before Win stepped forward holding out his hand, introducing himself. "Addicus Winthrop. Nice to meet you."

John shook it with no enthusiasm. He stared at Sarah for an

awkward moment, then averted his gaze and moved to the next group of people.

"What the hell was that?" Sarah asked.

"I have no idea."

She whispered, "He doesn't seem like the John we know at all, and what was with…"

She was interrupted by Divine when he shouted, "Peace."

His voice carried all through the room, even though he was standing at the head of the table several paces away from them. "Peace to you all my brothers and sisters. Have a seat, have a seat."

Everybody found a place at the table, with Divine at the head, and next to him, John.

He said, "I'm pleased to inform you all that you are in the company of God tonight. He has given me a great and powerful tool to help you all, and I will use it to move you all tonight." Everybody around the table clapped. Sarah and Win gave each other wondering looks from the opposing sides of the table. She mouthed, "The ring?" Win shrugged.

"My tool is right here," Divine said again and placed his hand on his own chest. Sarah and Win let out their air. "Tonight we are going to pray, we are going to give thanks, and we are going to look into the future. I am not long for this world, my friends, and that is why I need all of you. I need your youth, I need your spirit, and I need your souls."

Everybody other than Sarah and Win were fixated on his words. He spoke swiftly and loudly. His words were so sure. "I need you all to give everything of yourself to the movement. You need to give up the outside world, your possessions, and your future to the Divine. I need from each and every one of you a leap of faith. When you put all that you are into the service of God, he will put all he has into you. If you are ready for it!"

It's a damn cult, Sarah thought.

"Now what I have here is a man who is brimming with faith. A man brought to us by divine intervention. He has put his money where his faith is. He is going to take us to the next level. If everybody here had the faith of this man to my right, we would be in heaven tonight!" He pointed to John. Sarah and Win exchanged confused looks.

After introducing John, Divine went on with his sermon, which was peppered with words meant to encourage donations, words such as generosity and giving. At the conclusion of the speech the room came back to life. Tuxedo-clad men served soup and salads at each place setting. The waiters made rounds in the room offering wine.

After their food was in place, the room became noisy again with conversation.

"What do we do now?" Sarah asked.

Win answered, "I think we need to follow John and see what else he left out. He seems off to me."

John talked to Divine all through dinner. Divine and his wife laughed throughout the conversation.

The woman sitting at Sarah's side struck up a conversation with her. She was the same woman from the bus earlier. And something else seemed familiar about her as well, though Sarah couldn't put her finger on it.

"This is the best damn meal I ever had," the girl said. She looked to Sarah and asked, "How did you end up here?"

Sarah replied, "My friend was invited," she said, pointing across the table. "He brought me along."

The girl looked across the table and said, "Hello, friend. My name is Anita." Win stood up and reached across the table to shake her hand. Sarah realized that this was the Anita that she had helped get to a shelter all those years ago, but Win seemed oblivious.

"Anita, my name is Sarah," she said placing heavy emphasis on the first name. "I'm sorry, but haven't I met you somewhere before, like downtown?"

Win caught on and nodded at her.

Anita shook her head. "Sorry, you don't look familiar to me. I live at the Divine, and I don't go out much except to Reverend Divine's parties," Anita said.

"I must be mistaken. So what's it like living at the Divine? Doesn't it get expensive?" Sarah asked.

"I'm the church secretary. It's the world's greatest job. If Divine offers you a job, take it. You won't regret it. I get the best deal in town: free meals, free housing, and a nice salary to boot. And all I do is sit in an air-conditioned office typing up notes."

"That sounds like a good job. How'd you get it?" Sarah asked.

"I used to come in to the Divine for meals. My mom and I fell on hard times and Divine would always make sure we had three square meals a day and a shower once per week free of charge. A couple of years back my mom died, and Divine offered me this job."

"So, he's a good man," Sarah said.

"The best damn man walking the face of the earth," Anita said.

At the conclusion of dinner, desserts were set on the tables on the back wall by the windows. The waiters set out the desserts and then opened the doors. Everybody got up and started to wander around, chatting and noshing. Sarah continued to converse with Anita when she noticed John walking towards her. She tensed, wondering if he was going to stare at her again, but he walked right past her to Anita. She greeted him with open arms, and he nearly lifted her off the ground with excitement.

After he let her go, he leaned forward and whispered something in her ear. Anita nodded and the two of them walked out to the balcony. Win's back was to Sarah. She tapped him on the shoulder, and he turned around. She nodded her head in Anita and John's direction.

Win said, "Excuse me a moment," to the people he was speaking with, and turned to grab Sarah's hand and follow John and Anita out to the balcony.

A full moon lit the night sky. Anita and John had left the balcony and were walking toward the woods. Win and Sarah hurried down the stairs to catch up to them, jogging hand in hand. Anita and John disappeared into the woods just as Sarah and Win entered. They stood quietly listening for them and could hear the sound of breaking twigs in the distance. They followed the sound, stepping gingerly. They approached a clearing which opened to a pond. They couldn't yet see John and Anita so they stayed in the cover of the woods and walked around the pond. Sarah took a step and noticed the ground was soft. She looked down at her feet to see that she was standing on Anita's dress. She pointed to the ground and showed Win. They heard splashing and looked to the lake to see John and Anita entwined in the water. John's clothes were just a few feet further ahead of them.

Win and Sarah shared a look and turned to walk back into the woods. As soon as they were sure they were out of earshot they started to whisper to each other.

129

Sarah said, "Did you know he and Anita were together? Like together, together?"

"No," he said. "John was always interested in her well-being, but he just said she was an old friend."

"I think John left out some of the story." Sarah said.

"That would appear to be the case."

"Well, how do we spend our night?" Sarah asked.

"There isn't much we can do tonight. I think we should go back, make sure we don't miss the bus, and go over what we know when we get back. Try to figure out our next move."

Sarah agreed, but before they could move they heard branches break behind them. They stayed motionless. Sarah turned and looked back at the lake. She could still see two figures floating in the water. She thought the noise might just be a small animal, but then she heard it again. This time it was closer to the lake. Win reached out for her hand and gently pulled her with him toward the sound.

They moved silently, tucking behind trees as they went. Looking back at the water, Sarah now saw the silhouette of a man between the two trees. Win noticed it too, and squinted in the dark, trying to see who it was.

Win looked to Sarah and mouthed the name, "Jim."

She nodded her head. Then Win took a step backwards, and the sound of a twig snapped under his feet. Jim turned around, and Sarah heard him take a quick step towards them. She hooked Win's arm with hers, and with her hand tapped the ring. The two of them were swept back to her room at the hotel.

CHAPTER 19

"I am not one to swear, but what the hell was that about?"

Sarah rubbed her chin between her fingers lost in thought. She walked to nightstand next to her bed and pulled out a pad of paper and a pen etched with the name Hotel Divine on it. She sat on the bed and started scribbling.

Win moved over to the bed and sat next to her. She wrote furiously then passed the page to Win.

1. John and Anita are a couple. Why did John keep that a secret?
2. Jim is following them. Why?
3. Is Divine as good as he seems?
4. What happens to Kirby?

"These are the questions we need to answer before we make any decisions, Win. This is what we need to figure out to decide what we should do. We have two days left. I say we start with John."

"Let's split up. Tomorrow you go to John's and follow him. I'm going to follow Jim and find out what I can about him."

"Agreed."

2002

Darrius and Carol awoke the next morning to find that their foster mother, who said to call her Mama Cassie, had big plans for them. First, they were going shopping, and then off to the pool at the County Rec Center. She made them waffles and bacon, and the two ate heartily again.

They left for town in Mama Cassie's oversized Green Cadillac. It had tan leather seats, which were cracked but still comfortable. The two sprawled out in the back seat as they drove through town to the post office and then made a stop at the bank. Mama Cassie handed the teller a check, and he counted back to her fifteen twenty dollar bills.

"Wow, what's all that for?" Darrius asked.

"It's for you. Sarah thought you could use some new clothes and issued you a stipend."

"Awesome," Darrius exclaimed, and he shook Carol's arm with excitement. "All new clothes. Can you believe it?"

They pulled into the mall and bounded happily alongside Mama Cassie to a department store. They shopped for Carol first, filling a cart with frilly pink and purple skirts, dresses, and shirts adorned with sparkles and glitter. Her favorite find was a pair of shiny Mary Janes with butterfly clasps and a brand-new pair of neon and black adidas sneakers. She also grabbed several bags of socks and a pink and white Minnie Mouse bikini.

Darrius snagged four pairs of jeans, a tie, and button-down shirt, a plain blue pair of swim trunks, and three pairs of sneakers. He told Mama Cassie he would rather buy all new sneakers and no clothes, but she insisted on more shirts. He obliged, and by the time they were to the register, the cart was overflowing. Mama Cassie had kept a calculator by her side, keeping precise calculations of their purchases until they maxed out the clothing stipend.

Darrius and Carol couldn't hide their ear-to-ear smiles as they rung up their new purchases, it was more clothing than either of them had ever owned at one time. Darrius hugged each pair of sneakers before handing them to the cashier to be rung up.

After every last item was through the cashier total flashed $299.84.

"Perfect," Mama Cassie said. "I need two copies of that receipt."

"Why do you need two copies?" Darrius asked.

"One for me and one for Ms. Davis."

"Why do you need one?" Darrius asked.

"In case we have to bring something back after we give Ms. Davis the receipt," she replied.

"No way," said Carol with a grin. "If something doesn't fit I'll make it fit."

They walked out of the store and back to the Cadillac, where Mama Cassie put the bags of clothing in the back seat next to the kids.

"Now pick your favorite outfit out of the bags," she said.

They dug through the bags, Darrius pulling a brash pair of

orange sneakers, jeans adorned with silver thread and a plaid shirt. Carol picked a pink frilly dress and her shining pair of Mary Janes. Mama Cassie dug out the swimsuits and put the clothes the children had picked and the swimsuits in one bag and the rest of the clothes stuffed into three others. Then she tucked one receipt into a bag and put the other in her glove box.

She pulled the bags out of the car and told the kids to follow her back in.

"What are we doing?" Darrius asked.

"Follow me and don't ask any questions," she said. "If you act up I'm taking it all back."

CHAPTER 20

1964

The next morning Sarah dressed quickly and went straight to the breakfast room. It was on the first floor and eye level with the street. She didn't see Win there. Divine and his regular entourage were conspicuously absent, too. As Sarah was scanning the room, Rosa saw her and came bounding over. The two of them walked through the breakfast line together and shared one of the four-top tables near the window. They watched people passing on the sidewalk as they ate.

"Whatcha doin' today?" the little girl asked.

"I thought I would go visit an old friend," Sarah replied. "How about you? What are you doing today?"

"Well, first I have to go to Bible study with my mom. It's a Friday so they usually let us out early. But after that I'm going to Pep's 'cause my dad's going to play the horn there tonight."

"What's Pep's?" Sarah asked.

"Daddy's jazz club," Rosa said, beaming. "My dad's the best jazz player you ever saw. Momma says he plays the horn like the devil gave him his fingers."

Sarah smiled. "I hope you have a great time, Rosa." She desperately wanted to say more, such as always remember what a great man your father was, or never forget how much he loved you. But she feared saying those words might be enough to be considered intervention, and she would be sent back. So she bit her lip and said nothing more.

"You should come with us," Rosa said, chewing her toast.

"I'll think about it," Sarah replied.

As she was leaving the breakfast room she ran into Win in the lobby. He said he was waiting for Jim.

They agreed to follow their charges until lunch, and then meet again at the hotel. Sarah wished Win luck as she walked down the hall to the ladies' bathroom. All of the stalls were empty when she walked in so she went to the farthest one from the door, thought about the shed near John's house, and tapped the ring.

The ground beneath her yielded, and up under her came the roof of a wooden shed. Her legs were at the apex of the roof, and she nearly fell off because the ring had set her right where she had asked to be, on top of the shed, not in it. She had neglected to picture the inside of the shed.

She concentrated on a space on the ground near a tree and tapped the ring again. Concealed by the tree, she examined the house. She didn't observe any movement, but she was too far away to get a good view. She ran to the windows of the study and stood to the side. Those windows were heavily draped with window coverings leaving little visibility from the outside. She peeked quickly inside the study and saw no signs of people. She went around to the dining room windows, which were full-length, and looked in again. Again she saw nobody. She went around to the rooms of the house she knew well, the kitchen, her room, the main foyer and saw nobody room after room. The only sight worthy of notice was the décor, which was dark, old, and greasy looking.

She went back to the study and confirmed with a glance there was nobody in the room. When she was sure it was empty she touched her finger to the ring and willed herself inside. She went to the drawers first and started pulling things out. She found old photos of John and his brother and mother. She couldn't find any photos of his father.

Their relationship must have been strained, she thought. He had hinted at that when they were talking about how his father got the ring.

The drawers in the main room of the study revealed nothing. She wondered if there were any hidden rooms. She touched her finger to the ring and asked, "Are there any secret rooms?"

Nothing happened.

I guess it's not like a magic eight ball, she thought.

She walked along the rows of books and had an idea. She looked at the bindings and found the books were alphabetically ordered. She ran her fingers over the books until she found one out of order,

Plato's Republic. She grabbed the top of the book, pulled it forward and heard a click on the side of the bookshelf. She pushed, and it opened to reveal a secret room.

She walked cautiously into the dark, windowless room. She felt along the wall until she found a light switch. She was in a tiny space with just enough room for a small bookshelf and a single desk in the middle. She looked at the books on the shelf. They were about mythology, magic, and witchcraft, and on the bottom shelf was a row of Bibles. She pulled one of the Bibles off and its weight surprised her. It was too light. She opened it and discovered, like her family Bible, it was not a Bible at all, but a game board. She pulled more and more of the books off the shelf and each and every one of them was a Bible hiding a game board. The last book she opened said "Property of P.D. Pentwater."

She closed them all back up and rearranged them on the shelf. She went back to the desk and pulled out the drawers. In the top drawer were stacks of papers and a ledger for construction projects. There were bids on installing plumbing and electrical updates to the home.

She found another ledger for public construction projects. Sarah was taken by surprise when she noticed that John had commissioned the construction of the park across the street. He had made specific instructions for the trees, pathways, and even the fountain. She noticed there was a box built into the fountain behind the plaque. In the notes it said the box was made of copper. She thought that box might be a planned hiding place for the ring.

Tucked into the ledger was an endowment he had given to a local park committee intended to fund the park for several years. The charity predicted it would fund the maintenance of the park into 2035. She took a mental note to tell Win about the park endowment so he could fund it later, as John would have passed by then.

She continued rummaging through the desk and found the blue book, the one John had given her when she first came to his house, with a record of all of his jump dates in it. She pulled it out of the desk and opened it to the first page. It was different from the first page in her book. The color of the pen in hers was consistently blue, the color of the pen on this page was black. There were several dates written on the first page. She looked around for a pen and a stray piece of paper to take down the numbers, but she couldn't find any loose paper. It was all bound in books. She feared removing one of the pages in case John noticed it had gone missing. She found a fountain pen in the center drawer and started writing the dates up her arm.

The first ones she took notice of were all in 1929, starting with October 24, 1929. She went on adding number after number.

She dug further into the desk and found a small blue book similar to the rule book he intended to give her, but it was not the same. Hers was spiral-bound, and this one was held together with copper brads at the edges. She opened it and noted the rules in this earlier edition were more basic. It said things such as, "don't leave the ring touching your skin," and "don't wish to bring people back from the dead." She wondered how he knew that one. She continued to flip through the desk, and the only other item of note was a black and white headshot of Anita. Her large almond eyes blazed through the photo. They were softened and made more beautiful by her thick lashes. Sarah thought back to the day she met Anita at work, guarding her roach-infested trash bags and wearing tattered clothes. She wondered how John could ever let that happen to her.

She closed everything up, put it back in the desk, and started for the exit. Before she reached it, the door started to creak. She thought quickly about touching the ring to take her to the hotel, but she didn't want to risk appearing in front of an unsuspecting housemaid. Instead she tapped the ring and, without knowing if it would work, thought the word invisible. In the same moment the door was fully open she disappeared. The man who walked in was not John. He looked like John, only taller and with a longer nose.

He started a quick search of the room. He scanned the outer wall away from the desk, moving his hands up and down it and checking all cracks in the wainscoting. When he was to the edge of the desk, Sarah backed away from him, making sure she took soft steps. He rummaged through the desk and pulled things out quickly. He didn't look through the paperwork as she had. He looked under it and around it. He bent under the desk and knocked on the inside walls of it.

When his search didn't turn up what he was looking for, he went to the bookshelf, flipped through the books, and tossed them behind him. One nicked Sarah's shoulder and fell to the ground. She didn't make a sound or move, but the man flipping through the books noticed that the book didn't travel far enough to hit anything. He stopped his tossing and turned, looking straight at Sarah. The four books he had just thrown were on the floor by the wall, but the last book was on the ground at Sarah's feet, away from the wall. The man looked to the ground where the book fell. He had not made a move yet, and Sarah found herself holding her breath. But she had the thought of the shed in her mind and was prepared to touch her ring if the man took another step towards her.

"Who's in here?" the man said, reaching out in front of him. Then a sound rang out from the other end of the house. The man looked at the desk and hastily threw things back into place. While he was in a fervor around the desk, Sarah slid into the space under it. The man stepped over to where Sarah had just been and reached out through the air, searching for her.

"I know what you have and you won't get to keep it to yourself. We all have to share. Even the miracle man had to share." Then he walked back out and shut the door.

Once he left the room, Sarah breathed easier and crawled out from her hiding place. She tiptoed out from under the desk, staying invisible.

The study was still empty, and she walked as quietly as she could across the creaky floor. Her heeled shoes were making quiet clickety-clacks, so she kicked them off and held them by their heel straps. When she got to the door, she put her ear to it to see if anyone was coming. There were still no sounds in the house. She heard the roar of an engine from the other end of the house near the garage and went to the window to see who it was. The garage door opened, and she saw John and Anita drive away in a convertible. Anita's arm was draped over John as he drove; her blue and white scarf fluttered in the wind. After they were out of sight she saw the tall man who had ransacked the secret room walking down the lane towards the gate.

Sarah took the opportunity of an empty house to snoop some more. She had not seen the second floor, so she walked up. There was a uselessly large hallway with a wide red rug running the length of it. There were more rooms than there were purposes for them. Two of the rooms she entered just had Victorian sofas facing each other.

Even more rooms had no furniture at all and there were at least another two spare guest rooms. Finally, at the end of the hall she found John's room. Like the rest of the house, it was bigger than it needed to be. One end of the room had a fireplace large enough to walk into, the other end was furnished with an imposing four-poster bed. Sarah thought the distance from the fireplace to the bed made it nearly useless for warming anybody in the bed. The walls were adorned in thick paneling. The room was bare of any other furnishing save for two lamps near the bed. It made her think of a place that was just moved into, where the occupants hadn't finished unpacking. There was a closet built into the paneling at the back of the room, and when she opened it she found several men's suits and a tuxedo next to a handful of women's dresses.

She was no closer to figuring out why John kept Anita a secret, but now she knew that the relationship was more than a one-night fling. Anita was living with him.

2002

Darrius and Carol worried as they followed Mama Cassie back into the store. They were closer to a full wardrobe of clothes than they had ever been. Darrius kept a close eye on the bag with his shoes as the three went back to the service department.

Mama Cassie placed all four of the bags on the counter, where a disinterested clerk looked them over.

"Whadya want?" the girl asked.

"Return these three bags," Mama Cassie said and Darrius and Carol both started crying.

"Or we can take it all back?" she snapped and the whining came to an abrupt stop.

The clerk went through the items, ringing the chosen outfits back in and making notes on the receipt as she went. When she was finished she handed Mama Cassie back the marked up receipt and a handful of cash.

"Now take this bag," she said handing the cashier the last bag of clothing and the receipt again. "And use this coupon to mark down the items. I want the difference."

The clerk rolled her eyes but rang up the coupon and went through each item one by one calculating the difference and giving

Mama Cassie another stack of bills.

The kids walked back to the car staring at the ground, feeling defeated. Darrius looked at Carol and saw tears streaming down her face.

"It's okay, Carol. We still got new clothes. At least we got to keep the best ones. I can't wait to wear my new shoes. As soon as we get home we can try 'em out."

She looked at her brother and sniffled, then nodded her head in agreement.

They walked back to the car in silence, and when they were buckled back in Mama Cassie put the clothes in the trunk.

"Can we at least look at them?" Darrius asked.

"No," she replied. "You're not wearing them until Ms. Davis comes for her next visit."

CHAPTER 21

1964

Sarah went back to the hotel looked at the dates on her arm and wrote them on one of the small note pages left in the hotel drawer. It filled two sheets of the tiny paper. She double-checked her dates to make sure she had written them all correctly, then went to her bathroom to wash off the numbers. She tucked the papers into her pocket and headed to the elevator that led to the top of the hotel.

She walked into the dining hall and saw no sign of Win. The room was half empty, a far cry from the bustle at lunch the previous day. Again, Divine was not present. One of the other parishioners from the church stood to give the lunch sermon, though it was lackluster compared to Divine's fiery speeches.

Sarah picked at her food, too worried about Win to enjoy any of it. She tried to formulate an idea of where he was. The phones in the hotel room didn't have any type of answering machine. She thought she would go down to the desk if she did not see him arrive by the end of lunch. She saw groups of young professionals come and go through the dining room. Many of the needy stayed seated even after they were done, drank coffee, and looked out the windows. Sarah went to the coffee stand, poured herself a cup, and joined the watchers. After more than an hour and no sign of Win she went to the first floor lobby.

She walked to the blonde she had seen the day before and asked, "Do you have any messages for a Sarah?"

The girl opened a drawer under the desk and flipped through some little white papers. She shook her head. "Nothing, sorry."

"Have you seen the tall guy that I came in with yesterday?" The girl looked like she was thinking hard and told her no. Sarah went back to her room and called Win's number. She let it ring for several minutes before making the decision to see if her talisman could help her. She touched her finger to the ring and said, "Where's Win?"

Nothing happened. So she tried, "Can you show me where Win is on the TV?" Nothing happened again.

She touched it again and pictured Win's room. She was whisked up to his room and the sight of it startled her. It had been tossed into disarray. His mattress was leaning against a wall, all of the bedding was on the floor and his empty suitcase was open and sitting facedown. The clothes he had bought the previous day were on the floor, and all of the drawers in the room were open. She started to panic and was angry at herself for not checking the room sooner. She had no way of knowing how long the room had been like that. Her breathing grew labored. She sat one of the chairs taking deep breaths, as she tried to calm herself. She placed her head in her hands and started thinking. She wondered if Win was dead. What if he was? What would happen if she materialized by him? If he was underground, would she get stuck in soil? Or if he was tossed into a river, would she get stuck struggling for air in the water? She didn't know what to do. I can't leave him alone any longer, she thought. Her finger went to the ring and she said, "Take me to Addicus Winthrop."

She was whisked away to a dark place, and without any bearings she stumbled. She felt a hand reach out and touch her. It reached around for her face, and when it found it, covered her mouth. She started to turn her head back and forth, struggling to scream. Then she heard a whisper in her ear.

"Shhhh. It's Win. Get out of here now." She hooked her arm over his and went to touch the ring.

"No," he whispered and moved his arm. "You go. I'll explain later."

Sarah could hear movement in the distance. It sounded like somebody was walking towards them.

"Get out of here!" He whispered urgently, and she shook her head. He hurriedly said, "Go to the heart exhibit tonight. I'll meet you if I can. If I am not back by midnight tell the ring to bring me to you, not the other way around." The footsteps were closer and it sounded like a handle was turning. One last time she heard an urgent whisper in her ear. "Go." She touched her hand to the ring and was back in Win's room.

Her heart was beating out of her chest, and her forehead was wet with perspiration. She was frightened for Win. So frightened she could barely stand it.

She wished now she had thought of wishing him to her and not the other way around. Or that she had been smart enough to think of illuminating the area so she had an idea of what was going on. But it was too late now. Whoever was walking towards them would be there now, and if she were to materialize she would do it right in front of them.

She looked back at her list of questions. She still didn't know about John and Anita. Win was supposed to learn about Jones. That still left questions about Kirby and Divine. That I could work on, Sarah thought.

She went back to the first floor and walked around. She looked at all of the common rooms. The main hallway was polished white marble on the walls and floor, with a cascading staircase which led up to the second floor suites. The breakfast room was off of the main foyer and on the other side there was a music room. Near the lobby desk was a small snack counter with a young man working it. At the moment he was sitting down reading a newspaper.

In her time that snack counter was gone and the space was filled with mailboxes. The atmosphere around the Divine was relaxed and calm. Sarah leisurely strolled around and read the plaques, many about Divine. She learned that in the 30s he was jailed for holding a mixed race luncheon. He was ordered to serve one year in jail. On the first day of his sentence the judge who had ordered his imprisonment died. There was a quote in the article from Reverend Divine that said, "I hated to do it. I thought I just might let the truth touch his heart and the truth, rather than set him free, killed him."

Other articles talked about the charity work of Divine, feeding the homeless and paying the fines of those arrested for preaching civil rights. The hotel she stood in was an example of his charity work, the well-fed and cared for homeless were a far cry from the homeless she would know in the future. Whatever she thought of him personally, and the bad taste he put in her mouth with his practices, she did think that Divine's presence made Philadelphia a better place. She searched her mind for who might be a man as good as Divine, who would have been meant to take over in John's time before he gave so much influence to Jim, and her mind landed on Kirby.

She went to work on question number four. Find out what happened to Kirby. She had not seen him since that first day. After a thorough search and waiting around in the lobby, she went to the man at the snack counter to ask about him. He said that Kirby always walked Rosa Lee and her mother to Bible study in the afternoon.

"You know him well?" Sarah asked.

The man replied, "I known him a long time. He moved in next to my grandma over on Point Breeze about six years ago. I known him at least that long. How about you?"

"I just met him yesterday. Seemed like a nice man, and I had breakfast with his daughter in the ladies' breakfast lounge this morning. She invited me to watch him play in a show tonight, and I forgot where she said he plays."

"He plays in a lot of places," the man said. "He's good, too. He's damn good. If you head south out of that entrance you can go on and catch up with them. He wouldn't mind you finding them if it's to buy a ticket to his show."

"You don't think that's too forward?" Sarah asked.

"No, he a good man. He wouldn't think twice about inviting you to a show. And you got good instincts in you if you like Kirby. My grandma says he helps her every day. Gets her trash out, brings in her mail. He got me the job here when we was all in transition. Good man, Kirby. Good man."

She took note of his neighborhood. Point Breeze. She knew that area well. The roads were still wired for trolley cars, though they hadn't been used in years. Her memory of that area was even clearer because of what happened there. It was where she was nearly jumped and robbed. She knew she wasn't going to Bible study. She was going to Point Breeze.

❧◦❦

She jumped on the trolley in front of the Divine. The driver told her he stopped only a few streets from Point Breeze Avenue. When she got off the trolley she was in a row home neighborhood with deep set porches, comfortably appointed with wicker patio furniture and hanging baskets of cascading flowers. There were no bars on the porches like she knew in her time. She even saw open windows decorated with drapes. She remembered most of the homes in her time had sheets for window treatments or in some cases the same curtains she was looking at today, only faded. She stood in the street looking for a clue as to where she might find Kirby, and happened upon an older woman watering plants in her yard. She called her over.

"Hey, child, you need some directions?" the woman asked fanning her face as she stood.

"I'm looking for Kirby. He works at the Divine. Do you know him?" Sarah asked

"Oh, sure. I know Kirby, girl. You only two houses off." She pointed in the direction of the trolley and said, "Right there, sugar. The house on the corner."

Sarah walked down to the corner and saw a two-story brick home. It had coral geraniums in pots all along the edge and a wooden porch swing. The house number was set in aqua tiles.

She walked up to the house and knocked on the door. Nobody answered. Asking about a jazz show was a pretty thin motive for tracking down a man's home. She looked around and in the back saw a thicket of trees. She walked into the backyard and hid in the trees while she thought of what to do next. She wrestled with herself for a moment about going into his house knowing he wasn't home. But in the end decided it was justified. She was trying to save his life. Standing in the trees, she looked to a window on the second floor and thought, in there.

And there she went, into the master bedroom. It was neat and lightly furnished. The bed was made up neatly with a floral comforter. She checked the drawers of the dresser and found nothing that hinted at a problem with Kirby: no drugs or hidden liquor, not even a cigarette. Everything was faultlessly organized; socks in a row and belts tucked into tight circles. The home was impeccable. There was one pair of shined men's shoes and one pair of women's cream heels sitting next to the dresser. She went downstairs where there was a nicely appointed living room with a simple but clean sofa and coffee table, no television, but there was a large radio in one corner. The kitchen was a Formica dream: Aqua Formica countertops and a Formica table with white vinyl dining chairs and a black and white checked floor. There was not so much as a crumb on the ground. On the wall next to the fridge was a calendar, and written on it for tonight was "Pep's" and for the following day "Divine Party, Country Club." The only other scheduled items for the month were hair appointments and church functions. Sarah closed her eyes to remember back to the file. She couldn't remember it exactly. What was the day he was reported missing? She thought, closing her eyes. She knew he was last seen in August on a Saturday. She couldn't remember the date of the Saturday. There were only two left in the month, so he would either last be seen at the Divine Party or the next Saturday. She had a feeling she knew the answer. She heard a creak behind her and whipped around. There was a woman sliding a key in the lock of the kitchen door. She heard mumbles from the other side of the door and saw a woman's silhouette through the sheer curtains. She quickly reached to her wrist and thought about the trees in the yard.

When she got to the trees she could see Kirby's back as well as Rosa Lee and a woman who was obviously her mother. She was holding a grocery bag.

As they walked into the house, Kirby reached forward and squeezed her plump buttocks. She turned around and smacked him on the hand. He had the silly soft smile of a kid caught with candy. Rosa Lee stood between the two of them hugging both of their legs as they came together for a kiss. Sarah touched her hand to her ring one more time and thought about her hotel room.

When she was back she ran to her phone and dialed Win's room again. No answer. She ran back to the elevator and down to the lobby. The blonde was on the phone when she got there, and Sarah stood waiting, tapping her foot. The receptionist covered the phone and whispered, "He hasn't called if that's what you're asking. Don't let him know you care so much or he'll think you're desperate, sweetie." Then she turned and continued her phone conversation.

Sarah let out a huff and noticed a pamphlet sitting on the counter listing the social events for the month and found that a bus was scheduled to leave for the heart exhibit opening that evening, with semi-formal attire requested. Sarah had less than an hour before the bus was scheduled to leave. She searched the hotel one last time and came up empty-handed. Resigned, she returned to her room to change for the heart exhibit. She and Win had purchased several outfits with advice from the man at Wanamaker's. She had taken note of what was considered formal and semi-formal when the man explained it to them. All of it would be formal by her personal standards. As far as she could tell semi-formal was like formal except the clothes were lighter. Formal was almost always blue or black, and semi- could be white or any number of light colors, but the fabric still had to have a shimmer or some embroidery. She slid into a fitted silver satin dinner dress and accented it with a pair of clustered rhinestone earrings. When she was dressed, she set off for the elevator and found it filled with people dressed to the nines, as she was. They crowded together to make room for her, then when it reached the ground, spilled into the lobby and as a jolly group went out to the lawn of the Divine to wait for the bus. She saw Anita looking around and made a point to stay out of her line of vision. She did not want to interfere with Anita and possibly change something. But she did think, if Anita is coming, I'll see John again tonight.

2002

Darrius and Carol rode silently back to Mama Cassie's house, though Carol could not contain her tears.

As they got out of the car Darrius asked, "What happened to going swimming?"

"We'll go swimming next weekend during the DHS luncheon at the center."

"Can't we go this weekend too?" he asked.

"No, it's not free this weekend, and there isn't anybody there to see you swimming."

"So what do we do today?" Darrius asked.

"I don't care. Go play in your room."

When they arrived at the house, the children ran down the hallway to the room at the back of the house. As soon as the door was shut they began a conversation in low tones.

"I don't like this lady very much," Carol said. "I guess we got to keep some clothes, and she feeds us pretty good. I've never had a new swimsuit."

"It's still not right," Darrius said. "We've got to call grandma."

"Or that Sarah lady," Carol said.

Darrius began, "I think we should…" he stopped talking when

he heard steps down the hall coming towards them. Mama Cassie flung open the door and threw the new bag of clothes at Darrius and Carol.

"Put these on. The police are coming."

"Why?" they asked in unison.

"I don't know. Get dressed and behave."

She toddled off to the kitchen and left them with the clothes.

They smiled at each other and got to the task of pulling tags off of their clothes.

By the time the police arrived a fresh tray of cookies was arranged on the coffee table in Mama Cassie's neat living room, and the smell of coffee was in the air. She had run a comb through each of the kid's hair, washed their faces and made them brush their teeth.

When they ascended the stairs, the police were waiting at the door. As soon as Officer Trudge saw the children he said, "I hardly recognize you guys." He turned to Mama Cassie and said, "You must be taking good care of them."

"I do my best," she smiled. "We just went shopping this morning. They got a whole new wardrobe."

"Sure did. Now we have double the clothes we came with," Darrius said. Officer Trudge knew they came with one outfit and looked like he was about to ask for clarification when Darrius saw Mama Cassie flare her nostrils just out of site of the officers. Darrius smiled sweetly at the officer. Trudge thought Darrius might not understand quantity.

"Yup, double," Darrius said.

Trudge turned his attention to Mama Cassie and said, "Can we take a look at what the kids got?"

"Well, it's too much to pull out now," she gritted her teeth and walked over to her purse pulling out the receipt. "But you can see here what all they got."

She handed it to Trudge who looked it over. "This is a bit more than double, Darrius," he said smiling. "You guys are going to be the best dressed kids in town, next time you..."

Detective Cooper interrupted, "We found your caseworkers wallet and phone down by the Divine. I wondered if you kids might know why she was down there."

They shook their heads.

Trudge asked what had happened when Sarah chased after Darrius a few days prior, and what happened to his flashlight. Darrius knew she had hit Runty with it, but the two of them ran off so fast afterwards they didn't know what happened to him or the light. And he didn't know why Sarah would have gone back to the hotel.

"Nothing," he said.

Carol bumped his shoulder, imploring him to say more. She knew they had had a confrontation, but she would not say more than her brother.

"Well," Cooper said, "if you think of anything we should know call me here."

He handed a card to Darrius and one to Mama Cassie. He asked her to excuse the kids so they could talk. Darrius and Carol ran down the hall to the back bedroom.

"Darrius," Carol yelled. "Go tell them about Runty. What if he took her?"

"No way. We can't trust these guys. Some detectives they are. He didn't even ask more about that receipt. Stupid cop missed a theft right in front of his face. There are new socks on that receipt and look at the holey mess we got on our feet. If Runty has her, I don't trust those guys to take care of it. She got herself into trouble helping me out. I gotta man up and help her myself."

Carol wanted to burst through the door and tell the police all she knew but she dared not defy her brother.

He put his ear to the door to see if he could overhear the conversation with the police, but no sooner had he put his ear to the door than it swung open hitting him hard.

"Get those clothes off. We're going back to the store," Mama Cassie shouted, throwing the plastic bag from the store on the floor.

"Why?" Carol pleaded.

Darrius was still on the floor holding his hand over his ear, trying to get it to stop ringing.

"Because Darrius is pulling stunts and Sarah's gone. She's in a lot of trouble and nobody else is coming by to check on you now. Dinner's cancelled. Get those clothes off right now."

The doorbell rang, and she looked over her shoulder to the door.

"Stay here," she spit.

The moment she stepped away from the door Darrius sprang into

149

action. He grabbed their other set of clothes, their shoes and the aquarium holding his frog. He handed Carol her pinwheel and stuffed the handful of mints he had taken from the IHOP into his pocket. He tucked Sarah's number and the number from the police officer in his other pocket and said, "We're getting out of here."

He ran to the back window, pushed it open and knocked out the screen.

CHAPTER 22

1964

The bus pulled to the front of the Franklin Institute, its airbrakes announcing their entrance with a loud whoosh. The imposing Greek revival building sat at the end of the Benjamin Franklin Parkway which featured three other similarly styled buildings. One was the city free library and the other building Sarah knew very well: it was the family court building. The Institute matched the other two buildings in style, but its sheer size and raised setting made it the crown jewel of the parkway.

Sarah walked into the building and was greeted by a smiling twenty-foot tall statue of Benjamin Franklin in the large, domed foyer. The main lobby would probably echo each step she made, except that it was full of people. Sarah followed the rest of the group from the Divine to the second floor where the main reception was happening. There was a line to get in, and while Sarah stood in the wide hallway overlooking the statue of Franklin, she scanned the room for Win. After several minutes standing in the unmoving line to get into the exhibit room, Sarah saw him stumble in the door and jog past Franklin. She waved frantically down at him and noticed how dramatically her body relaxed. He came bounding up the stairs towards her, and as soon as he was at the top, she vacated her place in line to run over to him. She nearly jumped up to hug him, but stopped herself. When she got to him she said, "Are you okay?"

"I'm fine," he said.

"What happened?" she demanded. "I've been worried sick."

He looked over his shoulder and scanned the room. Then leaned forward and in a low voice said, "All I can say here is that somebody else knows about that thing we have," his eyes went to her wrist. "And they thought I might have it. Now they're sure I don't."

She said, "Who?"

"As soon as we get back and can talk in private, I'll tell you more," Win said. "Let's go see what we can learn tonight."

The two stood in line for nearly half an hour before reaching the main room. Once inside, Sarah understood what was taking so long. Each group of guests was paired with a guide who walked them through the various exhibits. The first was a display showing preserved human hearts in varying stages of decay, and with chunks removed to show the inner workings. Their guide, Robert, an intern from the Children's Hospital of Philadelphia, wore a long white coat and enthusiastically showed off the preserved hearts in the main room. His enthusiasm for looking at what were once the hearts of patients at his hospital was astonishing. He talked about hearts as one might his favorite model train. He bent to one of the hearts that had particularly bad yellow caking in it and said, "This is advanced Atherosclerosis, and if you look closely down here you can see that the restriction here in the arterial blood vessels is likely what killed him."

He had a story for each heart and talked about their owners with no decorum at all. Sarah thought of how patient privacy rules would never allow that in her time. After multiple breaches of doctor-patient confidentiality, he took them to the newly refurbished two story heart, meant to be walked through. As they approached, Robert said, "Now this is where the fun really begins. Follow me to my cave, or inferior vena cava if you will." He cracked himself up with the pun and ushered them through what Sarah could only describe as the blue thing on the back of the heart.

"Now I know what you are asking yourselves," he said as he turned around to watch them making their way up the tight corridor inside the model heart. "Why are some of these corridors blue and some of them red?"

Sarah whispered to Win facetiously, "How did he guess?"

Robert must have had stellar hearing because he answered, "It's one of the most common questions so far tonight, ma'am. See, the blue veins are blue because they don't have any oxygen yet. The arteries already have their oxygen. You can remember this because artery and away start with the letter "A." Then he sang in an awkward tune, "Artery away with your blood with oxygen, yay!"

When neither of them responded he said, "Neat, huh?"

They replied, "Yeah, neat."

When they finally reached the peak of the heart, they had a full view of the packed room. Sarah saw John's mother standing near the buffet, greeting guests. But she did not see John. Anita was standing by herself eating appetizers. Win saw something and stood straight upright. He looked at Sarah and said, "Meet me back at the hotel. Don't talk to me here or come near me for any reason." Then he turned and pushed past the next set of people making their way up the heart. Robert tried to stop him, but Win was too fast; Robert never got a word in. He turned his attention back to Sarah with a puzzled expression on his face.

"He said he was getting faint thinking about all the hearts and blood and stuff," Sarah said.

"I've seen it before. He can't handle the sight of blood," Robert said shaking his head. "*Vasovagal syncope* is the technical term for what he's going through, poor guy. I hope he gets past the blood exhibit before he loses consciousness."

Sarah continued down the other side of the heart with Robert. He pointed out features and veins as they made their way out.

When they were out of the heart, Robert turned to her, "Now I leave you to your own devices, dear lady. Please enjoy yourself and remember *hearting* is such sweet sorrow." Again he suppressed a laugh at himself. Sarah thanked him and started walking towards John's mother.

Mrs. Vandevelt was impeccably coiffed. Her auburn hair was set high in a bouffant, and her elegant cream dress skimmed the floor. Sarah made her way to her by way of the buffet line. She filled her tiny plate with shrimp and cheese and when she was at the other end Mrs. Vandervelt reached out her svelte hand to Sarah. She took it and noticed the woman's skin was incredibly soft and her grip very loose. Sarah thought she looked like a wisp of a person, made up of more hair than body.

"Hello, dear," Ms. Vandervelt said. Her tone belied her appearance. It was filled with warmth.

"Hi," Sarah replied. "You're that lady from the newspaper. I saw your photo. You helped with the restoration effort, is that right?"

"Yes, my dear," she said. Sarah noticed she had crooked teeth. The teeth made Sarah feel more at ease with her, and something about her manner was more approachable than she thought it would be from her photos.

"What made you decide to refurbish it?" Sarah asked, trying to keep her talking to see if she could glean some amount of information about John.

"We are patrons of the museum, my dear sons and I. We will partake in any endeavor which seeks to improve our fair city. We support many charities. You are the recipient of some of our generosity, I believe. Aren't you here with the group of young persons from the Divine Hotel?"

"I am," Sarah said. "And…" She couldn't think of another thing to ask. Mrs. Vandervelt looked beyond Sarah. A large line was forming behind her to see Mrs. Vandervelt. Sarah was being nudged out of the way but managed one last question. "Is your son here?"

Mrs. Vandervelt nodded her head in the direction of the tall man that Sarah had seen earlier that day in John's secret room. He was wearing a white dinner jacket and thin black tie. When Sarah examined his face, the resemblance to John was clear. Sarah walked near him and waited for him to turn around. When he did, he bumped her, and she feigned surprise. "Oh, my gosh," she exclaimed. "I'm so sorry. I was coming over to ask if you are the Mr. Vandervelt who helped refurbish the exhibit."

"Yes, I'm Astor Vandervelt," the man said with a bright toothy smile. His smile was not as imperfect as his mother's, and his manners were unlike hers. He did not put her at ease. "Pardon me, madam. Do I know you?"

"No. I'm with the group from the Divine," she said. "I was just talking to your mother about why you decided to refurbish the exhibit. Who came up with the idea to do it?"

Before making a reply, he looked Sarah up and down. He stared in the region of her chest longer than she was comfortable with and then returned to her face looking disappointed. "This little refurbishment, as you call it, is one of my brother's schemes. Perhaps you have had occasion to meet him. He skulks around with the Divine crowd on a more frequent basis than is advisable."

Astor's manners were so stiff it made John seem like a kitten. Astor looked as if he had smelled something rotten standing near her. Then something caught his eye across the room. He uncrossed his

154

hands and walked right past Sarah without a parting word. Sarah spun around to see what had Astor had perked up. When she turned she saw Anita in his line of vision. She noticed Anita's chest was far more ample then hers and thought, I guess mine weren't worth talking to.

Sarah tried to move closer to Astor and Anita to eavesdrop. Astor was doing most of the talking. He kept moving closer to Anita, but her body language made it clear she didn't want him any closer.

Sarah heard him ask, "Where is my dear brother this evening?"

Without looking at him Anita said, "Helping Reverend Divine get ready for tomorrow's party at the country club."

"Shouldn't you be with him?" Astor asked.

Anita rolled her eyes and Astor continued. "It seems like John does a lot of things without you, Anita. Maybe he's up to something."

Anita rolled her eyes and then whispered something so quietly Sarah couldn't hear it. Anita walked away from Astor, and he was left with an agitated look on his face.

Sarah went to the window and looked out on the city. The sun had set, and she had a clear view of the Parkway fountain. The dim lights from the street lamps were mellower than the florescent ones she had grown used to. The light looked more natural and softened the hard edges of the concrete. She saw a couple sitting on the edge of the fountain dipping their feet in and splashing each other. It was a warm summer night and seemed perfect for a city stroll. She had always wished she had a person to take a stroll with. She let out a sigh and headed back to the hotel by mortal means.

৵৽৽

Sarah didn't see Win again until she was back at the hotel. She went straight for his room, ignoring the no ladies order and banking that enough of the men were out on a Friday night that nobody would notice her there. She was right. She didn't see a soul on her way to his room. When she arrived she knocked, and the door whooshed open.

"Why did you go through the hallway?" he asked angrily.

She was miffed at his tone. "I don't care about the modesty policy, Winthrop. And there is nobody around, anyway."

"I'm not angry about the modesty policy," he shouted. "Jones

155

saw us using the ring last night, and he has been trying to find the person using it. I was trying very hard to keep us separate so he wouldn't associate you with the ring. That's why I left you at the reception."

"But if he saw us use the ring, why didn't it change the future and send us back? That should have been enough to change the future, right?"

"No," Win said. "If he had just learned that you had the ring it might be enough to change the future, but he knew about it before last night and he didn't know who had it. He was starting to suspect John or Anita. He was following them trying to find it, when he heard us and saw us disappear. Well an outline of us anyway. He knew it was somebody else, somebody close to them."

"Then he must never have learned it was John," Sarah said. "If we set him off of the trail of John and Anita and we didn't get sent back then it must have been something that was going to happen anyway."

"But who was going to set him off the trail?" Win asked.

"John's brother, Astor," Sarah suggested. "He's looking for the ring, too; he thinks John has it. I never thought to ask John about his brother."

"I remember in the rule book, one of the rules is not to talk to Astor. I don't know why. But John never told me his brother knew anything about the ring."

"Well, where's his brother in the future?"

"I've never met him. I think he's dead."

"Why were you in a closet?"

"I was following Jones this morning. He went to a church in the city and set up a big meeting in the basement. He went in and unfolded chairs and set up a podium. I followed him down and walked past the room over and over again, watching him. Finally, it was getting obvious so I hid at the end of the hall trying to think of what to do next, when Jones just left. I took the opportunity to sneak in and hide in the closet. He came back with another man. I couldn't see them, but I heard them, and he told the man that he had seen somebody other than John and Anita performing miracles that night. He said it like they had been searching for this person for a long time. The two were going over the guest list at the Divine party discussing who might have had it.

Jim said he would be late getting to the party. He was going to have to sneak in as he'd had a falling out with Divine the night before and been disinvited. He gave the man a list of people to watch. We weren't on it. Then the man left. In the end they decided their number one suspect was Father Divine himself."

"But why didn't you want me to get you out of the closet?" she asked.

"You came later," he said. "After the sermon, and it was a long one, he talked a lot about taking over the Divine. He said that Father Divine was in bad health and the time was coming for a new leader. He might be awkward when he's just walking around, but when he starts giving sermons he seems just like Divine, Sarah. I believe John really thought he was a good man if he saw what I saw today. He appeared to genuinely want to carry on the good traditions without the restrictive rules Divine has. He said he wouldn't require people to give up their money to join him. He wanted more civil rights involvement. He almost seemed like a good man. Even knowing his future, I still saw a glimmer that I thought maybe was destined for something better. When you came in he had just begun discussing his plans for the Divine and starting his own church. I was intent to listen and see if we could get useful information out of his plans. But when you arrived, and subsequently left, Jones heard me and flung open the door and ended his sermon. He and the rest of the congregants interrogated me, thinking I was a spy for Divine. One of the other men suggested they beat the truth out of me, and Jim held him back, but not before the other man slapped me across the face.

"After a long period of questioning me, Jones told them to strip me and lock me in the closet. I assume Jones was attempting to see if I had the ring on me, but the others were angry. I was in there for some number of hours before one of the congregants came back with my clothing and let me out. He made me promise not to tell Jones who let me out."

"So, why did you say to call you back at midnight?" she asked.

"I didn't know how long I was going to be in there or what would happen to me, and I didn't want us to be separate."

She thought for a moment before phrasing a question to him. "So you would have saved yourself and possibly ruined the future for

157

everybody else by having me call you back at midnight?"

"I'm sorry, Sarah. It seemed logical," he said hanging his head.

"It's okay, Win," she said. "You're not a perfect person and neither is John. I don't think either of you were the right person to have the power of the ring," she said acidly.

CHAPTER 23

Without saying another word to Win she tapped the ring and whisked herself back to her room. She was furious with him, so much so that her teeth were involuntarily grinding. She took a moment to figure out why she was so angry. Then it dawned on her. This was the first time Win's character had been tarnished in her eyes. Through all that happened with John and all of the people she met, Win felt like a person she could trust. He had told her that he was weak when he told her how he had used the ring. But it was a weakness for his mother. It was not selfish, and she couldn't fault him for that. She was weighing the pros and cons of the interactions she had with him and was trying to decide if he was still a good man when her phone rang. She knew it would be him.

She stomped over to the phone and picked up the receiver, "What?"

"You're mad at me," he said. Not a question, just a statement.

She took a breath. "Of course, Win. You could have made me lose Ruth, you could have lost John, you could have blown everything and for what? For your own skin, that's what."

The line held for a moment and he replied calmly, "Sarah, I had been in that closet for quite some time when you arrived. I had much time to ponder what might happen to me. Let's discuss what might have happened. First, if I had been killed I might have been found dead in that room the next day, which would have changed somebody's future. We fail. Or I could have been alive and being tortured which could change Jim's future trajectory. We fail. Or I would still be sitting in there quietly with nobody being any the wiser. As it was, the other man let me out, and I was free to go, no intervention required. I had many considerations to make. My own skin was a small one. But Sarah, recall that I asked you to bring me to you and not the other way around. I could not see you in any danger in any of these scenarios. Do I get any credit for that?"

She digested what he said, hovering on the last part where he said he could not see her in danger. Then he continued without her response. "Sarah, we are none of us perfect." She huffed into the phone and he continued. "I don't wish to upset you, but can I please remind you that you showed up there without knowing what you would see or where you would be? Your curiosity or concern for me led you to will yourself to a place which you had no way of knowing the safety of, or if you would be hidden from sight. Had you appeared at my side just a few moments later you would have been the catalyst for the fail."

That knocked the wind out of her, and she knew he was right. After she realized it she said, "I'm sorry, Win."

"Sarah, I want more than anything for us to be successful. I think to do that we mustn't turn on each other. We only have one day left before we will be forced back. You are all I have here, and I am far more vulnerable than you. Please bear with me."

"I know," she said. "Let's try again. Hang up the phone and call back in one minute."

He hung up the phone as did she. Then she took off her shoes and unzipped her dress. She stepped into the robe provided by the hotel. She fluffed up her pillows and sat on them, pulling the covers up to her waist. When the phone rang she picked it up and said, "Hello. May I ask who is calling?"

"This is Addicus Winthrop," he said. "I am calling for Miss Sarah Davis. Is she available?"

"This is she," Sarah replied.

"Where did you go to college, Ms. Davis?"

"Don't you know?" she asked.

"Humor me."

"I went to U Penn," she replied. "How about yourself?"

Win replied, "I went there as well. I graduated before your time, though."

"Do you have any real questions? Questions you may not know the answer to?"

"Sure," he replied. "I have had one question on my mind, but I have been afraid to ask."

"Go ahead," she said.

"How is it that when you were given your first bit of power, your mind did not go to your parents? For me it was involuntary."

She thought on the question before replying. "I loved my parents. But I don't think I could handle seeing them again and not get to keep them. Maybe knowing your story kept me from thinking about it."

"That's a good answer," he said. "That was only half of what I had to ask. The other question is bolder."

"Go ahead," she countered.

"Are you lonely?"

Without a word Sarah let out a long exhale and held the line out. She returned the receiver and replied, "Yes. Are you?"

"I thought I must be the loneliest man on this Earth. I miss my family more than I can stand at times. When I met you I felt like a fool about it. I was at least always safe, well insulated from the outside world by money. You were not afforded such luxuries."

"Do you think about your parents often, Win?" she asked.

"I do. After all these years when I see raspberry jam I think of my mother. It was her favorite. She had raspberry jam on her toast every morning. And when I smell mint it reminds me of sitting on our back porch drinking lemonade mixed with crushed mint leaves. Or sometimes, I will hear her laugh. It's a high pitched laugh that I am sure a million women must have, but when I hear it my heart leaps and I am sure I will turn to find her. But I never do."

As he spoke, Sarah remembered her own parents. Mustard made her think of her father. He put it on everything. The smell of acetone made her think of her mother and the days they spent on her front porch painting their toes. After their toes were finished they would lie in the shade of their awning but leave their feet in the sun to help the nail polish dry.

Her thoughts brought gentle tears. She turned onto her side leaving her right ear on the pillow and her free ear to the receiver. It had gone quiet. She said to Win, "Tell me more about your family."

∂∘⊸

Sarah was roused the next morning by a busy signal blaring from the receiver. It was lying on the bed, the cord wrapped around her arm. She had fallen asleep listening to him talk. She couldn't say it gave her energy, but it made her feel close to somebody. Close in a way she hadn't been in a long time.

She hung up her phone and called Win's room. When he answered she felt her heart beat quicken. It took her by surprise.

"Hello," he repeated, when she failed to answer the first time.

"Good morning," she replied. "I'm going to breakfast just now. If you want to, you know…"

"I'll meet you there," he said.

She met him in the breakfast room and found herself smiling in his direction involuntarily. She noticed he kept glancing back at her too, as they walked through the breakfast line. Sarah put a croissant on a napkin and poured herself a generous cup of coffee. Win did the same but added some sweet pastries to the top of his napkin and balanced them on his way back to the elevator. The two of them shared the elevator up and agreed to meet in Win's room.

Sarah grabbed the paper she had written her questions on the previous day and made her way up to Win's room. Once there, she found the stationary in his desk and put the names of all the players on separate sheets of paper, laying them in neat rows along the dresser. She wrote people's names, their character traits and any future information she and Win could remember about them. She filled Win on all she had learned about John and his family as she filled out their pages.

Then she told him about her side trip to visit Kirby's house. "I can't help thinking that Kirby is really important to all of this," she said. "I know that John said he has been tricked by bad men who seemed good before, but I feel like something is different about Kirby. Something important that we are missing about him. I met his grandchildren the day before we came here. That can't be a coincidence. Remember how I told you he disappeared? His whole family fell apart after he went missing."

"Kirby might be important," Win said. "But I don't think he is the most important. I think we need to focus on Jones. He is much more important to our history. We have to make sure we change his narrative. I don't know if we will be able to fix the Kirby problem and the Jones problem both this time."

"There won't be another time," she said. "This is Kirby's last night. And if we go back into his past further it could negate any changes we make now, assuming we get it right."

"What change do you suggest we make?" Win asked.

"I don't know yet. I don't know exactly what happens with John and Jones. I'm thinking we could try to steer Jones away from the party, like you said he was uninvited. Maybe we can make sure he gets kicked out or send him somewhere John might not see him again. I don't know. I could touch the ring and send him to Bora Bora or something, drop him there and hope John never finds him."

Win shook his head. "John will have the ring and can easily ask it to take him to Jones."

"I have to think more," Sarah said. "But if I don't find a good solution we are going to warn younger John not to give Jones any money, show him the ring, and then hope it's enough."

"I don't like that plan, Sarah. It leaves too many unanswered questions. And it could create a paradox. Two rings in one place can't be right. And even if we don't destroy the world, we will have no way of knowing that he will believe us. Maybe seeing you with the ring will make him think you stole it from him, and he will be even more determined not to listen to you."

She flipped through the cards of people and tried to formulate a different plan.

"There's another sure way to make sure Jones doesn't get the money from John," Win said.

Sarah looked at him, "Oh?"

"Kill Jones," he said.

Sarah replied, "I think that's the worst possible use of this ring that there is. I would never, ever kill somebody with it."

"I hate to say it, but you don't have to kill somebody with a ring, Sarah. There are old-fashioned ways to do it."

"I can't believe you would even suggest it," she said furious.

"He is going to kill nearly 1,000 people, Sarah. Would you kill Hitler if he was right in front of you?"

"I don't know. That's different."

"It's not that different. We may have to…"

She held up her hand to stop him. "There is no 'we' about this one."

"Fine. I may have to kill Jones."

"I would place that at the very bottom of the list, below telling John."

The two of them went back and forth trying to decide what was important and what wasn't. After a morning full of coffee and Sarah's hand cramping from writing, they decided to take a break. Then Sarah remembered the dates from John's secret book. She pulled the piece of paper she had been carrying and showed it to Win.

"I forgot I found these in John's secret room. These dates are not written in any of the books he gave me. Do they mean something to you?"

He looked carefully over the paper and checked the first date a few times searching his head for something. "Do you think this first one was a Tuesday?" he asked. She scrunched her face at him. "Why does it matter if it was a Tuesday?"

He looked up to the wall and appeared to be counting something on his hand. "Meet me in the library on the second floor. It's to the right of the elevators. I saw it when I was following Jones."

CHAPTER 24

The library was a long room with red carpeting and oak bookshelves. There were reading nooks under each window. In the center of each room was a tall table with reading lamps and two sets of chairs on either side. At the far end of the room was a fireplace flanked by two wingback chairs. Win walked to the wall and tried to make sense of the order of the books. He told Sarah they were looking for the "B" encyclopedia.

They walked up and down the room looking for it. Sarah bent down near the fire place and found an entire set of *Encyclopedia Britannica*. She pulled the volume and said, "I found it."

She carried it to the center table where Win spread the pages and flipped until he found it. "Black Tuesday" was the entry. The first line after the mention of Black Tuesday was the date October 29, 1929. He looked at the piece of paper in his hand, which read 10/24/29.

"Phew," he said to Sarah. "I was worried there for a minute."

"What did you think it was?" she asked.

"I thought maybe he had something to do with the stock market crash. That was the only date on this list that looked vaguely familiar, but I had the day wrong. I was thinking it was the twenty-fourth, but it was the twenty-ninth."

"So, did anything happen on the twenty-fourth?" she asked.

"Nothing I can think of. We will have to search the internet when we get back to see if the dates mean anything."

"Or ask John," she said.

"Yes, or that."

Win took a seat in one of the chairs by the reading table, leaned his head back and let out a big breath. "I need to clear my head for a minute."

She sat in the chair opposite him and started cracking her neck. "I think I saw a water ice store by the river. Food and air might do us some good."

"Agreed," he said, sitting back up in his chair.

They put the book back and left the hotel. The heaviness of their task felt lighter with the warm afternoon sun beating down on them. They walked side by side on the street, closer than they had walked the day before. They didn't talk, but the back of their hands would graze with each step and when they did Sarah felt a spark travel up her arm. She fought the urge to reach out and grab his hand. She was thinking about his hand when she noticed a man cross the street and head towards them. He was clean cut, wearing a bell-bottomed sailor suit. He had a bag slung over his back. When he got to them he asked, "Do y'all know the way to Fairmont Ave?"

Win stopped and gave him directions, sending him down the way they had just come. The man thanked them tipped his head and started down the street. Within seconds Sarah's wrist started to pull, the wrist with the ring. She felt like the bracelet was going to pull her away. She grabbed Win and said, "Something changed."

"What do you mean?" he asked then noticed the look of panic on her face. The pull was getting stronger.

"What's going on?" he asked.

"My wrist. It's pulling me. I feel like I'm going to get pulled away any second." Ahead of them they could see a woman standing over the edge of a bridge. She was facing the water with her back to the rail. Nobody took any notice of her. It looked like she was about to jump.

Win looked ahead and noticed it, too. "You can't get involved, Sarah. It was supposed to happen. It's going to pull you if you do."

Sarah's arm was already pulling. It was getting harder by the second to keep her feet on the ground. "No, Win. It has to do with the man. Go get the man. Hurry, bring him back."

"Sarah, no," Win said.

She turned and grabbed Win by the face and pulled him down to her. She was more sure of what she was about to do than she had ever been of anything. "Trust me. Win, go get him now, and bring him back here no matter what. Run."

He turned and ran, and Sarah ran for the girl on the bridge. The girl's strawberry-blonde hair was blowing in the wind. Her eyes were closed, and her bright white skin glowed in the sun. She held onto the rail of the bridge with her hands, letting the rail hold her up while she leaned forward. Sarah's wrist was pulling hard as she ran. Watching the woman lean farther over the bridge Sarah finally yelled, "Stop." The woman turned her head to face Sarah. A look of terror spread across her face. And Sarah watched, as if in slow motion, the woman's hands released from the bridge and she fell forward. Sarah's arm started burning and without giving it a second thought she ran to the spot where the woman had been on the bridge and jumped over the railing. She didn't look to see what was below.

She had no idea how high she was and before she could think she went face first into the water. She got her bearings and managed to get her feet under her. She kicked up hard from the ground when her feet hit the bottom and searched for the woman as she made her way up. The woman was not far away from her, but she was floating face down near a branch. Sarah tried to swim to her, but the current was carrying her farther away. She tapped her hand to the ring and pictured the woman face up. The woman rolled in an unnatural way. Sarah kicked to her with all of her might but made no headway. She started to panic when a form fell in front of her, splashing her face and causing her vision to blur. She wiped her eyes to get the water out and noticed her arm was no longer pulling. When her eyes were again clear enough to see, she noticed the young sailor had grabbed the woman and was pulling her to the shore. She kicked hard to try to catch up to them and finally she felt ground beneath her. She breathed a sigh of relief and walked to the shore. She looked up to see Win at the top of the bridge, holding the sailor's bag. Sarah walked over to the sailor and woman and asked them if they were okay. They nodded, and she ran past them up the embankment to Win. He was standing with a throng of people who had amassed on the bridge.

2002

Darrius and Carol were well-rested after a night sleeping on benches at Suburban Station. The remodeled grand station with high ceilings, oak benches, and bright hanging pendants was an ideal spot to stay warm for a night. Darrius had correctly assumed that dressed as nicely as they were they would remain undisturbed through the night.

Upon waking Carol looked at her stomach. It was aching with

hunger as they were nearing twenty-four hours since their last meal. Darrius heard her stomach rumble and gave her the two mints from his pocket. They quickly left the station and set off in search of a flea market.

There was a small gathering just a few blocks off. Unlike the market in their part of town, this one took place completely on the sidewalk and catered to tourists. Darrius approached a vendor selling new clothes and showed him the swimsuits. He was given a low offer and rather than haggle Darrius walked away. The vendor called after them and adjusted his offer to a fair price. Darrius also procured a small amount of money for the gently used Dora Shirt and knock off Ralph Lauren polo.

"Are those shoes new?" the man asked.

Darrius reluctantly pulled one off, exposing his grubby grayed sock, and showed it to the vendor. The offer from the man was too much for Darrius to turn down knowing his sister was hungry. He sold the shoes and netted enough from his sale to feed them well and pay for bus fares. They left the market and headed back to the Main Street. All they had left was a small amount of cash, a pinwheel, and Darrius' frog, Kermit.

CHAPTER 25

1964

Adrenaline coursed through Sarah's veins. She was so full of energy she was practically running back to the hotel. She left a trail of water in her wake and Win struggled to keep up with her.

"Slow down," he begged.

"I figured it out, Win. I can't believe I have been so stupid. John has been wrong about how the ring works the whole time."

"How do you know?"

"It's hard to explain. It's a feeling," she said without turning around. "John told us that the ring pulled him back when he gave Jones the money. Bad consequences, he said. When he talked to your dad and suggested he start a youth program the ring sent him gently back, good consequence. So, it would seem like the ring sends you back nice for good or harsh for bad. That's not it. The ring jolts you back when you make it do stuff that's not supposed to happen. I could feel it warning me. Something about the pull toward the woman was telling me that that *she* was what was about to change. She was supposed to live, and when you talked to the man he walked away. I just knew he was supposed to be there. Something made me feel I had to get him."

"How do you know it's not a good versus evil thing?"

"Because we had no intent when we gave that man directions, or toward the woman, and I could tell the ring was pissed. The reason that the ring worked with your father with such little coaxing was that your father meeting your mother was what was supposed to happen. It just sent John back so it would have a new start point. Each time you make a great change you need to go back for a reset. But you do something that was supposed to happen you just go back all nice and easy. When you do it right it's not hard at all."

"How do you know you're right?" he asked.

She turned to face him. "When your mother accidentally died early did the ring send you back?" she asked.

"Yes," he replied.

"Harsh or soft?"

"Soft," he said.

She turned back around and continued her fast walk back. "I knew it. The ring did not jolt you back because her dying was going to happen anyway. When you mess with destiny for real the ring gets pissed—well whatever power it's wielding gets pissed. And now I know it warns you before you do something it doesn't like, but John ignored it. I have to figure out why he would ignore it and what was supposed to happen."

They reached the entrance to the hotel, and Sarah pushed the door open with Win still jogging to keep up with her.

"Go to your room and get dressed for the party," she said. "Pack up, wipe down your room, make sure you collect every piece of paper we have written on and burn it. Meet me at the bus. It's leaving in forty-five minutes. We need to leave here without a trace."

"I have more questions, Sarah," he said.

"We're running out of time. We need to get ready, and I need to think."

Sarah ran away without saying another word to Win. She hurried to her room and stripped out of her wet clothing. She turned on the water in her claw foot tub and let it fill while she collected her dress, a navy blue floor length gown that hung off the shoulder with a thick band of crystals along the sleeves. She hung it in the bathroom near the tub. The steam would help smooth out any wrinkles. Then she lowered herself into the tub.

She thought about John and why he never told her that the ring would warn her when she was about to do something wrong. She tried to figure out his motivation. If he was a good man, he was truly motivated to help the bank manager all those years ago and was doing a terrible job of it. If he was a bad man, he would have had some other motivation to help Jones, but what? John didn't need money. John didn't need more power. He already had all the power a man could ask for, and he appeared to be happy with Anita. So what was left to motivate him to ignore the ring's warning and give the money to Jones? She closed her eyes and tried to clear her mind. It wandered to Win, his mother and his father. She had never met or seen Win's mother or father, but she had clear pictures of them in her head. She wondered if the pictures were accurate. She closed her eyes tight again and nothing. The picture was lost.

She closed her eyes to try again when her phone rang. She opened her eyes to see it was dark out. She jumped out and threw the towel around herself. She made her way to the phone and found Win on the other line.

"Are you ready?" he asked. "They are allowing people to board the bus. We're leaving in fifteen minutes."

She ran to the mirror, which she had moved to the floor two days ago and touched her finger to the ring, picturing herself in the dress she had hung in the bathroom. She tapped the ring again and her hair went up. She thought of Audrey Hepburn's hair from My Fair Lady as she did. She hastily evened out her complexion with the cover up from her bag and used a light line of eyeliner and mascara. She surveyed the room, taking note of each out of place item and tapped her ring to make it all disappear. She pictured it at the bottom of the ocean. All of her dresses, the papers she had written on, and her bags were gone. She slid the mirror away using the ring and did a quick walkthrough. She picked up her purse and left the room with little more than she had come with. She locked the door to her room behind her and took the elevator to the lobby where she handed off her key to the blonde behind the desk.

When Sarah turned she saw Win running behind her. He was wearing a black tuxedo with a blue cummerbund and bowtie. He had his own key in his hand.

"I forgot to turn this in," he said sliding the key over to the woman. She gave him a flirty smile and waved with her fingers.

He looked to Sarah and said, "You look beautiful." He placed his hand on her back to steer her toward the bus, which made her shiver. She hadn't realized that the back was so low cut on the dress until his fingers touched her. The woman behind the desk made a tsk tsk after Sarah turned around, and Sarah thought Win would remove his hand but instead he turned, raised his eyebrows at the woman, held his finger to his lips and said "Shh."

She smiled at him and waved her hand as if to say, "Go on."

The two of them boarded the bus with the other guests. Anita boarded. She wore a fitted, silver sequined dress with spaghetti straps. Her hair was high and adorned with a bow that, had Sarah not known who Anita was dating, she would think had fake diamonds. Anita sashayed as she walked in her gown. When she saw Sarah she ran to her, excited.

"I'm sitting with you, girl," Anita said, hopping into the seat next to Sarah. "A familiar face is a sight for sore eyes."

The sight of Anita well-dressed and well-fed reminded her of the great task ahead of her. She smiled warmly at Anita and had to fight back tears. Behind the smile she was thinking, I hope I save you tonight.

2002

The children took a bus back to their old neighborhood and had only a few blocks to traverse to get to their regular flea market. Darrius found the vendor who had sold him Kermit and asked the man if he would watch him until the market closed. The man agreed and asked Darrius when the frog had last been fed.

"Uh, what should I be feeding him?" Darrius asked.

The man pulled out a pack of pellets and slid a few into the square aquarium.

"Two times a day you give him these," He said with a smile. "No worries, young gentlemen. I'll give you some pellets to take with you when you pick him up. Then I'll expect you to find a pet store and make sure you feed him regularly."

Darrius promised he would. The vendor asked why they were alone. He was the first person to question them in all their travels that day.

"Our grandma is busy today," Darrius replied.

"What about the woman from the other day?" the vendor asked.

"She's our caseworker," Darrius said. "We haven't seen her for a while. Have you?"

"No," the vendor said, "But I'll ask around."

The two walked the market looking for familiar faces and asked if anybody had seen Runty. The few people in the know about Runty's stolen loot getting impounded told Darrius and Carol to steer clear of him.

Darrius knew he wasn't going to let Carol come with him back to the Divine and it was time for him to tell her. He gave her five dollars and said, "Get some lunch here and save a dollar for bus. Stay in the market by all of these people."

He pulled the police officer's card out of his pocket and handed it to her. "If I'm not back by the time the market closes, get Kermit, go back to the city, and call the policeman."

She watched him walk away from the market. He only looked back once to make sure she wasn't following him. She could see the Divine towering above the other buildings in the distance. She stood at the edge of the market watching him go farther and farther away until he disappeared entirely.

Darrius approached the Divine, a place he had called home for many years, with a fear he had never before felt. He stopped at the man sleeping on the bench and asked, "Have you seen Runty?"

The man nodded his head and pointed to the building.

Darrius took a deep breath and walked into the lobby. It was dark and quiet. He moved slowly through the building, checking around corners before he rounded them. First, he walked back through the out of use hallways and looked in the molded room and the trash room. He saw the board he had used to help Carol cross the hole on top of the trash pile.

The open space in the old hallway echoed and amplified every noise, which made its silence conspicuous. He pushed open the door in the alcove of the molded room and looked out on the courtyard. The only thing he saw was the Maglite from the day before. He jogged over to it and picked it up. He clicked the button and to his surprise found it still worked.

He walked into the building through the old hallway and back to the main foyer. He started a slow climb to the top of the building. With the light of the flashlight he made quick work of it. He stopped at his old floor and walked down to his apartment. It was sealed with a large orange sticker from the police department that was still intact.

Darrius continued down the passage and looked through the cracks in the boarded up window at the end. He couldn't see anybody outside. He walked back to the stairwell and continued up. When he finally reached the top he heard voices. He walked slowly through the outer room which led to the dining hall doors that were chained shut. Only the farthest door was unchained. He looked through the crack and saw Runty pacing in the center of the room. He was lit by a camping lantern placed on the floor. Darrius could make out the outline of a person in the corner of the room, just on the edge of the lantern's light.

"Sarah," he whispered. He tiptoed to the farthest door and held his breath as he put his hands on the center of the door. He pushed it with all of his strength and the doors swung open with a bang.

CHAPTER 26

1964

After a quiet ride, Sarah and Win disembarked with the rest of the passengers at the country club. This night did not hold the same type of excitement as their last Divine trip. Sarah was tense. She found herself shaking out her shoulders like an athlete getting psyched up for a big game.

Win noticed and walked over to her. She was standing near the steps of the clubhouse, lightly illuminated by the lights from the entry. "Do you feel it?" he asked.

"I do," she said. "Something's in the air tonight, Win. Like it's all about tonight."

"Have you made a plan?" he asked.

She nodded her head. "I have, and it starts with John."

"Can you tell me?" he asked.

She shook her head. "I want you to follow Kirby. He should be around the back. He is playing with the band. Whatever you do, keep him safe."

"But, Sarah?" he said.

"Don't doubt me. John thought I should have the ring, and now I know he's right. No matter what, promise me you'll keep Kirby safe?"

"I will," he said. He turned to walk away then turned back to her. "We need a plan in the event that you have to leave me here. In case things don't go well."

"I can come back for you if I'm forced to leave," she said.

"You will have to leave me for three months at least. On John's next visit to this time he gives Jones the money and stays for three months. He helps get Jones established. Don't worry. I can manage three months. Meet me in the Divine if you lose me. I will go there every day for lunch. With my financial situation being what it will be in this time, I'll need to eat there if I'm to eat at all."

She thought for a moment. "Is there something we can do to get you some money from this time so that you don't end up homeless?"

She glanced to her wrist thinking about removing one of the diamonds from her bracelet. Win mistook her meaning, thinking she was looking at the ring. He reached to her arm and pulled her to him. "Never again, Sarah. You were right. We should never have used it for our material gain. No matter what, Sarah, don't compromise who you are."

He kissed her hand. Caressed it with his eyes closed, and then pulled her to him.

"It was always you," he whispered in her ear. As she turned to face him they were nearly touching. They stared at each other for a moment before he moved forward and met her lips with his. He gently held her at the base of the neck, and she could feel electricity from his fingertips. He kissed her deeply, and she had to stand on the tips of her toes to return his passion. She wrapped her arms around him and lost herself for a moment. She felt the kiss all over her body, warming her breasts and her cheeks. She finally pulled away when she needed to take a breath. He continued holding her for a moment, then eased his grip and smiled down at her.

In a stupor she stuttered, "We have to, you know."

"I know," he said and laid another gentle kiss on her forehead before saying, "Let's do what we came here to do."

Then he started for the clubhouse.

She stood in a fog for a moment. She felt tingles all over her skin where he had touched her. She held her hands to her cheek feeling the warmth, and then thought on what he had just said. "Did you mean I was always the one for you, or for John?"

Her turned around, smiled at her and waved.

She could still feel his kiss on her lips and wanted nothing more in that moment than to do kiss him again. But she just huffed and walked up the clubhouse steps. She pictured Ambrose Winthrop's story as she walked the steps and saw the little boy making the trek up them to be a caddy. She saw it as if it were midday and dusty. For the second time in a night she saw a clear picture in her head of a boy she had never met and a day she hadn't experienced.

When she reached the top of the steps her mind snapped back.

The porch was lit with hanging lanterns. She walked into the clubhouse. Men in tuxedos with tails held the doors open for her. They didn't acknowledge her as she passed through the doors. What she noticed was a much larger entrance than it was in her time. This foyer had a more imposing chandelier hanging in the center, an overstated showpiece. And while there were large crystal and brass chandeliers hanging throughout, the appearance was much darker. The walls were dark green with wood paneling. She was trying to remember when Win's father started his golfing program. She thought it must not have started yet, but was about to. It occurred to Sarah that it was an odd thing that the country club allowed Divine's party, given the exclusive attitude that prevailed before Ambrose Winthrop's golf club.

Sarah walked into the main ballroom, which was full to capacity. The stage was the centerpiece of the room, and the band was playing *Accentuate the Positive*. Women spun around the room in spectacular dresses, and Sarah felt completely at ease with her attire. The man from Wanamaker's had dressed her perfectly for the occasion with his exceptional taste.

She scanned the room looking for John and found him near the bar. She made her way over and overheard his conversation with the bartender. "Rum and Coke," he snapped without looking at the man. The bartender didn't move. John placed a five-dollar bill in the man's cup and said, "One rum and Coke, please."

She stood behind him, and when he turned, he said, "Ms. Michigan. It's you again. Where have you been hiding?"

"I haven't been hiding. I've been at the Divine. I've seen a lot of your lady friend, Anita, there."

"You and Anita are friends, are you?" he said. He looked at Sarah's neck again which made her uncomfortable.

He slugged his drink, and Sarah opened her mouth to speak, but the room broke out into loud applause drowning out her words.

Divine took the stage. He was in full regalia, a well-tailored tuxedo with tails and a top hat. The singer stepped away from the mike and yielded it to Divine who jumped forward to address the crowd. "Accentuate the positive. Ain't that the truth, my brothers and sisters?" he said. "Who needs to sermonize when you have my words immortalized?"

Laughter spread through the room like a wave.

"Now I have no need to go on," he said, turning away from the crowd. He took two steps then spun quickly around and grabbed the mike again, pulling it to his face. "But I will anyway. We are here tonight to celebrate togetherness. We are here to come together in unanimity and say that we will not find the fruits of our labor plucked before the season is ripe. We are here to celebrate the resurrection and not the crucifixion..."

His sermon continued with a rapt audience looking on. Sarah turned her attention to John, who had slipped away. In his place was a tall slim man with a bucktooth smile. He leered at her, and she could feel his eyes trying to look down the back of her dress.

"Hello," he said, slurring. She didn't respond. The man ran his finger down her arm, and she pulled away from him.

"That's too forward, sir," she snapped.

The man closed his eyes and shook his head. "You don't need to be like that. Don't you know me?"

"No," she said taking a step away.

"Dr. Robert Glacier, the second," he offered. Sarah's coincidence meter went off and the hair on the back of her neck stood up. She had just been talking about Dr. Glacier with John at the club a couple of days prior and nearly four decades in the future, and here he was. She turned back to him. "Are you a doctor or is your father Dr. Glacier?"

"Both," he said with an idiot's grin on his face. "You should be extra nice to me. My dad's on the board. He can pull a lot of strings when he needs to. You will have him to thank once that pool out there is done. They are pouring the concrete tomorrow and by this time next week you and I can be the first ones to christen it with a skinny dip."

"Ugh," she uttered. She wanted to walk away, but she needed to know if there was more to this coincidence, so she coaxed him into conversation. "This is a nice party."

He looked around and made a startled face. "You know what? You are right. This is pretty nice."

"I'm surprised Rev. Divine would have a big shindig way out here when they could have just had it at the Divine or at Rosemont, Divine's house."

"Well," he slurred leaning forward into her. "They could have, but that John guy booked the space for Divine. Divine's not even a member. That doesn't sit well with a lot of people around here and you want to know a secret?"

"Sure," she said leaning closer.

"My dad hates him," Glacier whispered.

"Your dad hates Divine or John?"

Glacier hiccupped and leaned forward. Sarah took a step back and another man stepped forward and caught Glacier before he fell forward.

"Sorry about Bobby. He hit the Jack a little early."

Sarah took in what she had just heard. It was another piece of the puzzle. This party was at the club because John had made it so.

She knew she had to ask John why he was helping Divine in the first place. She found John in the crowd again, making his way up the steps, balancing a drink in each hand. When Sarah looked up the steps she saw Anita smiling down at him. Sarah ran through the crowd and bounded up the stairs towards them.

"John, I need to talk to you," she shouted.

Anita raised an eyebrow.

"What do you want?" John asked.

"It's a private matter, about some very special jewelry."

"I knew it," he spit.

"What's going on?" Anita asked.

He kissed her on the cheek and teased, "Don't be jealous, my sweet. It's just business."

She softened her expression. "Go on you, but make sure you get him back to me."

Sarah walked to a quiet corridor away from the other guests. She started to feel a twinge in her hand from the ring. John followed behind her.

As he walked behind her he looked to see if they were followed and asked, "Where's that tall fellow you had with you the other day?"

He held his hand up to approximately Win's height, and Sarah noticed his hand. There was a tiny burned circle in his palm. She drew in a sharp breath. He already had the burn from the ring. He had lied about how he got the scar. He didn't get it from giving money to Jones. He already had it.

"Are you okay?" he asked.

She pointed to his hand and blurted, "How did you get that scar?"

Her own arm started to burn under the weight of the accusation. And she knew she was making a change. Her question immediately put him on alert. His hand flew back down.

"None of your business," his spat. "What do want?"

She could barely concentrate for the burning in her hand. John moved his hand down to the watch on his wrist, waiting for her to answer.

"I just wanted to ask…" her wrist tugged at her again throwing off her train of thought. She knew she had to stop questioning him or she would make her intervention right then and there and she would never be able to help Kirby. She made sure not to look down at the ring. "I wanted to ask if you had proposed to your lady friend. If not I was going to recommend you come visit me at the jewelry shop I work at, Fernando's. I can get you a good deal on a ring."

As soon as her lie was out, the pull on her wrist eased and John took his hand off of his watch.

"Oh, that," he said. "It's in the works. I'll make sure I look you up. Where can I find you?"

"Jewelers' Row" she replied. "Near Eighth Street."

"Sure," he replied, and she watched him roll his eyes as he turned away from her.

She started thinking about this new information. If John hadn't gotten his injury giving money to Jim, he had gotten it doing something else. She wished she had learned more about the other dates in his book. A young man carrying a tray passed her quickly, and she asked, "Do you have a library?"

2002

As soon as Darrius whipped open the doors to the dining hall, Runty was waiting for him.

Darrius kept his eyes fixed on Runty as he jumped over the hole and walked towards the center of the open room. He held the Maglite in front of him across his body. A warning gesture, that he would use it as a weapon if he had to.

"What are you going to do with that, little man? You planning to throw it?"

Darrius shook his head. He still didn't have a good view of the other person in the room.

"Is Sarah okay?" Darrius asked pointing to the corner.

"Sarah?" Runty asked. "Who do you think is over there?"

"My social worker."

Darrius turned on the light and flashed it in the corner towards the figure, but Runty stood in the beam.

"I don't know where she is, but if I find her she's going to pay for messin' with my business."

Darrius stepped to the side and tried to sweep the light behind Runty.

He blocked the beam again, pulled out a gun and fixed the barrel on Darrius.

"Do you want to see how that light works against a bullet?" Runty asked.

"What do you want from me?"

"Nothin' you're going to want to give, Darrius. Your mother was supposed to hold onto some property for me and just when I find a buyer, she gets that shit locked up. I did all this work. I found the property. I arranged for storage. I arranged a buyer. Now all my work's for nothing. Who's gonna pay me?"

"I don't know."

"Nah, you don't," Runty replied. "I don't think letting you run around after your family screwed me over is going to send the right message to people who want to do business with me, you know what I'm sayin'?"

Darrius was about to speak when a creak near the stairwell startled him. They both quieted and focused their attention on the one open door. Runty held up the gun and walked towards it. Darrius took the opportunity to flash the light into the corner, and felt his heart sink when his eyes finally focused. In the corner was Officer Trudge, holding Carol.

Without a thought about what he was going to do, Darrius ran to her, and Trudge pulled his gun. "Don't come any closer."

"Why are you doing this?" Darrius yelled.

"I was the buyer," Trudge said. "And I need to protect my reputation. Everybody knows Runty is my informant, and if you'd mentioned it in front of the detective my career would have been over."

"I didn't tell him, and I won't. So why don't you just leave us alone?" Darrius said.

"I can't risk it."

Runty jumped over the hole and walked through the door. He yelled back, "I don't see anybody out here."

"Let's get it over with," Trudge yelled.

Darrius was thinking frantically. He had just walked up those stairs and through that door without a sound. Whoever had just made a noise had opened a door on the floor below them.

He started to jump in place and Trudge fixed his gun on him.

"Put that away, man," Darrius said. "You know you ain't gonna shoot no kid with your service weapon."

"I said, knock it off."

Carol followed his lead and started pounding her feet.

"What are you doing?" Trudge yelled.

Darrius shouted, "Carol, remember the board, chicken?"

"Yes," she shouted.

"Let's do it," he yelled back.

The floor below them started to shake. Trudge looked down, and Darrius whipped the flashlight hard at his face.

As soon as Darrius heard it clunk, Carol ran to him, grabbed his hand and the two of them darted as fast as they could toward the door. They saw Runty running toward them, but before he could aim his gun the two of them jumped into the hole. Bullets whizzed by them as they fell and fell and fell.

CHAPTER 27

1964

Sarah found two men in the library engrossed in conversation and smoking cigars in the corner. The older of the men motioned to her that he would put out his cigar and she shook her head.

"Carry on as if I'm not even here," she told them.

She walked straight to the shelves and perused them, looking for a set of encyclopedias. She didn't find anything and huffed in defeat.

"Excuse me," the older of the two men in the corner shouted. He walked over to her, and she noted his magnificent mustache. He reminded her of Colonel Mustard from the game Clue. "What are you looking for?" he asked.

"I was looking for an encyclopedia to settle a debate, but I'm not sure what I'm looking for."

"Well, my dear you're in luck. I happen to be a historian, and I love nothing more than settling debates. My friends know me as Orwell, and after I settle a debate for somebody I always consider them a friend." He reached for her hand and kissed the back of it.

She perked up. "Well, a friend and I were musing over some dates, October 29 1929."

"Black Tuesday," he interrupted.

"And October 24, 1929."

"Black Thursday," he interrupted.

"What's Black Thursday?" she questioned.

"Well, it's the Thursday that directly preceded the stock market crash on Black Tuesday. It was the first day the market started to fall, but the delay in reporting, and technology being what it was back then, nobody knew yet quite what was happening. The slide started on Black Thursday and reached critical mass on October 29, 1929, Black Tuesday."

Then she knew what Win had thought about that date the first time was correct. John had crashed the stock market.

"Excuse me, miss," Orwell said bending forward. "What's the question?"

"Oh, I forget." She took a step towards the door. Before she reached it she turned around and thanked him for the information. She passed a Bible on her way out the door and stopped in her tracks.

"Does the name P.D. Pentwater mean anything to you?" she asked.

He thought for a moment and shook his head.

She walked briskly back down to the main ballroom. She couldn't wait to tell Win all that she had just learned to see what he made of this new information. She lingered in the ballroom, checking every face that passed without any luck. Then she went through all of the side halls and open rooms, but still she didn't see Win or Kirby.

Kirby should have been playing with the band, but the stage was empty. She stepped into the kitchen and asked, "Where's the band?"

"A couple of them are out back having a smoke," he said pointing to the rear kitchen door.

She pushed through the door, rushing to the back when she felt her wrist start to pull. But she wasn't doing anything. She thought, it must be Win.

She found the band. They were smoking in a circle near the back railing of the porch, which looked out over the woods. They were wearing matching powder blue tuxedos with ruffled shirts.

She shouted at them, "Hey, Kirby?"

They all turned around but none of them were Kirby.

"Do you guys know where Kirby is?"

One of the men said, "Kirby wandered off about ten minutes back, said he had to run to the van."

"Where's his van?" she asked.

The man pointed behind her. "It's parked out by the back hoe digging up that pool. The pool, she thought, and Dr. Glacier.

She knew what was about to happen to Kirby.

"We couldn't park any closer with all that construction. We had to lug all the horns and those drums all the way through that construction, past all those trees. Lady said she didn't want us dragging instruments through her parking lot. Believe that?" The other man next to him said, "Shit naw, man. Divine parks his Rolls out front, and we park in the back."

Sarah felt her wrist pull again. It was starting to burn, and she knew Kirby was about to die and Win was about to interfere, but he wasn't going to succeed. She took off running down the steps. One of the men shouted after her, "Be careful. That ground is tore up. You're gonna break your leg."

She didn't slow down. She ran so fast she lost both of her shoes in the muck. When she got past the fence blocking off the construction site she saw Kirby in the distance. He was on the other side of the pit that had been dug for laying the foundation of the pool, and he was surrounded by a small group of men, five by her count. She didn't see Win among them.

She ran along the fence trying to make her way around the pit. The only light was that of the moon, so she knew her movements weren't visible to them. She heard the men yelling, but she couldn't make out what was said. The hem of her dress was soaked with mud, and she could feel the front of her dress hitting her shins with muck, but she didn't stop. She was about to round the corner near the pit when her toe caught on the hem of her dress and sent her tumbling forward.

She was disoriented for a moment when a pair of strong hands hoisted her up and pulled her through a break in the fence and into the woods. She turned around and saw that those strong hands belonged to Win. She let out a sigh of relief, and he beckoned her to follow him.

The ring was still tugging her.

"What's going on?" she whispered.

"The three men there." He pointed to the three white-haired men folding their arms and nearest to Kirby. "The oldest one, he's Dr. Glacier. That guy in the middle, they call him Judge, and the little guy was the one who pulled me out of Jones' closet. He's Dan Paddy."

"Fanny Paddy?" she whispered. Then she wondered if he was related to Fanny and Trish? Could it be another coincidence?

"What?" he questioned.

"Nothing," she replied. "What are they doing?"

"These were the men who were at Jim's sermon at the church in the city. I think Divine offered Kirby a spot on the board of the church, and they wanted it to go to Jim."

He pulled her with him through the woods, and they crouched behind the fence, looking through gaps in the chain link.

They heard Glacier shout, "You're going to step down. And if you do I'll make sure you're fairly compensated."

"I'm not going to back down," Kirby yelled. "Divine already gave me the spot."

"That's the wrong move, Kirby," Glacier said. "Divine's days are numbered. You won't have his protection much longer. And if you want assurances for your safety and for that of your daughter and your pretty wife, I recommend you tell Divine you've had a change of heart."

"Don't you threaten my family," Kirby shouted wagging his finger in Glacier's face. The other two men reached up and pulled him back holding his arms behind him.

"You're too stupid to understand what's at stake here, son," Glacier said and reared back his fist to punch Kirby. He hit him so hard in the stomach that he fell to his knees. Win moved to help him, and Sarah's hand burned. She reached out and pulled Win back.

"Not yet," she whispered.

"We aren't going to let another black man take over," Glacier shouted. "Not when there's a perfectly good white man ready for the job. There's been enough of this bullshit. Do you know Divine's parked in my space right now? How long am I supposed to put up with this?"

He reared back his fist again and punched Kirby in the head. Win looked at Sarah and pleaded for her to let him go.

"The ring is telling me it's not right. It's pulling. I don't know what to do," she whispered. They looked at each other but could hear the thumps falling on Kirby beyond the fence. She remembered the ten dollar trick, and knew what she had to do. "I'm going to distract them. You get Kirby away and run like hell. No matter what happens to me, you save Kirby."

The ring stopped tugging.

She pushed a loose bit of fence in front of her forward and crawled through. She made her step unsteady and swayed back and forth.

"Who's that?" Glacier yelled. The two men who were holding Kirby let go and walked towards her. She thought she was making the right move, but her hand started to pull again. Paddy got to her first, grabbed her arm and pushed her towards Glacier.

"What are you doing out here?" he asked.

She tipped back and forth and giggled. "I'm supposed to meet Bobby out here with a bottle of Jack?"

She trilled. "Oh, Bobby!"

"Where's the bottle of Jack?" Glacier asked giving her and icy stare.

"Gee, I forgot," she laughed.

Paddy said, "I've seen her before. She hangs out around the Divine with this one and his daughter."

He pointed to Kirby.

"Is this one your lover?" Glacier asked, pointing to Kirby.

"No," she slurred.

"What are we going to do with her, Judge?" Glacier asked.

"I say there's plenty of room in that pool for two," Judge replied. "Grab your gun, Paddy."

"I didn't sign up to kill a woman," Paddy whined.

She tried to put her arms together to touch the ring, but Paddy had too tight a grasp on her. Her wrist pulled harder. Something was about to happen to send her back. The pull was getting stronger by the minute. She thought, Kirby was already going to die tonight so that's not the change. Then she realized she was the change. They were going to kill her, and it would change everything.

"Paddy, get out your pistol," Judge shouted.

Her arm pulled so hard that Paddy felt the force of it and shouted, "Somebody help me hold her. I need to get my gun."

Judge came around and grabbed her arm. He, too, noticed the great pull.

"I can barely hold her. She's bucking like a bull," he shouted.

Glacier walked over to Paddy and pulled the gun off of his hip. "I'll take care of it if you won't."

"No," Paddy shouted. Sarah knew she had to do something that would change the trajectory of the moment, and she had to do it without the ring. She thought of all she had been taught and all of the times she had been powerless. She thought of Fanny and Trish and the dogs.

"What would Fanny say?" Sarah yelled at Paddy.

"What," he stammered.

"Do you want her to have a father who's a murderer, Paddy?"

Her hand stopped pulling, and all eyes were on her. She tilted her head to Win, giving him his cue to get Kirby.

"He doesn't have a daughter," Glacier shouted.

"But," Paddy stammered. "I do. Nobody knows. How did you...."

She saw Win bend over Kirby, pull him from the ground and support him as they limped away. Glacier started to follow her gaze and she shouted, "And what about your Bobby? How will you face him?"

Paddy's grip on her arm had loosened as did Judge's. They were both looking to Glacier for their next move. She seized the opportunity and twisted away from them. Paddy scrambled to grab her again, but only grazed her arm with his nails. Her hand was pulling again, but a gentle pull. She started after Kirby and Win, but stopped when she saw them walking back towards her with their hands in the air.

Before she could say anything she felt a sharp kick hit her right between her hips, knocking her forward. She put her hands out to catch her fall and landed on her hands and knees. She saw Win and Kirby both reflectively move forward towards her. Then she heard screams and a shot, and in slow motion, just like with Ruth and John, she watched the bullet whiz towards Kirby, only before it made contact Win jumped in front of it and took it square in the chest.

Sarah scrambled to Win. He stumbled for a moment then fell to the ground. She dropped with him and grabbed his hand. The world went quiet around them and dark. The pit and the men faded away. She scanned the grounds for Kirby, and just before the last of 1964 faded she saw him running at the edge of the green. Run, Kirby, run. They'll never catch you now.

CHAPTER 28

2002

She looked down at Win and was terrified by his wound. She could see his heart beating in his chest. She reached for the ring, and Win reached up to stop her. "You can't stop it, Sarah." She gently pushed his hand away and put her hand back to the ring. She thought of her trip to the heart exhibit. Step into my inferior vena cava. It was the blue thing at the back of the heart. Win's was ripped. She pictured the fibers of his inferior vena cava rejoining and realigning just like the model. There was still blood leaking out from a red vein. She remembered the rhyme, *Artery Away*, and pictured the red artery reattaching to the top of the heart. Then she pictured the tissue of his chest coming back together, and when it was solidly back she placed her hand over his chest and put her head over it. Without touching the ring, she said a silent wish.

They were surrounded by darkness and all she could hear was Win's heavy breathing and the sounds of crickets in the distance. She kept her head on his chest for several moments until she felt his hand reach up to her head and run his fingers through her hair.

She sat up to look at his shirt. With only the light of the moon she had to sit to the side not to block the light. His shirt was soaked in blood, but when she looked under the hole torn in the shirt, she saw that the injury had disappeared. His skin was light and pink without even a scar to indicate the injury. She had healed it. He held his hands to his heart, savoring each beat.

He moved his hand from his heart back to Sarah's face. He could only see it in shadow as the light was behind her. He could feel the wet of tears on her face as they slid onto him.

"It's okay," he assured her. "We did it."

"It felt right, didn't it?" she asked. "Did you feel the air when we returned? Something in it felt right."

"I didn't feel much, other than the dying," he told her.

"You were almost dead, but not quite," Sarah said as she helped him sit up. The two sat alone in the grass looking at each other with the dimly lit night.

"How did you save me?" he asked.

"Step into my inferior Vena Cava," she said. "Remember?"

He nodded his head. "So if you know how a physical repair is supposed to look you can do it with the ring?" he asked.

"So it would seem," she said placing her hand on his chest again. They sat in silence for a few more moments while Win caught his breath.

"Why aren't we in the car with Ruth and John?" Sarah asked.

"Because," Win said, "we changed the future too much. We aren't in the same place."

Win looked to Sarah and asked, "Are you sure Kirby was the answer?"

"Yes. I don't think Jim mattered at all. Kirby was the key. John's hand was marred when I saw him at the party. Something he had done before he gave the money to Jim gave him that scar. It was what he did before that changed the future the most. It wasn't about stopping a bad man. It was about helping a good man."

Win looked around the club. "Something is changed. The pool." He pointed to the space which was just the pit for the pool. "It's gone."

"Then Kirby's alive."

"Why?" Win asked her.

"Glacier knew that the concrete for the pool was being poured the next morning. That's why he was going to kill Kirby that night. So he could bury him in the pit and then the pool would be built over him and nobody would ever know what happened to him."

Win nodded. "All that time Kirby was buried under the pool. Glacier wouldn't let them tear down that pool even though he knew it was falling apart. He knew if they ever dug up that pool they would find Kirby."

"We have to go see what else we did. I need to find Ruth and see if she is okay and find out what happened to John. Where do we start?" Sarah asked.

She looked down at his torn bloody shirt and her mud soaked

gown and said, "Well sooner rather than later we are going to have to find some clothes."

He smiled at her and pointed to the clubhouse. "Maybe there will be something in there. And they have a computer. We can use it to see what happened to everybody."

Sarah helped him sneak in without breaking anything. They went in the front door and quietly padded in the down the back hall to the manager's office. Sarah stood watch outside the office while Win turned on the computer.

They heard steps on the upper floor of the clubhouse, and she hurried Win. He quietly clicked away until he connected to the internet and the familiar screech of the modem connection startled both of them. The steps overhead quickened.

Sarah ran into the office and closed the door behind her. She watched Win type Jim Jones into the search engine. After a short wait, the result was an almost infinite number of entries for Jim Jones. There were so many people with the name Jones, that there was little way of differentiating one Jones from another. Win used the words "religious movement" with the name and had a few hits. He clicked on one and read it aloud. "The founder of a small Bronx-based religious movement was found dead in his apartment on August 12, 1968. He, along with three female parishioners, were discovered after a neighbor called police regarding an odor in the apartment. A note was found that indicated the group committed suicide together. Police are asking...." He yelled triumphantly to Sarah, "We did it."

When he turned to face her he saw that she was drenched in tears, though she was smiling. He stood, and in two strides he was at her side. He picked her up and twirled her around.

"We need to find Ruth." Sarah said. "And I want to check on Kirby." Win turned back to the desk and pulled out a drawer. In it he found paper and a pen. He pulled them out and started typing.

"What's Ruth's last name?" he asked.

"Kingston" she replied. He typed again and after a few moments wrote something on the paper. He typed in Kirby Holt and again wrote on the paper. They heard steps down the hallway and Sarah whispered, "Let's go."

Sarah walked around the front of the desk and cracked the window. She saw a man rounding the steps. He had just turned on the light.

"I'm going to check one thing," Win said, typing feverishly.

Sarah ran back to him, and he scribbled down something on the paper, ripping it off the pad just as the door of the room whipped open. Sarah reached down grabbed Win's hand and thought about the clearing outside. They passed effortlessly through the building and back to the grass.

"Where do we go now?" she asked.

"Let's go find Ruth and Kirby."

They walked down the driveway of the clubhouse and down the street toward town. Win recalled seeing a payphone at a gas station nearby. It was open, and Sarah went in to buy Win a shirt while he stood at the payphone outside and called a cab.

The only shirts in the gas station were for NASCAR and they were mediums. She bought him a shirt, a bottle of water, and a pair of scissors. Then she met him at the curb. She threw the shirt to him. He pulled off his bloodied one, balled it up and threw it away. The shirt was too tight, but it looked better than the bloodied one. While they sat at the curb to wait for the taxi, she cut the muddied hem off of her own dress.

While they waited Sarah told Win all she had learned about John and the lies she suspected he told.

"Why do you think he told us giving the money to Jim caused all this trouble?" Win asked.

"Maybe he thought that was the worst of what had happened from his actions? I just wish I had saved the list of dates so I knew what else he had done."

"But wait," Win said. "If you still have the ring, how did you get it?"

"Huh," she said. "We'll have to find out."

The taxi pulled up, and Win passed the man the first address on his sheet of paper.

"Ruth doesn't live in the city anymore. She lives in Manyunk," Win said. "Have you ever been there?"

She shook her head.

"It's in the hills. There is a big bike race there every year. And it's by the river where the rowing teams practice. I never biked, but I rowed by there a few times."

"Did you find anything on the internet about what happened to her?" she asked.

"She's now called Dr. Kingston and works at Chestnut Hill College as the dean of the social sciences program."

"All of these changes are so amazing," she said. "Will we ever figure out how we did it all?"

"I don't know," he replied.

They drove parallel to the water. The road sloped upwards, but the homes were level up and down. The driver slowed the car in front of a three story brick house. From the street light in front of the home they could see dark shutters and colorful red and blue flowers in a box underneath the windows. The home's interior was brightly lit, affording them a clear view of the living room beyond the windows. The walls were decorated with paintings and sculptures. A breeze caught the gauzy curtains that flanked the window causing them to billow in and out. Sarah's heart leapt when she saw Ruth walk past the window. She was wearing a white tunic and mixing something in a bowl with a large wooden spoon. She danced as she walked. She looked fit. This life took years off of her face and body. Sarah took notice of the changes, and it hit home that she did not know this Ruth.

She felt a pang of hurt realizing that Ruth was her closest friend just a few days ago, and now she was known only by Win, who was practically a stranger. The person closest to her in the world would not know her if they passed on the street. She shook off the sadness. I will know Ruth again, and I have all the time in the world to do it, she thought.

"She looks happy," Win said.

Sarah nodded her head in agreement, and another pesky tear escaped her.

"You'll be friends with her again. Don't worry. We'll find a way."

She closed her eyes and steadied herself. She took a deep breath and said, "Can we get a car somewhere?"

Win gave the driver an address in town, and he drove them to an office building in the city.

Win and Sarah got out of the taxi in front of a parking garage next to the office building. Once the taxi pulled away Win told her, "It looks like I'm working as a lawyer again."

193

As they walked past the garage, the attendant tipped his hat to Win and asked, "Do you want the Mercedes?"

Win looked behind him and then said, "Me?"

"Yes, sir. I almost didn't recognize you two dressed like that." Sarah looked down at her tattered dress and at Win's NASCAR T-Shirt.

"The two of us?" she questioned.

"Yeah, rough night?" the valet asked.

"Oh, yeah," they replied in unison.

The man pulled around a black Mercedes, and the two gladly jumped in and breathed a sigh of relief.

Win rounded the block and headed towards Center City.

"We're going to Chestnut Hill, to find Kirby," he told her. It occurred to Sarah that she might see Darrius and Carol again. She hoped that whatever changes they faced were for the better. Win rolled down the windows for the drive back to the city. It was a warm night, and the air was light. They held their hands out the windows and let the fresh wind run over their fingers.

With the windows down they could hear the whiz of the car slowing when they pulled in front of a white brick row home, affixed with a historical marker on the front. It was wide for a row home, with a walk-up to the entry, which was an arched double door. The windows on the home were tall and topped with stained glass smaller windows. The sidewalks were brick and there were street lamps all along the tree-lined street illuminating the walkways. Win parked his car in front of the home, and they kept the windows down while they watched the house, looking for signs of movement. The lights were off and nobody appeared to be home.

"Do you want to roll up the windows and walk the block a couple of times?" he asked her.

"Sure. If we don't see them after two rounds around the block, we can come back tomorrow," she said.

They got out, and Win offered her his arm. She slid her arm into the crook of his. While they started down the street, Win reached into his pocket and hit the chirpy chirp button on the car. The neighborhood was gleaming with immaculately maintained row homes dripping with historical detail work. They passed another couple walking in the night and gave them a nod. When they rounded the corner there was a silver Range Rover parked behind the Mercedes. A woman got out of the front passenger seat and made her way to the back of the car. She pulled out a large instrument and carried it into the house.

An older man with a hunched back and slow walk slid out of the driver's seat, went to the side of the car facing the road and opened the door. He reached into the back seat and helped out a young girl with braided hair who was wearing a silk dress and shined shoes. It was Carol. Darrius followed behind her wearing a tuxedo and black dress shoes with wingtips. He jumped out and chased his sister down the sidewalk toward Sarah and Win. Carol giggled and bumped Sarah as they ran past. She looked up to Sarah to say she was sorry, but then stopped in her tracks, stared at Sarah, and smiled. Sarah stared back at her and had a strange feeling Carol remembered her.

"Do you need anything?" Sarah asked.

"No," she said, a knowing grin crossing her face. "I'm great. Thanks."

Then she ran off with her brother. The two of them played happily in the street, carefree and surefooted.

The older man padded towards the playing kids. As he approached, it was clear that the man was Kirby. Only a bit of grey had touched his temples. "Sorry about my great-grandkids. They are a little rambunctious."

"No, it's okay," Sarah said. Kirby was only a few feet away, and when he heard Sarah speak he searched her face.

"I know you," he said.

She shrugged her shoulders.

"Well, the feeling like I know you is a good one, so we must have met under positive circumstances," he said holding out his hand. "My name's Kirby, and I'm just going to squeeze past y'all if you don't mind and..."

The kids ran past the two of them again, their dress shoes clicking along the sidewalk. Sarah tried to mask her emotions. The woman who had pulled the cello out of the car was dragging it into the house. Win shouted, "Can I help you with that?"

"No," Linda said smiling. Her smile was bright and inviting. "I've gotten used to the weight of it after all these years. It's practically attached to me."

"You must play well," Sarah said.

From behind her she heard Darrius yell, "She plays the best!" Then Carol parroted, "The best, the best."

Linda rolled her eyes, "Little boasters, aren't they? Come along, you two."

The two children whizzed past them up the stairs and past their mom into the house. She turned and carried her instrument down the hall. Not far behind them Kirby strolled by and up the stairs when he reached the door he turned, nodded his head and said, "Good night, folks."

When he closed the door, Sarah looked to Win and grabbed her heart. "Did you see how Carol looked at me?" She asked. "It was like she remembered me.

"No," he said. "It's not possible."

"The important thing is they're safe. Before I left, Ruth said to me, 'You want to do right by them, and so you will' and Win, I really did. I never dreamed in a million years it would be this right."

CHAPTER 29

"I saved the best for last," he said.

He drove out of the city and onto the turnpike. Sarah fell asleep on the drive. She was almost in REM cycle when Win reached over and shook her. They were parked in the roundabout of a sprawling three-story stone home, built with the styling of a cottage. It was both grand and cozy. The walls of the home were softened by ivy clinging to the walls. All of the windows of the home were tall and made uniform by lattice work. There were flowers hugging the perimeter of the house and the front door was a heavy wood. To the side of the home was a three-car garage with oak doors to match the entrance. Sarah wondered what kind of cars were on the other side of those doors.

"It's beautiful," she said. "What is it?"

"It's our home," he said.

"Our home?" she questioned.

He handed her the piece of paper he had been holding. It contained four addresses and under the last one it said, Sarah Elizabeth Winthrop, married 1998.

"How?" she didn't know where to begin. She looked down at her left hand.

"I can get you a big diamond to wear on your finger if you like," he said teasingly.

"Don't be ridiculous. You probably already have," she said. He nodded his head in agreement.

"Knowing me, I probably did."

They looked at the house together in the dark. She asked, "Did you live in a place like this before?"

"No, I stayed with John. Should we go see it?" Win questioned, and she nodded.

They exited the car and walked around the front of the house.

Win looked down at the car keys and saw that he had a full key ring. He tried all of them until one clicked the lock. They walked through the door and were greeted by the beep of an alarm. Win ran over to the pad and said, "What date do you think it might be?"

Sarah gave her birthdate and the beep continued. He put in his birthdate and again in beeped.

"One more try," Win said.

"How about the year of our wedding?"

He punched in the numbers and the beep stopped.

Sarah turned on the light in the entry way and barely had a moment to look around before a thought crossed her mind.

"What is it?" Win asked.

"Something was bugging me, and I just remembered what it was. It was the Bibles. When I went to John's house and looked around, he had a secret room. It had a shelf full of Bibles just like the one I had growing up. They had secret compartments that held games. Why would John have so many of those Bibles?"

"Where did you get the Bible?"

"It was a family heirloom passed down from my great-grandfather, to my grandfather, and then my father. When my parents died I inherited it."

"Do you think it's here in the house?" Win asked.

They ran up the stairs and started opening doors.

"Guest room," Win said.

The next one was their bedroom, and then another spare room, a library and an office.

Win told her to check the library, and he went to the office. She strode around the room looking through stacks. Then she looked at the ring, touched her finger to it and thought of her Bible.

From the next room she heard Win shout, "I just heard something thump."

She ran into the room touched the ring again, and she heard it too. It was coming from the floor. They pulled back the rug under the desk and felt along the floor. Sarah wedged her finger into a crack and pulled. Nothing happened. Win saw the crack and grabbed a letter opener off of the desk to pry it. It would not yield. Sarah looked at the shelf behind the desk and saw an oversized Faberge egg on the bottom shelf. She crawled over to it. When she tried to pick it up, the top opened on a hinge and she found a fingerprint scanner inside. She touched her thumb to the scanner, and the wood slid back to reveal a box made out of copper. She unlatched the top, slid it open and found her Bible. She opened it and looked through its contents. It was the same Bible she'd always had.

"Why did I lock this up?" she said to Win. "I used to leave it on my bookshelf in my apartment."

They searched the rest of the copper box and found nothing. Sarah slid the fake Bible back into its hiding place and locked it back up.

৵৽৽

"I think I'm hiding the Bible from John," she said. "We need to find out what else he lied to us about without telling him what we know. I don't think he knows I have the ring."

They changed their clothes and started down the stairs. They were headed back to the Mercedes, but before they reached the car Sarah stopped and looked at Win. "Wait, John had a copper box just like that one placed in the fountain in the park across from his house. The Bible didn't come out of the copper box when I summoned it. The ring can't penetrate copper, and John knows it."

"So?" Win said.

"So, go find some tools. We're going to see what he hid in that copper box in the fountain that he doesn't want us to see."

They climbed back into the Mercedes and drove into the city.

They parked in the street by John's house and walked over the uneven cobblestones which were dimly lit by distant street lamps. The fountain held statues of fish sprouting water into the pool around it. Sarah walked to the plaque on the front of the fountain and crouched down. She looked at the screws. They were all copper. She motioned for Win to give her the screwdriver. She tried the first screw and after it refused to yield she handed the tool to Win. He unscrewed them all, and after all of the screws were free she dug her fingernails in behind the plaque and pulled. It didn't give way without a fight. She pulled hard and when Win helped her, the plaque finally relinquished its place and they both fell backwards. The copper box had tarnished to a dull green. She pulled it from its place. Dust swirled and cobwebs

199

escaped as she pulled the box free.

They put the plaque back on the front and took the box with them back to their car. Win drove them a few blocks over and parked under a street lamp.

"What is it?" he asked her.

"John funded the building of this fountain around 1963. He only provided enough money for it to be maintained for seventy-five years, into 2035. I saw the ledger for it in his home when I was following him. I had a feeling there was a reason he provided for it to stand only so long as he was alive. There must be something he wanted us to know, but only after he died."

"You didn't tell me about that."

"I didn't think it was important at the time. I didn't know about the copper boxes."

She brushed dust off of the top of the box. Under the dust she could see that in perfect stenciled letters were the words Property of Sarah Davis and Addicus Winthrop.

Sarah tugged at the corners and finally noticed it was hinged at the back. She pulled it open and it creaked as it relented. In the box was a Mylar bag which contained several pieces of paper neatly folded and tucked into an envelope. Sarah pulled the paper out and smoothed it. It was filled with elegant handwriting and addressed to "My dearest Sarah and Addicus."

Sarah read it to herself while Win looked on over her shoulder:

If you are reading this I will have passed from this life into the next, and I must relieve my soul of a burden that I have been carrying for many years. I don't know if I will know you or if you will even know me by the time this letter reaches you, but there is something that you must know. That gift that I once gave you, Sarah, as you may by now have figured out, was always meant for you.

I was not truthful when I told you what I had done with the gift. That was a selfish fabrication. The truth of the matter is that I was born into poverty in a small hill town in the upper peninsula of Michigan.

I did not grow up, I endured. We survived some of the harshest winters the north had ever known in a drafty cabin. I shared my first home with my mother, brother, and on occasion my father. With my father's regular absence, my mother worked herself nearly to death.

200

Her fingers were dark, scarred, and hard like that of a man after years of hard labor.

Our life did not truly fall apart until the day my father met, "The Miracle Man." On a particularly cold winter evening a house near town caught fire. My father was nearby and watched as many people ran from the building. One woman screamed that there were still children inside and begged the fireman to go after them. When they refused, she darted in herself, but was held back at the precipice of the home by her husband and the chief of the fire brigade.

The fire chief told her that to enter at this point would mean certain death. Flames engulfed the home, and it was about to fall back into the earth when, unexpectedly a willowy figure emerged holding a baby. It was a young girl holding her infant brother. Everybody declared it impossible. The home was too taken over by the flames. The infant was swaddled in a loft far above where the young girl could reach. But my father saw something the others did not. From his perch on a hill near the home he saw a man in the fire holding tight to something in his fist. The man in the fire inched to the edge of the door, and when he saw the children safely away from the home, he disappeared.

That day my father dubbed him The Miracle Man. *Seeing such a thing might have driven better men to religion, but it drove my father to the wish to possess that power. He ran to the door and called to the man, but he was quite gone. My father started his life-long quest on that day to chase down The Miracle Man. He wandered from town to town racking up debts gambling and drinking away what little he could get his hands on as he searched. His habits left people to call upon my mother to assume the debts. My father's methodology was simple. For twelve years he chased stories of miracles, feats, and amazements, and for twelve years he came back empty-handed.*

His travels took him to Texas where he heard he could get good work on an oil rig. But when he got there, the rush for the jobs was over, and he couldn't find work. He drank away the last of his money and decided to make one last attempt to find The Miracle Man. He snuck onto the rig and set a great fire, one he was sure would be grand and terrible. He did this in the faith that The Miracle Man would appear and save everybody. Half of that assumption was true. The Miracle Man came, but not before the loss of many, many lives.

My father saw The Miracle Man and rather than give him a chance to disappear again, he attacked him and tore open his palm. In it was the ring which he wrestled away. The man calmly told him to return that which he had taken, but my father refused. The man assured my father he had no idea what he was getting involved in. He told my father that his bloodline alone had been entrusted with the ring, and that nobody else could wield it. My father refused to give it up and when the man lunged to retrieve it from him, my father touched the ring and wished the man dead. You can surmise how that turned out.

My father never told me who that man was. But after all my troubles, I decided to find out. I searched the names of the dead at the great Texas Rig fire and found a mention of a man Joseph Nathanial Davis, found dead on the bank. His death was a mystery. Not so much how he died, it was assumed he died from inhalation, but local authorities were baffled by his presence. He was a middle-aged farmer from Michigan, who by all records had no reason to be there. His hometown was named in the report, and I went there to search for his descendants. Davis being a very common name, I followed many Davis families. In the end it was you. Of course, you know this. When I came upon you, your family was in great peril. In my own patched up way, I tried to save you. I am very sorry Sarah, but my attempts to save your family were fruitless, and in the end my actions took your parents too soon. I decided to save you, at least, by mortal means, so that I would not destroy you, the last of the Davis family. I made sure you were the recipient of a scholarship, which brought you to Philadelphia and under my watch. I was not lying when I said I watched you through time. While you put yourself in dangerous situations I was always nearby making sure that you would not perish. I knew I would need you one day.

This leads me to the worst of my actions and an admission that I owe you both. I always knew how to fix it all. But I could not bring myself to do it. The truth of all these journeys I took through time was me trying to correct my initial mistake made in 1929. I went back, before my birth, and made sure my family was exceedingly wealthy. I wished for money and did not realize that the money I wished for had to come from somewhere. I made the wish for my family. The moment I wished for the money, for my father and mother, the ring threw me back to my actual time, burning my hand in the process. My new life was a great adjustment for me. I was no longer of limited means. I would never know cold or hunger again, but my actions had evaporated great sums of money, causing a great crash that nearly ruined the country. Nobody could figure out where the money went. In taking that ring and using it so carelessly, I had set off a chain of events that nearly ruined a nation. Further, they almost ruined my Anita. She and I met at a shelter in Pittsburgh long before I came to hold the ring, and when I changed my fate I lost her. I lost her over and over again, breaking my heart. I changed the world and moved the moon and the stars to save Anita and bring her back from ruin. But nothing I did could bring her back to me as I had known her.

So, why tell you this now? Why admit all of it? The truth is I need you, Sarah. I need you to make sure that you can repair as much of my damage as you can. I left you with the notebook of all of my actions, and I would like to ask that with whatever time you have left in this world you would try heartily to fix this world that I have left you with.

I am the villain here, Sarah, and for that I am truly sorry. But I must defend myself on some fronts. When I was a young man, only a teenager, my mother called me home to tell me my father had died. I had made my way as far as Pittsburgh and was just starting work in a mill. I received her letter and came back to find that my father was to be given a debtor's burial. The county mortician put him in a used pine box, which had the week before been used to transport fish. They moved him to the county church for a meager service, attended only by my mother and myself. When I saw him, he was aged beyond his years. The skin of his face was loose and weathered. I didn't know of what he died, and I didn't know what he had done with the ring, but my mother never benefited from any of it. When I came to the church that day to meet her, I found she had grown pale and sickly thin. The black muslin dress she was wearing looked like a shroud over her white, bony frame. I knew it was only a matter of time before she would be in the same place as my father. I knew all that my father had left her was a bad name and a legacy of bad debts to haunt her for the rest of her short life. She deserved better. She had worked throughout my childhood to keep me out of factories. I was lucky in that sense. But my brother was not. The cold northern winters took him when I was very young. I hardly remembered him.

When I held her shoulder at the service, her bones were cold in my hand. She was so weak she could scarce stand. I went to my father's body and punched it square in the chest. Nobody stopped me or even protested. When I pulled back my hand it stung. It stung as if I had struck steel instead of a man. When I looked at my knuckle I saw it was adorned with a red circle. I looked at his body and saw the outline of a circle in his pocket. I reached in and found the ring there. I knew what it was, and I took it.

Please forgive me, my dear Sarah and Winthrop. Winthrop, you were my life, and Sarah, I pray that you will be my salvation. If I have planned this correctly, you will have fixed the Divine and I will have died none the wiser about my previous misdeeds. I could not live knowing what I had done, but I was too much a coward to give it up. For that I'm sorry.

Please forgive me,
Johnathan Vandervelt (Pentwater)

She looked at the second piece of paper. It was a list of dates and times starting in 1929 and spanning through 1990.

"What do we do with it?" Win asked.

"We fix it," she said. They looked down the list. Win tried to match the dates with events he knew in history, and Sarah did the same. They were interrupted when they heard a phone ringing. Sarah opened the glove box and found nothing. Win opened the center arm rest found a car phone. He picked it up. His eyes went wide, and he held his hand over the receiver. He looked at Sarah and said, "It's for you. It's your mom."

ABOUT THE AUTHOR

You may know Nicole as the syndicated humor columnist, "The Starter Mom," or from her Best-Selling Saints Mystery Novels, which have had more than 100,000 downloads as an e-book. Because of the series' popularity, Amazon chose it for their Stipend Program to be turned into an audiobook at Amazon's expense.

An award-winning journalist and author, Nicole was recognized by Writer's Digest as a top fiction writer in 2015 and won honorable mention in genre fiction from the Writer's Digest annual publishing competition for her Saints Mystery Series.

Nicole writes for two daily newspapers in the greater Philadelphia area and as a columnist for Happenings Media. Prior to working as a writer, Nicole was an Agency Social Worker for the Philadelphia Department of Human Services, where she first learned about the subject of her latest novel, Divine Hotel.

Nicole grew up on a rural farm in Southern Michigan, but she was always a city girl at heart. She still has a penchant for straight-from-the-dairy cheese, but otherwise prefers to spend her days in New York and Philadelphia and her adopted hometown in Bucks County. The mother of two, she is a soprano in The Bucks County Womans Chorus and an amateur pianist.

Nicole loves mysteries. Her favorite female sleuths were dreamed up by Charlaine Harris and Janet Evanovich. She also draws inspiration from the classics such as Sir Arthur Conan Doyle and Edgar Allan Poe. While Divine Hotel is historical fiction, fans of Nicole's Saints Mystery series will by happy to know that her knew book also features a spunky heroine and a mystery to solve.

Acknowledgements

It's hard to make sure I mention everybody who has been a part of making this book possible, what a wonderful problem to have.

I have to thank my first readers first. They are the poor souls who tirelessly read my drafts, with barely a comma to be found and a glut of run-on sentences. Those early readers are Jamie Tirrell, Janet Sykes Germiller, Linda Utter, and Travis Silvas.

My editors Erin McNelis, MFA and Kourtney Wojciechowsi come in next to polish my work and make me sound smarter than I am. I could never do this without those two ladies.

Others who have contributed freely are Professor Brian Lutz, who gives regular literary therapy and PR Specialist Alyson Komyanek, who forced me onto social media against my will.

I also greatly appreciate Genevieve LaVo Cosdon, who brings an artist's eye to all of my stories

I would never have known Philadelphia as I do today had it not been for Natalie, Elizabeth, and Joe.

Lastly, thank you to my publisher Karen Hodges Miller. Her encouragement and faith in me have been both terrifying and inspirational.

THE REAL DIVINE

A note from Author Nicole Loughan

The Divine Hotel is a real building that sits at the corner of Fairmount Avenue and Broad Street in North Philadelphia. It was designed and constructed between 1892 and 1893 by architect Willis G. Hale, according to the National Register of Historic Places (NRHP)

The NRHP further talks of the importance of the building, outlining some of its history. According to the register it was purchased by Father Divine, the leader of the Divine Peace Mission Movement, in 1948. For fifty years the movement owned the hotel and served as the center of the movements religious, civil rights and social programs. Its importance in history is cemented by many factors. It was the largest piece of property owned by an African American at the time and employed many African American Philadelphians. Following Father Divine's death in 1965, the Peace Mission continued to own and operate the Divine Lorraine until 1999.

This fictional account of the Divine contains many exaggerations and purists may notice the addition of an elevator to the fictional Divine and some embellishments on location. It was my intent to capture the feel of the building and the 60s as shown through photos, but for much of the architecture I had to guess, based on the photos.

There are also cameos in this book from Father Divine. I toyed with the idea of leaving him out as merely a mythical figure whom we never meet, but it felt wrong to write about the hotel without bringing in its most seminal figure. For the few lines I gave Divine I listened to multiple sermons, trying to capture his cadence and a picture of what the people who met him must have felt. He is a controversial historical figure in many ways. Among the accusations against him he was said by many to be running a cult who required money and celibacy from his followers. There is no doubt that he is important to our history as a nation and to the Civil Rights Movement.

There is also an appearance by the notorious figure Jim Jones. In his own way he is also part of our history. Jones is known best for founding a cult in Guyana in South America which ended with the suicide of more than 900 of its members including children. It was reported at the time that they died by drinking Kool-Aid laced with Cyanide.

A play by play of Divine's history and his interactions with Jones are chronicled in a World Religions and Spirituality Project compiled by Virginia Commonwealth University. In the article authors David G. Bromley and Michaela Crutsinger discuss how Jim Jones was said to have been inspired by Divine and even made an attempt to take over the Peace Mission Movement, but was prevented by Divine's widow, Mother Divine.

The International Peace Mission is still active today. Tours are offered of the estate, known as Woodmont, where Divine is interred. Free tours are offered on certain Sundays. The International Peace Mission website reminds potential visitors of the modesty policy, still in effect today: "no smoking, drinking, obscenity, vulgarity, profanity, undue mixing of sexes, receiving of gifts, presents, tips, or bribes. Dress Code requires modesty – no shorts or sleeveless tops, ladies should wear a dress or skirt."

This is just a bit of the history which can be found about Divine and the Hotel. I hope more than anything this book has aroused your curiosity about the real history of The Divine and the themes of justice presented in the book.

Nicole

Further reading:
The World Religions and Spirituality Project.
www.wrs.vcu.edu/profiles/FatherDivine.htm
Father Divine's International Peace Mission Movement
peacemission.info
Divine Lorraine – Run by new owners of the hotel
thedivinelorrainehotel.com/

www.ingramcontent.com/pod-product-compliance
Lightning Source LLC
Chambersburg PA
CBHW020406150626
46554CB00012B/381